PRAIS

Something to Prove

"*Something to Prove* is a heartwarming story about a bad girl returning to her small hometown, finding romance, and discovering that you can go home again. Loved it!"
—*New York Times* bestselling author Linda Howard

"Lang's latest contains smooth, modern storytelling filled with lighthearted touches. . . . The town of Magnolia Beach is the true highlight of this story, though, with its distinctive charm and its colorful residents; it's sure to appeal to readers. *Something to Prove* is a truly delightful read."
—*RT Book Reviews*

"In this contemporary, we have Ryan Tanner (super hot) and Helena (former wild girl) getting together after years apart, and it's adorable. Watching these two had me smiling and blushing. When I'm in the mood for a contemporary, Kimberly's one of the first authors I go to."
—Happily Ever After-Reads

"[A] wonderful romance with a story line that had our interest from start to finish. . . . [It] pulls on your emotions and never lets go until the end."
—The Reading Cafe

Also by Kimberly Lang

The Magnolia Beach Novels

SOMETHING TO PROVE
ONE LITTLE THING

Everything at Last

A Magnolia Beach Novel

KIMBERLY LANG

A SIGNET ECLIPSE BOOK

SIGNET ECLIPSE
Published by New American Library,
an imprint of Penguin Random House LLC
375 Hudson Street, New York, New York 10014

This book is an original publication of New American Library.

First Printing, January 2016

For more information about Penguin Random House, visit penguin.com.

ISBN 978-0-451-47104-8

Printed in the United States of America
2 4 6 8 10 9 7 5 3 1

PUBLISHER'S NOTE

This is a work of fiction. Names, characters, places, and incidents either are the product of
the author's imagination or are used fictitiously, and any resemblance to actual persons,
living or dead, business establishments, events, or locales is entirely coincidental.

For Judith—

*Partly as an apology for my inability to
not call you by your nickname in public,
but mostly because you're an amazing friend
who will eat Mexican food with me anytime I want,
even if it does require us to actually leave our houses.*
Tischdecke, hummer *and* prost*!* Du bist toll!

Chapter 1

It's nearly impossible to keep a secret in a small town. But *nearly* impossible means it is still possible. It was just damn hard to do it.

Molly Richards felt like she knew most of the secrets in this particular small town. She wasn't a therapist, preacher, bartender, or even a hairdresser, but running a coffee shop—the *only* coffee shop in Magnolia Beach, Alabama—had to come close. People didn't have to tell her secrets. She overheard them at Latte Dah—whether she wanted to or not.

But she wasn't a gossip. She never repeated what she heard, never even dropped hints, because everyone had something they'd rather other people not know.

But she also never forgot those overheard tidbits, either, and it gave her a more complete picture of this town and its people than most folks who'd lived there a lot longer than the two and a half years she had.

In a way, it made her love Magnolia Beach all the more. Not only did she know *what* was going on, she also knew the *why*, the *who*, and often the *whoa-you-won't-believe-this*. It was a quirky little place, and the key to appreciating it fully was understanding it.

The buzz today was all about the engagement of Sophie Cooper and Quinn Haslett, but that was *news*, not gossip—literal news as Quinn had announced it himself on the front page of *The Clarion*.

That's one benefit of owning the paper, Molly thought with a giggle.

There were sighs over the romance, speculations over the timing—they'd been together less than a year, after all—and a bit of jealousy from the younger single set that Quinn had been taken off the market, but it made Molly smile all the same.

It was spring and love was in the air. And she was a sucker for a love story. She'd once thought that her own failed marriage would—or at least *should*—sour her on all relationships, turning her into one of those crotchety types grumbling at romance. She'd even gotten a cat in preparation for that day, but it never happened.

Even after everything, she still believed that everyone deserved a happily-ever-after. And she got to see lots of relationships start, grow—and occasionally end, too—over cups of coffee in the overstuffed chairs of Latte Dah.

Jane, who'd been with her from almost the day she'd opened her doors, blew her blue-streaked bangs out of her eyes as she passed carrying a tray full of dirty coffee cups.

"There are three applications under the register. Hire someone, or I'm going to quit."

"I will," Molly promised. In addition to Jane, Molly had two part-timers, but they were high school kids, so the hours they could work were limited. And while it was very nice to be busy enough to need another employee, she was enjoying the security of the extra cash after two years of just making ends meet. Right now, she was in a good position—she'd invested in the shop and padded her savings a little bit—but that cushion could deflate quickly. She couldn't risk losing Jane, though, and they'd only get busier once the summer season started. She tugged the envelope with the applications out and opened it as she followed Jane into the kitchen. "Any of these you particularly like?"

Jane didn't look up from loading the dishwasher, but Molly saw the triumphant smirk. "Samantha Harris or Connie Williams. Patrice is a little flighty."

Molly knew *of* both Samantha and Connie, even if she didn't know them personally—Magnolia Beach was pretty small, after all—and she didn't have a strong feeling either way. "I'll call them both back for interviews, and if they're good, I'll see who can start next week."

"*This* week," Jane insisted. "I'd like to have a life, too."

Molly sighed. "Fine. Can you call them and see if they'll come in this afternoon? Maybe one at four and the other at five?"

"Thank you. Now I won't have to poison your coffee today."

She grinned. "Then thank *you*." A glance around told her the morning rush was officially over. "I'm going to run out for a while. I'll be back before the Bible study group arrives."

"Bring back change," Jane called from behind her. "We're low on fives and ones."

Molly nodded as she hung up her apron and then held the door for a mother pushing a stroller with a sleeping baby. Outside on the sidewalk, she took a big breath of non-coffee-scented air and turned her face up to the sun. Late spring was quite possibly one of the best times of year here weather-wise: warm days, and nights that were just cool enough to require a light jacket. But the frizzing of her already unruly curls meant summer—and its humidity—were right around the corner.

It might be an odd little town, but there sure wasn't a much prettier place than Magnolia Beach on a bright spring afternoon. The town was practically a movie set labeled "small-town Americana"—tidy buildings set along clean, narrow streets and flags waving lazily in the breeze. Even the newer buildings intentionally had that older aesthetic, giving the impression the town wasn't necessarily stuck in the past, but instead rather gently resisting change wherever it could.

That feeling was part of what drew tourists to the area. That, and the water, of course. Magnolia Beach was locked in on three sides by water: Mobile Bay to the east, Heron Bay to the south, and Heron Bayou to the west.

The Yankee snowbirds had already left town for their northern cities and climes, but in a few more weeks the town's population would nearly double in size as all that water drew folks down to the coast. The Mobile Bay shore—called "The Beach" by the locals—had white, sandy beaches, perfect for sandcastle building and walks along the water, while the Heron Bay shore—called "The Shore" to avoid confusion—offered fishing off the jetty and a boardwalk along the rockier, man-made beach. Add in a marina full of boats to charter, airboat tours into the bayou, and long, hot sunny days, and Magnolia Beach was a summer paradise.

While the tourists looking for wild parties would head over to the east side of the bay to Gulf Shores and the Florida Panhandle, families and those folks wanting a more low-key vacation would come to Magnolia Beach. And when they weren't on the water, tourists had a full selection of restaurants, quaint shops, and family-friendly activities right at their doorstep.

Trapped as it was between the water and unable to sprawl, the town was rather compact, making pretty much everything within walking distance. The tourists loved that perk, and Molly liked it herself, leaving her car at home except on the most miserable of days. And since she tended to nibble at the pastries—strictly for quality control purposes, of course—she needed all the exercise she could get. That would be another perk of a new employee: she could find the time to start running again before the winter weight became permanent.

More importantly, though, she liked the walk. In the early mornings on her way to open Latte Dah, the whole place felt quiet and still, and that was better for clearing her mind and relaxing her soul than any kind of meditation. In the afternoons, the streets were busy and active, but not stressed and crowded, and there was always someone to stop and speak to, making her feel like a real part of the town. Making it feel like *home*.

Only better. She had no desire to really go home.

Fuller, Alabama, was only six hours away, but as far as she was concerned it might as well be on the other side of the planet. She was proud of what she'd built here, and the person she'd been just a few years ago seemed like a stranger. Eventually she'd have to go back—her day of reckoning would come—but until then, it was easy enough to forget Fuller even existed. *This* was where she wanted to be.

The bank, post office, and grocery store were quick, easy errands and she made it back to her place, a tiny guesthouse beside Mrs. Kennedy's house, in plenty of time for her own lunch and maybe a short nap. Even after over two years of getting up to open the shop, that five a.m. alarm was still hard to handle sometimes.

She dropped to the couch and kicked off her shoes, and Nigel jumped into her lap with a purr. Threading her fingers through his soft gray fur, Molly closed her eyes with a sigh.

And—of *course*—there was an immediate knock at her door, followed by Mrs. Kennedy calling, "Molly?"

Nigel hissed in the general direction of the door, voicing her feelings quite nicely. While the place was clean, cozy, and affordable, her landlady had boundary issues and a rather interesting interpretation of the tenant-landlord relationship.

Grumbling, she moved Nigel off her lap and rolled off the couch. Knowing Mrs. Kennedy could see her through the glass window in the door, she pasted a smile on her face as she opened it. "Hello, Mrs. K."

Eula Kennedy was welcoming warm weather with a bright fuchsia sundress and a color-matched faux hibiscus in her carefully coiffed white hair. Molly could only hope that forty years from now she'd have the nerve and ability to carry off something like that.

"Hello, dear. I'm *so* glad I heard you come in. I was about to head to Latte Dah to find you."

"I just came home for lunch." *As I do most days.* Her schedule wasn't a secret or anything.

"Well, I won't keep you but a minute."

Molly had no choice, really, but to open the door wider for her to enter. Mrs. Kennedy was carrying a bulging grocery sack from the Shop-N-Save, but it didn't look like groceries. As she set the bag on the coffee table with a sense of satisfaction and purpose, Molly had a bad feeling she wouldn't like the explanation of that bag.

"I got a call from Jocelyn last night."

Jocelyn was Mrs. Kennedy's niece, currently pregnant and living over near Destin. Molly nodded absently while she eyeballed the bag. Oddly, it looked like it was full of notebooks. "I hope she's doing well."

"The doctors have put her on bed rest. Worries about an incompetent cervix."

That got her attention. Molly had no idea what that diagnosis might mean, but Mrs. Kennedy looked worried, so it probably wasn't good. "I'm sorry to hear that. Please let me know if there's anything I can do," she said automatically.

"I'm so glad you said that," Mrs. Kennedy said in a tone that had Molly wishing she'd stopped talking after "sorry." "There's no way Jocelyn can rest the way she needs to with two other little ones running around, so

I'm going to go stay with her and help until after the baby is born."

"I'll keep an eye on things at the house, no problem." She often looked after the place while Mrs. Kennedy traveled. It was one of the reasons her rent was so cheap.

"I know you will, and I appreciate it, but the house is really the least of my issues. I've got my Sunday school class and volunteer shifts at the library covered, but there's no one to take over the Children's Fair on Memorial Day weekend."

No. She couldn't possibly be thinking that I should . . .

Memorial Day marked the official start of the summer tourist season, and Magnolia Beach always went all out for the weekend with concerts and an arts and crafts fair downtown, a fireworks show over Heron Bay, services at the War Memorial, a parade, and, of course, the Children's Fair, which was originally Mrs. Kennedy's idea and her pride and joy. More importantly to *this* conversation, though, it was a huge undertaking, with a dozen different parts. Not to mention all the children. She liked kids—honestly, she did—but in small manageable groups, not large screaming masses. "Oh, Mrs. K, I couldn't. *Really.* I wouldn't know where to begin, and I'd hate to mess it up."

Mrs. Kennedy waved that away. "It's impossible to mess it up. Most of the heavy lifting is already done, and the folks involved are old pros at it by now, so it will mostly just roll along on its own. I just need someone to keep an eye on it."

"But—"

"Have you already agreed to volunteer somewhere else?"

Molly wished she could lie. "No, but—"

"Then this is perfect. A great way for you to get your feet wet."

Get her feet wet? This would be like jumping into

the deep end of the pool. With dumbbells strapped to her legs. And the pool would be full of small screaming children.

"I don't—" Molly started her protest, but Mrs. K just patted her on the arm—firmly, but kindly nonetheless.

"Everything you'll need to know should be in those notebooks, and if it's not, just ask Margaret Wilson or Tate Harris for help. They'll know. Now . . ." Mrs. Kennedy started unloading the notebooks as she talked, placing them in Molly's hands so that she was forced to either accept them or end up with bruises on her feet from dropping them.

Molly was being steamrolled and she knew it, but damned if she knew how to stop it. Mrs. Kennedy kept talking as if it was a done deal, with or without Molly's agreement, and Molly couldn't bring herself to interrupt a sixty-something-year-old woman. And since Mrs. Kennedy never seemed to stop to take a breath, she had no place to interject an objection.

The flood of words and instructions rolled on, interspersed with assurances of Mrs. Kennedy's confidence in Molly's ability to pull this off. Molly was still blinking in confusion and formulating her plan of resistance when Mrs. Kennedy gave her a quick kiss on the cheek and was out the door.

Leaving Molly with the Children's Fair literally in her hands.

"Damn it."

Nigel blinked at her from his perch on the back of the couch, then stretched out his neck to sniff disdainfully at the load in her arms. A second later, he pulled back quickly, ears lying flat against his head.

"My thoughts exactly."

She didn't have time for this. She had a business to run, and she was shorthanded right now anyway. Equally important, she didn't *want* to do this. She, too, was from a small town, and *this* was exactly how people got sucked into the volunteer pit, never to surface again. She was all for community spirit, but there was no way she wouldn't screw it up somehow. And since it was a big fund-raiser for . . .

Damn—she didn't even know where the money raised actually went. It had to raise a lot, though. Christ, she was going to mess this up *and* be the reason some deserving charity couldn't make its budget this year.

This was insane.

She was still standing there trying to figure out a graceful way to decline the honor when she saw Mrs. Kennedy go back out carrying a suitcase. She hurried to the porch, ready to claim illness, insanity, incompetence, *any* reason not to be in charge of this, but Mrs. Kennedy was very spry for her age and was already driving off with a honk and a cheery wave.

Damn it. She was well and truly stuck now.

Tate Harris stood under the shower and let the hot water beat the tiredness from his shoulders. After a long spell of nothing but checkups and routine procedures for weeks, it seemed every pet within a twenty-mile radius had decided today was the day for illnesses and accidents. He'd been on his feet all day, without even a lunch break, gone through multiple changes of clothes, and Mr. Thomas's Pomeranian, Florie, had taken a bite out of his hand.

It was days like today that made him wish he still drank.

With that option off the table, though, he stayed under the spray until the water ran cold and forced him out. He scrubbed a towel over his hair to dry it, then grabbed a clean pair of jeans and a T-shirt.

Now that the animal smells were washed away and out of his nose, he caught the faint scent of lemon furniture polish and bleach floating through the house, meaning Iona had come today—a day earlier than usual. Suddenly hopeful, he went to the kitchen and opened the fridge. There, in neatly wrapped and labeled packages, were his dinners for the next several nights.

He'd been not exactly dreading, but not looking forward to either, a cold dinner of ham sandwiches, so the sight of Iona's pot roast made his mouth water. Feeling better already, he stuck it into the microwave to heat.

A fresh pitcher of tea sat on the counter, holding down a note from Iona, explaining that she'd come today because she had a doctor's appointment tomorrow, and if he'd text her a list of any personal items he might need from the store, she'd take care of that on her next trip.

But the fact she'd signed that note with just an initial and a small heart—well, that was a little disconcerting.

When he'd hired Iona last year, he'd been drowning, overwhelmed by a busy practice and trying to have some kind of life while still having clean clothes, decent food, and a house that didn't look like the health department needed to intervene. Iona had laughed at her interview and said he actually needed a wife. He hadn't disagreed with her. And she'd been an absolute godsend, taking over and running this part of his life with ease. Unfortunately, the feeling that Iona might be wanting to take on the title as well as the job had grown stronger over the last few months.

It'd first become noticeable when his best friend, Helena Wheeler, had moved back to town last fall. The amount of time he'd spent with her ignited Iona's jealousy. He'd faced weeks of bland food and scratchy, wrinkled clothes. Once Helena had started dating Ryan Tanner, however, his life had gone back to normal.

That was enough to make any sane man think carefully before asking a woman out, however casually. Especially if he liked his creature comforts.

Then Iona had starting making him cookies. Specifically, her super-secret recipe peanut butter chocolate chip ones that he loved, saying he was too skinny and needed fattening up. He rubbed a hand over his belly absently. Those cookies would do it for sure.

Last week, he'd found a lacy pair of Iona's panties "accidentally" mixed in with his laundry, and now she was leaving notes signed with a heart.

It made him hesitant to eat the cookies, fearful of what Iona might read into it.

She managed to dance perfectly along the line of what was appropriate, never really crossing it and making it impossible for him to call her on it.

But he was going to have to do something. Soon. And he was selfish enough to not want to do it simply because Iona took such good care of him. If he rejected her, she might quit, and he didn't want to go through the trouble of finding someone else.

And if he *did* ask Iona out, he was only rushing that moment of truth along. He doubted Iona would accept payment for cooking and cleaning if she considered herself his girlfriend, and he couldn't not pay her for the work. He'd either have to marry her almost immediately or find someone else to take over at home—and he doubted Iona would like that much, either.

The whole situation was a disaster waiting to happen.

The thing was, there wasn't anything *wrong* with Iona Flemming. Cute, sweet, kind—she'd make some man very happy one day. But that man wasn't going to be him.

Taking himself out of the local dating scene entirely might seem an extreme step to avoid upsetting Iona and sending his life back into chaos, but it was a sacrifice he was perfectly willing to make right now. And dating outside the city limits wasn't *that* much of a hardship anyway. He had enough exes in Magnolia Beach as it was, and no matter what people said, it wasn't easy to "still be friends" with someone after you broke up.

He'd have to face the music with Iona at some point, but for now the price of domestic tranquility and delicious food was ignoring innuendo and playing dense as a tree when she flirted.

Working long, unpredictable hours didn't hurt, either. Maybe he'd hold off looking for a partner at the clinic for a little while longer . . .

He burned his fingers on the plate as he took it out of the microwave, nearly sloshing the rich gravy off the edge. The smell made his stomach growl as he carried it to the table. Now ravenous, he grabbed a fork, only for his phone to ring before his first bite.

Almost any other ringtone would have been ignorable, but not Sam's. Since her divorce had brought her home—and back to Mom's house—over a year ago, she'd been a little fragile. And he could talk to his sister and eat at the same time, rude or not. He answered with a "What's up?" and shoved a forkful of pot roast into his mouth.

"Guess who got a new job today?" Sam singsonged, obviously in a good mood.

"That's great," he mumbled around tasty bliss, then finished chewing and swallowed. "Where?"

"Latte Dah. I'm a barista now." She rolled the *r* with gusto.

"But you don't even like coffee."

"Doesn't matter. I know how to make it, and that's far more important."

He put his fork down. "What about the library?"

"I'll still have that, too, if I want it. But Molly's offering more hours and better money. That means I'll have the money to get my own place even sooner."

Sam didn't like living with their mother—not that Tate blamed her—but she wouldn't move in to his extra bedroom, either, however temporarily. He sighed and rubbed his forehead. "I told you I'd give you the money so you could move out."

"And that's very kind of you, but no. I don't want your money," she insisted.

Stubborn girl. "Then why don't you come work at the clinic instead of picking up part-time jobs all over town?"

Sam snorted. "Besides the fact that I don't want to work for you?"

He sighed. "Yes, besides that."

"If I had any training or experience in the veterinary business, or even any interest in learning, I'd consider it. But I don't want a pity job from my big brother."

It was times like this when he wished Sam was more like their sister Ellie: sweet, quiet, and much more persuadable—at least when he was doing the persuading. But Sam . . . Sam often made him want to pull his hair out. They were too much alike. "It wouldn't be a pity job."

"Then what would it be exactly?"

He thought for a moment, then grinned, since she couldn't see it. "Nepotism."

"Because that's *so* much better." He could almost hear her eyes rolling. "Thank you, but no," she added seriously. "I need to do this myself."

"Sam . . ."

"Tate . . ." she echoed in the exact same exasperated tone. "I called you because I wanted you to be happy for me."

"And I am. I just don't want you killing yourself when you don't have to." He wasn't rich, but he could certainly help his sister through a bad time. If she'd just *let* him do it, for God's sake.

"Put your cape away, Superman. I don't need rescuing tonight," she said, as if she could read his mind. "Look, I know the offer's there," she continued in a much kinder tone, "and I promise I'll take you up on it if it all gets to be too much or goes rocketing into hell. But let me at least *try* to fix my life by myself first, okay? I got myself into this mess—and, well, I have my pride, too."

It nearly killed him, but he reluctantly agreed. Then he ate more pot roast to keep himself from arguing with her about it as she moved on to other topics. He'd just have to start hanging out at Latte Dah more when she was working and make sure to tip well. He could slip her a little extra so she couldn't refuse it without making a scene.

He heard his mother in the background, followed immediately by a muttered curse from Sam before she said she'd talk to him later and left him holding a dead phone. Sam's pride really *was* running the show; otherwise she'd be begging him for a loan to get her out of that house.

Hell, he knew that was why she'd gotten married so young, but since she'd been burned by her poor choices, she was being more careful now. And here he was with the money to help assuage his guilt for leaving her and Ellie there with their parents while he went to school, and she wouldn't take it from him. This was his chance to make that up to her, and she wouldn't let him. It was frustrating.

Ellie, at least, seemed happy enough, up in Mobile, married to a marine biologist she'd met when he'd been down here studying fish or shrimp or something like that. He couldn't complain about Doug—much—and she had the kids and some volunteer work to keep her busy. She'd warned him that it was best to let Sam find her own way, but at the same time she wasn't here dealing with their mother or watching Sam barely keep her head above water.

He ate more pot roast, but his irritation at the orneriness of all women in general had sucked all the enjoyment out of it. He swallowed the last few bites and stuck the plate in the dishwasher.

There was nothing he could do about Sam or Iona or anyone else tonight, and in a way it felt good to just accept that. Anyway, after the day he had today, he deserved a lazy, brain-dead evening of doing nothing. He grabbed a couple of Iona's cookies and took them to the other room with him.

He'd certainly earned them.

Chapter 2

"**Y**ou can do it, Molly."

Molly wanted to throw a cruller at Helena. Instead, she took a bite and chewed slowly, waiting for the urge to waste perfectly good pastries to pass. "Everyone keeps saying that and totally ignoring the fact that I probably can't."

"Only because you don't want to."

Helena's reasonableness was really grating Molly's nerves today. But Helena Wheeler was also her best friend and the only person she could really complain to about this without risk. "Here, then," she said with a smile, pushing a pile of Mrs. Kennedy's notes across the table to Helena. "Why don't you do it?"

Helena used one finger to gingerly push it back as if it might have claws to grab her and pull her in to the event against her will. "I've got enough on my plate, thanks. I'm on four different committees already."

"Who knew *you* were such a joiner?" When Helena rolled her eyes, Molly understood. "I see. That's what you get for sleeping with the mayor, honey."

"No," Helena corrected her. "That's what your boyfriend's mother does to you when you can't tell the woman no because she doesn't need another reason not to like you. It has nothing to do with Ryan's mayoral duties."

"It's sweet to see you in fear of your future mother-in-law." As if dating the mayor wasn't enough pressure to conform and behave, the Tanner family as a whole was kind of a big deal in Magnolia Beach. Molly remembered all too well the expectations that came with aligning yourself with *the* family in town—and especially formidable mothers-in-law. She patted Helena's hand as she got up to refill their coffees from the urn behind the counter. The shop was empty except for her, Helena, and Toby Baker over in the corner on his laptop frowning at his Great American Novel as he did every Wednesday.

"I choose to view it more like purgatory." Helena sounded resigned to the fact. "I've got quite a few sins to atone for."

"And your penance is coordinating bake sales and charity raffles?" She had a few sins of her own to atone for . . . Maybe that was why the Children's Fair had landed in her lap.

"And the annual Best Dessert Contest and the church rummage sale. It's the eighth circle of hell, I tell you."

Molly bit back a giggle. Poor Helena—also known as "Hell-on-Wheels" in certain circles—still had a lot to live down. Their wayward youths were something they'd bonded over when Helena had returned to Magnolia Beach last fall, but Helena was facing down her past with strength and class—and succeeding brilliantly. It was a little annoying, really, when Molly thought about it. "I'm surprised they let you in the door of a church."

"They're not too picky when it comes to sacrificial lambs." Helena accepted the refill with a grateful smile. "I'm just surprised you weren't suckered into doing anything long before now."

"I keep a low profile," she admitted. "*Especially* around sign-up sheets. But because everyone sees me all the time in here and around town, they just assume someone else has their hooks in me and that I must be doing something somewhere."

"Lucky," Helena grumbled.

It was both the blessing and the curse of owning a coffee shop: she knew everyone and everyone knew her, but the relationships were all pretty superficial. At first it had been a relief, giving her a clean slate and a chance to create her own story in a town that didn't know anything about her. She'd enjoyed the anonymity and the freedom and the simplicity of it all.

By the time it started to feel a little lonely, Helena had arrived and became the first *real* friend she'd made in Magnolia Beach, the first person she'd gotten close to in the last few years. "To be fair, though, I thought you'd have to wrest control of the rummage sale out of Edith Mackenzie's cold, dead, arthritic hands."

"The old guard is getting, well, *old*. New blood needed and all that," Helena concluded grimly. "It was bound to happen eventually."

"While that is both true and reasonable, it doesn't address the fact that I have the entire freakin' Children's Fair to deal with. I called Mrs. Wilson yesterday and you'd have thought she'd never even heard of such a thing being done before."

Helena snorted. "That's because Mrs. Wilson wouldn't touch the Children's Fair with a ten-foot pole." Molly felt her jaw drop, causing Helena to laugh. "She and Mrs. Kennedy had a huge argument over it about fifteen years ago," she explained. "No one seems to know exactly what it was about, but it was a whole big hoopla. Mrs. Wilson still chairs the Memorial Day committee that oversees all the events, but the Children's Fair is its own thing."

Typical. The one piece of gossip that would have been immensely helpful to know was the piece she'd never heard. "How do you know all that?"

"My grannie, of course." Helena grinned. "Mrs. Wilson

and Mrs. Kennedy are still friends and still play bridge, but they just don't bring up the Children's Fair."

"Then why did Mrs. K tell me to call her if I needed help?"

"Sheer perversity?"

"Great." She'd spent hours going over Mrs. Kennedy's notes the day before, but they were disturbingly incomplete to have been handed off to someone with no experience. Hell, she'd never even set foot in the Children's Fair area. She didn't even know exactly what the hell she was organizing. "I'm so screwed."

Helena sipped her coffee. "You should talk to Tate. I heard his name pop up in connection to the Children's Fair at one of my committee meetings. I'm sure he could sort it all out."

Tate was Helena's best friend, second only to Ryan in the "great and perfect men" pantheon. But Tate was Helena's champion, not hers, and Molly didn't necessarily share her friend's complete and utter confidence in his charity-organizing abilities. "Mrs. K mentioned him, too, but I can't seem to figure out exactly *how* he's involved with this," she hedged. "I see he's signed some checks, but . . ."

"If he's got hands in the money, then he knows something about it. Does it really matter how he's involved, as long as he is and can help?"

"Well . . ."

"Then call him up. You have his number, right?"

"Actually, no, I don't." She knew Tate, of course; he was Nigel's vet and often came in for coffee. And she'd gotten to know him better recently since hanging out with Helena also often meant hanging out with Tate. But they weren't *friends*; they were more like friendly acquaintances. Hell, she'd gotten to know Ryan a lot better in the last few months, too, but she wouldn't feel comfortable calling him up for a favor, either. Beggars really shouldn't be choosers, but . . . "I don't know. I'd feel bad for dragging him into my new mess."

Helena waved that away. "That's what friends are for."

"Tate's really more *your* friend."

"He's your friend, too," Helena insisted.

"But we're not tight or anything."

"You don't have to be for something like this." Once again, Helena was being very reasonable, but Molly wasn't sure she was in the mood for reasonable at the moment. She wanted more sympathy first.

But Helena *was* sort of right, now that she thought about it. Since at least half of the money raised from the Children's Fair supported the county animal rescue— and probably explained Tate's involvement with the event—it made sense for her to involve him. But it didn't make her more comfortable with the idea of asking him. Admitting her inadequacies to Helena was one thing. Admitting them to Tate was something else. But the other half of the money went to the women's shelter—a cause she supported wholeheartedly—so she had really big expectations sitting on her shoulders. And she didn't want to screw this up.

Helena glanced at her phone and tilted her head in apology. "I gotta run. I'm meeting Ryan for a late lunch."

She had a small smile on her face, though, which made Molly think they wouldn't be having that lunch at Ms. Marge's diner. Helena and Ryan were quite possibly the strangest match in Magnolia Beach—a reformed hellion and the town mayor sounded more like the premise of a romance novel than an actual working relationship—but they were happy and that made Molly happy. Plus, without Ryan Tanner in the picture, Helena would have gone back to Atlanta last fall, and Molly would have missed her new friend terribly. "That's fine. Just leave me here." She sighed. "I wonder if a million paper cuts count as slitting my wrists . . ."

Helena met her eyes. "Seriously. Call Tate."

She shrugged. "I'll keep digging through this, see if I can make heads or tails of it first. If I can't . . ."

"Do you have book club tonight?"

"No." Her "book club" had first been a cover for her trips to Mobile to see her therapist and then for that self-defense class she took. Why she'd felt the need to hide it, even from Helena, she had no idea. This wasn't Fuller, and people weren't keeping tabs on her.

"You haven't been in a long time."

"It kind of fizzled out."

"I'm sorry to hear that. Let me know if you want to start one up here. My brain could use the exercise."

Helena wanted to join a book club. She really was settling in. Molly laughed. "Talk to me after Memorial Day, okay?"

"So if you're not busy tonight, why don't you come to Grannie's for dinner?" Helena offered. "Grannie knows everything about everything, so between the three of us—and Ryan, too—I'm sure we can figure it all out."

Sometimes she forgot that this wasn't Fuller, and she wasn't on her own anymore. She had a posse—however small. "That would be great. Thanks."

Helena waved good-bye and nearly sprinted out the door.

Molly felt a little better. Ms. Louise would be an excellent—and obvious, now that Helena mentioned it—source of advice. And if the three of them couldn't get it figured out . . . well, she would just suck it up and call Tate.

She'd sworn to never sacrifice her pride again, but failure wasn't an option.

Desperate times called for desperate measures.

"I have been brought here under false pretenses," Tate protested to Helena. "I was promised food."

He'd been a little surprised at Helena's sudden dinner

invitation, but he was beginning to regret accepting it. She was his best friend, and he adored her, but friendship had its limits, and surprise grill assembly was definitely crossing that line.

"Oh, I'll feed you," Helena said, standing over him with a screwdriver in one hand and a drink in the other. "But I can't cook it until you put the grill together."

"And why isn't Ryan doing this?"

"He was supposed to, but there was an emergency at the Kaufmans'. He's been there all day with Colby."

Tate snorted. "An emergency? Right." Ryan was a general contractor, for God's sake. "What? The cabinets don't match the crown molding?"

"They had a bad water leak. Their ceiling is now on their floor." She shook her head, trying to shame him. "They have eighteen-month-old twins, Tate. He has to at least get their house in a livable condition."

So now he felt like an ass. But he was hungry and needed three E-17s to connect to the regulator thingama-jig and nothing in the pile looked like an E-17. He'd been working on this for over an hour now, and the actual cooking of food was starting to look like a pipe dream. They'd all starve long before then. "Call for pizza. On me," he offered.

The screen door slammed and Molly came down the steps onto the patio. "Helena, Ms. Louise needs you inside." Then she looked at the pieces of what should have been a grill, and an eyebrow winged up. "This does not bode well."

"I offered to spring for pizza," he said.

"You're a well-educated man," Helena said with a sigh. "All that schoolin' and you can't put together a grill?"

"I'll remind you that I'm a veterinarian. Does any part of this look like a Labrador retriever to you?"

Helena shrugged. "Well, maybe Molly can help you figure it out. I'm going to go see what Grannie wants."

"I'd be willing to go halfsies on the pizza," Molly muttered as she knelt next to the mess of parts and frowned. "I can't help but notice that Helena isn't trying to put this together."

"That's because Helena couldn't put two Legos together and she knows it."

Molly laughed and picked up the instructions. "That's mean."

"But true."

"Who wrote these instructions?" The laugh gave way to a frown. "Is this even English?"

"I need three of these," he said, pointing to the picture of E-17. "Do you see anything that looks remotely like it?"

Molly gamely joined him in sifting through the pile. "Not really," she finally admitted. "Wait, this might be it."

"Nope. I've already tried that. It's an E-19."

"Well, hell," she muttered and pushed her hair out of her face. He'd noticed that when she wasn't at Latte Dah, Molly let her blond curls roam free, and without the restraint of her headband, a rogue lock fell right back to its previous position. It was cute, and it made her look younger than he knew she was. "What about this one?" she offered.

"Nope."

"Darn." As Molly sorted, she made little organized piles, something he'd given up on twenty minutes earlier out of frustration. Her eyebrows were a shade darker than her hair, and they pulled together as she compared and then rejected each piece. They worked in silence for a few minutes, and it wasn't uncomfortable or anything, but he felt he needed to say something.

"How's Nigel?"

"Fat and sassy," she answered, same as she always did. The fact he knew that probably meant he needed to come up with something new to ask her. He searched for a different topic. "I hear you're taking over the Children's Fair."

Molly made an odd snort-like sound, but when he looked up, her face was calm except for a slight twitch of the corner of her mouth. "News travels fast."

"So it's going well?"

She shrugged a shoulder. "As well as could be expected."

"Meaning?"

Molly hesitated. "Mrs. K didn't leave very clear instructions as to what was happening. I'm still sorting through it all, trying to figure it out."

Understanding dawned. "Now I know why Helena suddenly invited me to dinner tonight." *Not that I'll ever get to eat.* "And here I thought the false pretense was the grill."

"I didn't know this was her plan. She invited me over saying she, I, and Ms. Louise could brainstorm and figure it all out." There was an apology in Molly's big coffee-colored eyes. "She never said she'd be dragging you into this."

"I believe you. This is just typical of Helena." He sighed. "So what's the problem?"

Molly seemed to be debating with herself. "I'm in way over my head," she finally confessed.

I'm going to regret asking this . . . "How so?"

"Honestly, I can't make heads or tails of Mrs. K's notes. I've never even been to one of the Children's Fairs, so I don't have a clue what's even *supposed* to happen there."

He'd agreed to serve on Mrs. K's "committee" in the first place only because it was really a committee of one, and Mrs. K micromanaged every detail. At the same time, there was an edge of desperation in Molly's voice that was impossible to ignore. And since the thing had been dumped on her without warning, he'd have to be a real ass to not at least *offer* what assistance he could. "I can meet you tomorrow if you'd like, and see if I can help sort it out and point you in the right direction. I confess I'm mainly a rubber stamp for Mrs. K, but I do have a basic understanding of how it all works."

"That would be awesome." The relief that crossed her face as the tension left her shoulders made him feel like Superman saving the day. "Come to Latte Dah? I'll buy you a cup of coffee . . ."

"I'll have to double-check my schedule at the clinic, but maybe around ten or so?"

"I'm available at your convenience. You're doing me the favor, after all."

He rolled his eyes at their current project. "Well, I'll owe you since you're helping with this."

To his surprise, Molly dropped the piece she was holding and dramatically dusted off her hands. "Oh, screw this. I'm going to declare that piece E-17 does not exist, therefore this grill is not going to be put together today. Helena can cook chicken breasts in the oven the way God and the creators of kitchen appliances intended us to do."

He laughed. "All-righty, then."

"Unless . . ." she backtracked.

"Unless what?"

"Unless your ego is caught up in this now and you have something you need to prove by completing it."

Molly was clever. Even if his ego had been invested, there'd be no way to admit that now without sounding like a complete tool. "Not in the least," he assured her. "Ryan can deal with this mess."

"Good." She pushed to her feet and dusted off the seat of her jeans. "I'm going to go give Helena our verdict."

He wasn't going to argue with that. Chivalry didn't include sacrificing *his* head to Helena when Molly was willing to take one for the team. Friendship had its boundaries.

Helena and Molly were an odd pair. Molly was sweet and sunny and perky, and Helena was . . . well, she was none of those things. Helena had sharp edges to her personality and could be downright prickly, whereas he'd never seen Molly with anything other than a smile on her face. What they had in common, he didn't know, and how they managed to get along so well was beyond him, but he was glad to see Helena with a girlfriend for once. And while most people were still a little afraid to get on Helena's bad side, it seemed odd that perky little Molly was not cowed by Helena at all.

He put the grill parts back into the box and made it back onto the porch about the same time Helena came outside. "Quitter," she said, shaking her head at him in disappointment.

"I gave it my best shot. Your poor planning isn't my fault."

"Poor planning?"

"Waiting until it's time to cook before making sure you have something to cook on? *Tsk-tsk*, Helena. Bad hostess."

She shrugged. "I guess I didn't get the party-planning gene."

"Are you *sure* you're Southern?" he said in mock horror as he collapsed onto the swing.

"Bite me." She nudged him aside and sat as well, putting the swing in motion. "So how's life? I barely get to see you these days."

"Busy, same as yours, which is why we barely get to see each other."

"Well, I'm glad you came tonight." She cut her eyes at him. "Even if you can't put together a simple grill."

"It's missing pieces," he reminded her. "That's not my fault."

"It turns out I forgot to get a propane tank anyway, so . . ."

Good Lord. "It's a good thing I gave up, then, or I would've had to kill you."

Not the least bit scared of that possibility, Helena waved a hand dismissively. "Molly already read me the riot act about that, so you don't have to. But dinner should be ready soonish. Grannie was precooking the chicken anyway."

God bless Ms. Louise. "Should we be helping?"

Helena shook her head. "You know how Grannie feels about men in her kitchen. That's why she sent me out here to talk to you."

"You're going to make your grandmother and Molly cook our dinner?"

Sighing, she leaned her head back and closed her eyes. "They both *like* cooking. And Molly's much better at it than I am anyway. And," she added primly, "it would be rude to leave a guest alone to entertain himself."

"Most people consider it rude to invite a guest over under false pretenses."

"I've apologized for the grill."

"I meant Molly and the Children's Fair."

Completely unrepentant, Helena shrugged. "Molly didn't feel comfortable asking you, and you'd have said no if I asked you, so I just gave you the chance to make it *your* idea to help her out."

"What would you have done if I told her no?"

She snorted. "Like that was even a possibility."

He looked at her. "I have no urgent desire to work on the Children's Fair."

"I know that, but I also know that you can't resist the chance to rescue a damsel in distress."

"That's not—"

"Don't even try to deny it," she interrupted. "It's sweet, really. But it makes you easier to play than 'Chopsticks.'"

He was tempted to prove her wrong, but that wouldn't be fair to Molly. "Such Machiavellian maneuverings."

Out of the corner of his eye, he saw Helena biting back a smile. "Oh Lord, what now?"

"Nothing."

She was up to something and it worried him. "What?"

"Let's change the subject," she said, a little *too* brightly. "So . . . how's your love life?"

"Just great. Thanks. And yours?" The answer and the tone were intentionally noncommittal.

"The same, of course," she answered flatly. "You seeing anyone?"

"Nope."

When he didn't elaborate, she elbowed him. "And why not?"

"Between the clinic, my family, and the rest of my life, there's not a lot of time." That wasn't a lie, and it was a convenient, if not terribly pleasant, truth.

"But you want to. Date, that is."

While phrased as a statement, it was obviously a question. And a very loaded one, by the tone of her voice. "What exactly are you asking me, Helena?"

She hesitated in a very un-Helena-like manner, which immediately put him on guard. Pausing the swing, she turned to face him. "I think you should ask Molly out."

It could have been worse. "Why?"

"Because Molly's great."

"I'm sure she is."

"So . . . ?" Helena prompted.

He nudged her foot, releasing its hold on the porch, and set the swing in motion again. "I've decided not to date locally."

"So it's a location thing?" Her brow wrinkled as she looked at him. Then she shook her head. "That's just stupid. Or are the ladies in Magnolia Beach just not good enough for you?"

"It's because I've got enough exes in this town already."

"Three."

"Excuse me?"

"You have three exes—at least serious ones: Jennie Daws, Tamara Chin, and Kara Moseby. I don't know about any flings. If you've had any lately, you must have been very discreet."

No one could give him a headache quite the way Helena could. He pinched the bridge of his nose. "And your point?"

"One, it's not like you're a player with a trail of broken-hearted women, and two, why are exes such a bad thing? Everyone knows everyone else's business anyway."

That was part of the problem, but it was a fact of life in Magnolia Beach. "It's a little different when you've been emotionally involved with someone."

Helena sat up straighter. "Are you telling me one or more of them broke your heart? Who? I'll kill her for you."

"Down, girl. My heart's in one piece, and the break-ups were amicable enough." He shrugged again. "I just don't like to be reminded of my failures."

"A failed relationship does not make anyone a failure," Helena said, indignant on his behalf.

"It's still awkward as hell."

"You're so sweet, Tate." She patted his knee. "But you need to get back out there. Otherwise, I might start thinking you're still hung up on me."

"You wish." Helena merely grinned at him. "Seriously, get over yourself." He'd told himself last fall that he had to give it a shot. That he'd *owed* it to his teenage self to finally make a move on Helena, just to see. He now wished he'd ignored that impulse, even if the true surprise had been how wrong he'd been about his feelings all those years. He was glad that Helena had turned him down—though it had stung at the time—but now he wondered whether he'd ever live it down. "I've known you for over twenty-five years. In all that time, I made *one* pass at you. That's hardly a reason for even *you* to think I've got some unrequited passion going."

"True." She thought for a moment, then frowned at him. "You know, that's kind of insulting, now that I think about it."

He patted her shoulder. "You definitely need to work on that 'getting over yourself' thing."

"So ask Molly out, then. There's no better way to force me to get over myself than by taking out my best girl-friend," she challenged.

"Iona would make my life miserable," he muttered.

"What?"

He was not going to try to explain that to Helena right now. "Nothing. Anyway, when would I find time to date? I can only barely manage to fit seeing you—my best friend—into my schedule."

"You don't find time, you *make* time, doofus."

"Helena . . ."

"You two have so much in common, and I think you'd be great together."

"I'm aware you think that."

As terrible as this conversation was, it was almost worth it to see Helena's confused and embarrassed reaction to that statement. "Really?"

"You're not nearly as subtle as you think you are. You've dropped hints before—not that you needed to. On New Year's Eve you couldn't talk about much else. And then you practically threw Molly into my arms at midnight."

"Oh." Helena looked a bit sheepish. "I don't remember that."

He couldn't help but laugh. "I'm not surprised."

"Everything after about ten thirty is a bit blurry," she confessed. "Molly's never mentioned it, though."

"Since you had me backed into a corner for the better part of an hour, I doubt you had much time to give her the same rundown of how great we would be together. In fact, she seemed a bit shocked at your demand I kiss her."

Helena dropped her face into her hands. "Oh God. I should not drink champagne."

"Maybe not."

Her bout of shame didn't last long, though. "But that doesn't change the fact that I think you two should at least go out. Just to see if anything sparks. She's pretty and smart and owns her own business . . ."

"Enough," he snapped. "I'm not going to ask Molly out on a date, okay?"

"Ahem."

The interruption had both his and Helena's heads snapping around.

Molly was standing half out of the kitchen door, eyebrows near her hairline in surprise. "This is either a very good or very bad time for me to interrupt," she said dryly, "but dinner is almost ready."

Damn it.

"Now look what you've done," Helena grumbled as Molly went back inside. Then she smacked him on the arm.

"*Me?* This is not my fault." He rubbed his arm. That had hurt.

"You've probably hurt her feelings."

"Only because *you* were badgering me. And anyway, I don't think Molly has any romantic feelings for me."

"Well, *now* she certainly doesn't. But that doesn't matter. No one likes to hear that someone's *not* interested in them."

"Then don't try to fix people up, Helena. It's extremely annoying and leads to situations like this."

Surprisingly, all the snap went out of Helena's voice. "I'll apologize to her—"

"Good."

"But you should, too," she said as she stood. Then she disappeared inside the house.

Tate leaned his head back and cursed softly. He would apologize, of course, because he certainly hadn't meant to hurt her feelings. He hadn't even meant to sound *that* repulsed by the idea.

He could only hope Molly would be just as understanding this time as she'd been on New Year's Eve, when she'd simply smirked and rolled her eyes before offering up her cheek for a kiss. They'd never mentioned it again.

If he was lucky, Helena would confess to her hounding when she apologized, giving at least a partial excuse for what he'd said.

It wasn't as if he had something specific against Molly. He'd been dating Tamara when she first arrived in town, and by the time they'd broken up, it was already well known that Molly had turned down every guy who'd asked her out, and she was just "Molly-from-Latte-Dah" to him by then.

And she'd remained just "Molly-from-Latte-Dah" until she'd become friends with Helena—and, by extension, him, too—so she'd never pinged on his radar in that way.

But now Hell-on-Wheels had dragged him into yet another fine mess, and he was going to be the one trying to clean it up.

Again.

For years, he'd been the one standing up for Helena when other people said she was bad news. A troublemaker.

Right now, he agreed with them.

Chapter 3

Under different circumstances, this would've been quite funny. And Molly was pretty sure that at some point in the future she'd look back on this and laugh.

Right now, though, it was pretty awkward.

She'd already had words with Helena about Tate once tonight. Inviting him to dinner so things could *casually* come around to the Children's Fair was just plain manipulative, and she resented being roped into it. But now . . .

She hadn't felt this humiliated in years. At least it was contained to only three people, but that barely mitigated the situation.

She hadn't heard much beyond Tate's avowal *not* to ask her out, so she had no context for the statement, but, honestly, would context help? There wasn't much to misunderstand, with or without the rest of the conversation.

She could guess at it, though. Helena had, once or twice—including orchestrating the most awkward New Year's Eve kiss ever—made it clumsily clear that she would like to see Tate and Molly together, but the idea wasn't completely out of left field. She and Tate occasionally did things with Helena and Ryan, and logistics often split them up like two couples instead of one couple and two singles. And she also understood the urge to fix up single friends once you were in a relationship.

And considering how important Tate was to Helena, Molly almost felt as if she should be honored that Helena thought she was good enough for him.

If only Ms. Louise had sent her out to get them just a few moments later . . .

Helena had whispered an apology in passing and promised to explain later, but Molly was planning to claim a headache and go home before this night got any worse. Tate looked distinctly uncomfortable when he followed Helena in a few minutes later, but Ms. Louise had called them all to the table before anything had been said.

Now they were all paying for that one moment with extreme awkwardness. The presence of Ms. Louise and Ryan's arrival with his dog, Tank—however tardy they might be—precluded any conversation about what had happened, which Molly was rather thankful for. The more she thought about it, the more she knew that actually having that conversation would only make the situation worse and more humiliating and should be avoided at all costs. So they sat there at the table, making small talk while Helena kept shooting her apologetic looks across her chicken and Tate looked as if he was ready to strangle someone—probably Helena. Ryan, bless him, was pretty much clueless about the undercurrents, and while Ms. Louise was probably aware something was going on, she was much too polite to bring it up.

It wasn't that she *wanted* to go out with Tate, nor did she necessarily want him to want her, but really, there was no way not to be a little bummed to hear it stated so baldly.

And now that she knew, and he knew, and she knew that he knew she knew . . . *Ugh*. There was no way for it not to be awkward as hell.

Oh God. What if Tate thinks I put Helena up to it?

If Tate didn't strangle Helena, she just might.

The unable-to-be-addressed tension put a bit of a damper on dinner. And since Ms. Louise and Helena were the closest thing to family she had, she looked forward to these dinners. She didn't want it to be strained and weird for everyone.

"Helena says you've taken over the Children's Fair for Mrs. Kennedy," Ryan said with just the right level of interest for the mayor to have.

That only served to remind her that she was now going to have to swallow a heaping serving of humiliation in order to work with Tate. *I have a meeting with him tomorrow, too. Kill me now.* "I have," she managed to answer.

"That's a big job," he replied, obviously not realizing how fraught that topic was.

"It'll be good to have some new blood in there," Ms. Louise said. "Eula's had control of it since God was a child, and she's way too possessive of it."

"Grannie . . ." Helena scolded gently.

"I've said the exact same thing to Eula's face many times." Ms. Louise was not in the least bit contrite over her words. "That's how you end up killing things." She turned to Molly and smiled warmly. "I'm sure you'll do wonderfully at the helm."

"Thank you, Ms. Louise. I realize it's a big responsibility I've been entrusted with, and I hope I can run it half as well as Mrs. Kennedy."

"That's very diplomatic of you, dear." Ms. Louise bit back a small smile. "Make all the changes you want. Eula will get over it."

Remind me not to underestimate the cattiness of little old ladies. But it was nice to hear Ms. Louise had faith in her. It both buoyed her and warmed her. Ms. Louise wasn't one to offer empty flattery, so her words carried oomph. "Helena told me you might have some ideas you'd like to see implemented. I'd love to hear them—or any other advice you'd like to offer."

"Me? No. I don't think I've set foot inside the park during the Children's Fair in years. I'm happier over with the bake sales and things like that. I wouldn't have a clue where to begin."

So the whole evening had been a setup. *I'm going to kill Helena Wheeler.*

"Tate's going to help Molly get everything sorted," Helena offered.

Grannie smiled. "That's good. I'm glad to hear you'll be getting more involved with things, Tate. I'm sure the two of you will make a great team."

"Oh, I totally agree. They'll be wonderful together," Helena added, ignoring Tate as he quietly choked on his drink.

Molly kicked her under the table.

"Ouch." Helena gave her a look, and Molly stared her down, hoping Helena got the very real threat of bodily harm being sent telepathically.

"Are you okay?" Ryan asked.

"I'm fine. Just bit my tongue." Then Helena smiled the fakest smile ever as she turned to Tate. "Can we expect exciting and fun new things from you two?"

Molly wanted to kick her again, but her foot only found air where Helena's legs used to be.

"Probably not," Tate said. "It's a little late in the process to make too many changes. But speaking of fun and exciting things, did I hear you say that you and Ryan had set a wedding date?"

It was Helena's turn to choke as Ryan quickly looked at his empty plate as if he'd never seen it before. Ms. Louise perked up at that question, saying, "How wonderful!" as a huge smile spread across her face. Had she been closer, Molly would have given Tate a high five for turning the tables like that. She loved Helena, but that was completely deserved.

Instead, a glance at Helena's face had her standing. "I'll clear some of these plates away." She wanted to get out of the line of fire—just in case.

"I'll help," Tate added, jumping up and following her into the kitchen, leaving a hushed yet fervent conversation behind.

While she understood Tate's need to get out of there, she was a little worried about being alone with him in the kitchen. What if he wanted to talk about it now? She needed time to prepare herself, to figure out what the hell she was going to say before she had that conversation. She could only hope Tate would choose to pretend the whole thing had never even happened. That would be grand.

"Helena will kill you for that," she said, stacking dishes in the sink.

"Probably. But she deserved it." Tate leaned against the kitchen table and crossed his arms over his chest. "Look, Molly, about earlier—"

Damn. She grabbed at the first available topic to sidetrack him. "I wanted to talk to you about Nigel."

Tate took the change in topic in stride. "Is he okay?"

"Yeah, um . . ." Now she had to come up with a question. "I think he's starting to get a little chubby."

"His weight was fine at his last visit, right? Did I tell you he was getting into the danger zone?"

"No, but . . ."

"Pet him and see if you can feel his ribs. If you can't, he's overweight, and you'll need to put him on a diet. When's he due to come in again?"

"A couple of months." Tate's efficient answers suddenly had her wondering whether she'd felt Nigel's ribs recently or not.

"Unless you think he's really packing on the pounds,

it's probably not worth a special trip to see me. If it's just a little flab, cut back a little on the amount of food you're giving him and try to get him some more exercise. If you're worried, though, I'd be happy to check him out."

"I don't think it's that urgent." But now she was a little worried.

He nodded. "Good. So . . ."

She was searching for another topic to keep him from going back to the one she wanted to avoid when she was saved by Helena, hands full of dishes, sliding the door between the kitchen and the dining room open with her elbow. Helena shot Tate a dirty look. "You're dead meat," she threatened, sliding her load onto the counter. "You did that on purpose."

"Yeah, I did," he said, completely unrepentant. "It serves you right."

"What did I do?" Helena protested, all innocence.

"Embarrassing me and Molly like that?"

"Only three people at the table had any idea what I was teasing about, but now you've gotten Grannie's hopes up about a wedding that's not happening anytime soon. It crushed her when I told her you were just kidding. You should be ashamed of yourself."

"*Me?* You're the one—"

Molly eased toward the door. Usually it was amusing to watch Tate and Helena bicker, but she wanted to get out of there before the topic rolled back around to her. She was almost out when Helena glanced over.

"Wait a second . . ."

"I've got a busy day tomorrow. Thanks for dinner, Helena." She nodded in Tate's direction. "I'll see you later."

Saying good night to Ryan and Ms. Louise was not as easy, as Ms. Louise seemed determined to talk about wedding dates and Ryan seemed to be dodging the subject with some amazing verbal gymnastics.

"Are you not staying for coffee?" Ryan asked, the desperation clear on his face.

One benefit of owning a coffee shop was the ease with which she could refuse others' offers of coffee—either they assumed she was over coffee in general or they assumed their coffee wouldn't be good enough for her. Neither assumption was correct, but Molly wasn't above playing that card when she needed to.

"No, I can't. Thanks, though. Dinner was wonderful, Ms. Louise, as always. I'll see y'all later." She stopped long enough to pat Tank's head. He was a rather funny-looking dog, being hairless and all, but there was something irresistible about him, too—mainly because he thought he was a much larger dog than he was.

On the porch, she took a deep breath. Some people might consider this to be a cowardly retreat, but staying really wasn't an option. She understood why Tate had brought up the wedding, and it was a fair play, but she didn't have a dog in the fight. Helena's wedding date was not her business until Helena informed her it was.

She had very strong feelings about that, both because marriage wasn't something people should be rushed or pressured into—she knew firsthand exactly how bad a disaster *that* could be—and because she really tried to stay out of things that weren't her business.

Even if she didn't feel that way, a strong sense of self-preservation would keep her out of it tonight. Tate could risk his life in that mess all he wanted. *She* was staying the hell out.

Clouds had moved in as the sun set, cooling things down and making her wish she'd brought a sweater for the walk home. She'd run home, even in these shoes, both for the exercise and the heat, except she was way too full to consider that kind of exertion. She could walk fast, though. It wasn't but a few blocks.

It was quiet outside, with most folks home for the

evening, and the people in the houses were backlit behind their curtains as they moved around. A few folks were still out walking their dogs or taking after-dinner strolls, and she could hear the shouts and laughter of children playing nearby as a man's voice called them inside.

At the foot of Ms. Louise's driveway, she paused long enough to pull out her phone and check her mail—just long enough for Cindy Claris to spot her and break into a trot down the sidewalk, dragging her Chihuahua, Itsy, behind her as she tried to catch up. "Molly, wait!"

She did, and Cindy came to a stop beside her a few moments later, panting from the brief run. Itsy danced around her feet, seemingly delighted at the change of pace.

Cindy started in on a long, convoluted story involving Latte Dah, the War Memorial, and the Fourth of July parade, but Molly was having a hard time making the connection between the three things. Since she hadn't been drinking, she had to wonder whether Cindy had been. "I'm not sure I—"

She was interrupted by a loud barking, followed by shouts of "Tank! No!" and Itsy trying to climb Cindy's leg as a small dark smudge dodged around them in the twilight. Without thinking, she reached down and grabbed Tank's collar, stopping his pursuit, and scooped him into her arms, where he wiggled furiously and alternated between growls and barks.

Tate was only seconds behind, apologizing profusely at letting Tank past him and trying to soothe both the dogs and Cindy. Cindy, though, was convinced Itsy had suffered trauma—psychological, if not physical—from Tank's bolt in her direction, so Molly carried Tank back up to the porch, where Ryan was emerging to find out what was going on.

"Sorry, Cindy," he called in that direction, lifting Tank out of Molly's arms. Dropping his voice, he explained, "He doesn't like little dogs."

That was funny, since Tank probably weighed only six or seven pounds himself. "I don't think he got hold of Itsy," she assured him. "He just startled everyone."

"Damn," Ryan said, surprising her.

Looking over her shoulder, Molly saw Cindy stalking across the yard in high dudgeon. "Oh. Good luck with that."

At least she'd escaped Cindy's confusing conversation, she thought with a small twinge of guilty pleasure. Cindy would follow up eventually, but maybe when Molly wasn't so full of baked chicken and Ms. Louise's famous potato cheese casserole the conversation might make sense. Or she'd at least have more patience for it.

Tate was waiting at the end of the driveway where Cindy had left him. "You okay?" he asked.

"Fine. Tank didn't do any damage to Itsy, did he?"

He shook his head. "Nah, Itsy's fine."

"Oh, good. Well, good night, then." Belatedly, she noticed only Helena's and Ryan's cars in the driveway. Which meant Tate was on foot as she was. And since he lived two blocks past her house, he'd be walking in the same direction. If Cindy hadn't stopped her, she'd be far enough ahead to avoid Tate offering—

"I'll walk with you."

There was no way to politely decline, which meant the uncomfortable kitchen conversation she'd avoided was now simply going to be her uncomfortable walk-home conversation instead.

She scrambled to gather her thoughts. As she knew fine well, no one liked to hear, "I'm not interested in you," and, dinged pride aside, she saw no reason to throw something like that in his face out of petty revenge. Tate was nice, and cute, too—tall and broad shouldered with inky black hair and bright blue eyes. If she were shopping the market, he'd be an excellent choice. But she wasn't, so it didn't matter. Now she just needed to get back to the friendly-acquaintance footing they'd lost tonight due to Helena's meddling.

Please just let it die a quiet, non-embarrassing death.

No such luck. They were barely out of earshot of the house when Tate said, "Can I apologize now?" His voice was a mix of exasperation and teasing, and he wore a self-deprecating smile that was really kind of charming.

"There's no need. Really."

He sighed. "When Helena gets an idea in her head . . ."

"She's tenacious about it, I know. And I know she means well."

"Still"—his voice turned serious—"what you heard me say . . ."

"It's fine. My feelings aren't hurt." The need to strangle Helena was coming back full force, though.

"It's nothing personal. You're a very nice person. You're beautiful and funny and smart . . ."

"And you're not interested. I get it. It's okay." She tried to sound reassuring, but Tate just shook his head.

"I'm just saying it's not you personally, or anything like that."

"Good to know." Before he could go on any further, she moved in front of him and held up a hand. "Can we stop this now? I don't *want* you to ask me out."

Tate pulled back a little, and she felt bad almost immediately. She hadn't meant for the words to come out so sharp. But the surprised look that followed nearly made her laugh. He hadn't been expecting *that.* He might not want to ask her out, but considering there were plenty of women in Magnolia Beach—and the surrounding counties, too—who'd be more than happy to grab him right up, her words had to have been a shock. Considering he'd been an unwilling participant in the evening's farce, she'd give him a pass for including her in that bunch of women. But only this one time, and only because he was Helena's friend. Plus, she reminded herself, no one liked to hear something like that.

He cleared his throat. "That makes this easier, then."

"Exactly." It was still awkward, though, and after a few more throat clearings and random looks around, they finally started walking again. Quietly, this time, thank goodness. The breeze kicked back up and Molly ran her hands over her bare arms to rub the chill bumps away.

"You cold? Take my hoodie." He was already shrugging out of it.

She shook her head. "It's a little chilly, but I won't freeze between here and home."

"I don't need it," he insisted. "I only have it with me because Helena borrowed it last week and returned it to me tonight. Here." Tate held it out, gentleman-style, ready for her to slide her arms in, and further refusal would just make her look silly.

The hoodie held his body heat, chasing away the chill immediately. As she zipped it up, she could smell the spicy scent of Tate's aftershave. She'd noticed the scent before, but from a respectable distance where it had been only a faint aroma. This time, it surrounded her, filling her nose and lungs each time she inhaled. It was nice.

Unsettlingly nice, actually, and it took her a moment to figure out why. It was just so utterly, unabashedly *male*, and coupled with the warmth of his body and the loaning of his clothes, it pushed the right set of buttons in the right order to cause a little flutter low in her belly.

Maybe if Helena hadn't had matchmaking on her mind, therefore putting it in *her* mind, this wouldn't be happening. She'd never denied Tate was a hottie—she wasn't blind, after all—but she'd never let her thoughts wander past that to the man himself.

It wasn't that she hadn't noticed; she just hadn't noticed like *that*.

But it was a lovely evening and she was on a quiet walk with a good-looking, smart, and kind man who smelled nice and had the good manners to offer her his jacket.

It was downright *romantic*.

And now she seemed to be noticing him in a big way.

It had been so long since she'd thought—really *thought*—of any man in that way, she figured her ovaries were all but dust anyway. Finding out that wasn't the case was nearly overwhelming.

And very disconcerting.

Damn Helena for putting ideas in her head.

No longer even the least bit chilly, she unzipped the hoodie to midchest to let the night air cool her down at the same time she started walking a little faster.

Four more blocks.

If Tate noticed the change of pace, he didn't say anything, and his long legs easily matched her stride. She didn't realize she was mumbling under her breath until Tate looked at her oddly.

Keep it together.

"I wanted to say thanks for giving my sister a job," he said, choosing a new topic. "She's really excited, even if she doesn't know anything about coffee."

It was such a complete change from where *her* mind had been that it took a second for her to process the shift. Once she did, though, she grabbed on to the topic like a lifeline. "I'm glad to hear it. She's got the right personality and attitude for the job, and that's the most important thing. Everything else is teachable."

"Can I ask how much it pays?"

Molly nearly tripped over her own feet. She gave him a hard look. "Why? Are you planning to apply for a position?"

A smile twitched at the corner of his mouth. "No."

Nosy big brother. "Compensation is negotiable and

those negotiations are private," she said in her most businesslike tone. "Ask your sister if you want to know."

"Like she'd tell me."

"Then don't ask me to."

"Fair enough. But do me a favor and don't tell her I
was asking." There was that grin again, and she felt it all
the way to her toes. *Damn it.*

"Of course not. I think it's very sweet that you're so
concerned about her." She was still way off balance men-
tally, but at least she could handle this conversation.

"Can you convince her of that?" Tate shoved his hands
in his pockets and leaned in to her as they walked. "She
thinks I'm just being nosy," he admitted.

"Should it come up in conversation, I'll do my best,"
she promised.

The corner of her street, where she'd be able to turn
right, finally appeared like an oasis in the desert. "This
is my stop. Thanks for walking with me." *Please don't
let him be gentlemanly enough to walk me all the way
home.*

"My pleasure."

She reached for the zipper of the hoodie. "Here. Let
me give this back."

Tate's hand landed on hers lightly. "Keep it. You can
return it later."

The touch was brief and not at all inappropriate, but
it gave her a jolt, and the warmth lingered even after he
returned his hand to his pocket.

She needed to have her head examined. "Well, good
night."

"Good night, Molly." There was a moment of awkwardness before Tate nodded at her and left, disappear-
ing almost immediately into the shadows outside the
streetlamps' glow.

With Tate away, the tension dropped out of the air,

but Molly was still left with a reservoir of tingly energy in her belly she didn't want to examine too closely.

Because it would prove she was certifiably insane. She had no business getting those kinds of tingly feelings.

Once safely inside her house, with Nigel winding around her ankles, she stripped off Tate's hoodie and dropped it into a chair.

She could still smell him, though.

But alone in her kitchen, she could at least think rationally. In the two-plus years she'd been in Magnolia Beach, she'd never looked at Tate as anything more than just another guy in town, and he'd certainly never given her the slightest reason to. Just because she'd suddenly discovered she still had a functioning—or *mal*functioning, depending on how she wanted to look at it—libido, nothing good could come from acting on this newly discovered information. This was all crazy and needed to be stuffed back into the box it came out of.

She had enough on her plate and plenty of worries on tap.

This was something she simply couldn't contemplate.

Chapter 4

By the next morning, Molly had it all straight in her head.

She'd spent some time reading last night, and all her books seemed to say that the feelings stirred up were *good*, however inconvenient they felt now. It simply meant that she was healing, and when the time was right, she'd be ready to find someone, start dating, and maybe even fall in love again.

That was a good thing.

The Children's Fair might also be indirectly responsible, too. Being entrusted with a big job by people she respected—however scared she might be about that—was an ego boost, and her brain was just exploring that new confidence in different ways, one of them being the reawakening of her libido.

As for why her brain had picked Tate—well, that was explainable, too. Tate was genuinely nice, the complete opposite of Mark in everything from looks to personality. He was the good friend of a good friend and therefore trustworthy. He'd offered to help her in her time of need, and American culture had all but trained her to go all moony-eyed when Prince Charming rode up on a white horse to save the day.

It didn't hurt that he was damn cute, too.

And a good-looking, kind, trustworthy man who was willing to help her out of a tight spot without first negotiating for something in return ... *Of course* she'd be attracted to that. Who wouldn't be? Tate was just lucky she hadn't swooned into his arms last night from the shock.

She didn't need to worry about her sanity. The wires might be crossed in her head, but that was okay. Now that she understood *why* she'd had that reaction last night, she could deal with it. It wasn't completely Helena's fault—although she was still to blame—and Molly didn't need to worry about being around Tate now.

Her reaction had just been a confluence of many things. It would work itself out. She'd be fine. It was all perfectly normal, and, honestly, a very good sign.

She couldn't—and really shouldn't—act on any of it, of course, but it meant she was getting there.

Progress was often slow, but it was good, and once she progressed through *this* stage, the Tate-tingles wouldn't be an issue.

After so much thinking last night, she hadn't gotten much sleep, but she was in a good mood opening Latte Dah anyway.

She no longer had to dread her meeting with Tate. It was still going to be a little awkward and uncomfortable, all things considered. But she'd just act as normal as possible, treat him the same way she always had before, and this would pass.

A little after ten, the chimes over the door rang, and she looked up to see Tate.

"Sorry I'm a little late. Crazy morning," he added with a smile and a shrug of explanation.

There was definitely something residual from last night happening in her veins, but she ignored it. "It's fine. Is everything okay?"

"Just the usual stuff," he answered, as if she was supposed to know what that might mean. She didn't, but she nodded anyway.

"Can I get you something?" she asked.

"Coffee would be great."

She waited, but Tate didn't expound on his order. "Want to narrow that down for me?"

Tate laughed. "Guess I need to. Just plain coffee. Nothing fancy."

"That's easy enough." As she poured, she saw Tate looking around, a little crease forming between his eyebrows.

"Did you paint in here?"

"No. Why?"

"It looks different somehow."

She looked around, trying to see if anything was out of place, but it was just Latte Dah: sea blue walls loaded with old photos of Magnolia Beach she'd found at a church rummage sale, overstuffed couches, tables with mismatched chairs—also from the rummage sale—all shabby chic and intentionally homey. "I don't know why," she finally said.

"Maybe I'm just tired or something." He shook his head as if to clear it. "How's Nigel?"

"Grumpy. I think he knew I wanted to check his weight last night and wouldn't let me pet him."

He laughed. "They do seem to know, don't they?"

Tate seemed to be acting pretty normally, not showing any lingering effects of last night's debacle, but then why would he? *He* wasn't the one who'd spent the majority of the evening examining his psyche for cracks. If he wanted to forget the entire evening ever happened, she was good with that.

Tate accepted the coffee with a nod of thanks, and she gestured toward the table where she'd stacked all of Mrs. Kennedy's notes. "Let's talk about the Children's Fair."

He sighed. "I don't know why you're freaking out over this," he said calmly.

She was not going to dignify that with a list of reasons why freaking out was the exact correct response. Hell, back in Fuller everyone would be in a panic on her behalf. No, in Fuller, no one would dream of putting her in charge in the first place. They knew she was a screwup, too flaky to be trusted not to burn the whole thing down. And while she was trying to think positively, deep down she was afraid they were about to be proven right. There were still plenty of reasons for Molly to be worried. Tate was just obviously one of those people who *didn't* freak out about things, which was practically a guarantee he was going to grate across her last nerve very shortly. "Beyond the fact that this is quite an important piece of the weekend's festivities that needs to be done right if I'm ever to hold my head up in town again, the truth is I have zero experience planning anything like this."

"Attitude and personality are what's important. Everything else is teachable," he reminded her.

"You're real funny."

"I try." At her look, he lifted his hands in defeat. "Okay, joking aside, show me what you've got."

"Thank you." She led him over to the table where her carefully organized stacks of Mrs. Kennedy's notes lay, yellow sticky notes hanging off their edges where she'd written questions or notes to herself. Tate settled his lanky frame into one of the ladder-backed chairs and pulled the first stack toward him. "That, as far as I can tell, *might* be contact information for the people involved," she said.

Tate chuckled. "That would be my guess, too."

"But it doesn't match up to her list of vendors or volunteers, and *that* list doesn't match up to last year's site map"—she handed the map over when he held out a hand—"that shows where everything was set up. So I can't tell who's even supposed to be there."

"Can you call Mrs. K and ask her?"

"I *could*, I guess, but until I have a better grasp on what I've got here, I don't know what to ask." Plus, that would be admitting defeat before she even got started. She still had a little pride she wanted to hold on to. So far, Helena and Tate were the only people who knew how clueless she was, and she'd like to keep it that way for as long as possible.

Tate nodded. "Let's start with the site map, then. I can help you reconstruct the list of who was there last year." He met her eyes. His were blue—*really* blue, she noticed, before she forced herself not to. Tate didn't seem to notice her noticing at all, thank goodness. "I will say that I'm sure everything's in good shape," he assured her. "We're less than five weeks out, so most of this is probably in place already."

"That's my hope."

"Mrs. K has done this so many times, it's probably all organized perfectly—only all the details are in her head."

"Which doesn't help me much," she grumbled. But she was relieved to hear that nonetheless.

Tate pointed to a big area on the map. "So that's the petting zoo there. Cliff Hannigan brings the animals in."

"I've seen that name somewhere," she said, flipping open one of Mrs. K's notebooks as Tate made notes on one of the sheets. He was left-handed, she noticed, and moved his coffee cup out of the way. "He judges the dog show, too, right?"

"Yep. But that's not you."

"It's not?"

"No. That's Sunday after the parade."

"Yay." She drew a line through that item on her list. "One less thing to worry about."

Tate nodded but didn't look up, busy as he was labeling the map and annotating her list, occasionally pulling out his phone to look up a phone number or e-mail address and add it.

His confidence and no-nonsense, get-it-done attitude was a balm to her nerves, and she recanted her earlier assumption that he'd grate on her. She'd never spent much time with him alone before now, and she liked the efficient and organized way he worked. There was no unnecessary small talk, either, which made this easier for her.

She sat back sipping her drink and watched him for a minute. He had good posture, she noticed; although he leaned forward over the table as he worked, he wasn't hunched up, and his shoulders—broad like a swimmer's—were held straight, the green stripes of his shirt running almost perfectly parallel across his chest without a wrinkle. Dark hair fell over his forehead when he leaned over to look at something, softening the angular line of his jaw and prominent cheekbones.

There was that tingle again, but it was easier to mute today. She was making progress already.

She searched through her mental gossip file. Many a young lady had a crush on Dr. Tate Harris, and while he had a couple of exes, there didn't seem to be any drama there. The only woman he was ever linked to was Helena, and that, she knew, was platonic. From a purely objective standpoint, Tate Harris was quite the catch. Why, then, was he still single?

Suddenly, those blue eyes were staring at her. "What?"

She cleared her throat. "What what?"

"You're staring at me. It's making me nervous."

Crap. She searched for a reasonable explanation. "Just wondering how you got pulled into this."

An eyebrow arched up. "You were all damsel-in-distress last night, remember?"

She sat up straight, a little indignant at the comparison. "I do *not* damsel-in-distress."

"Then I'll just saddle up my white horse and ride out of here." He pushed his chair back from the table.

"I do appreciate your coming to my aid, though," she said quickly to mollify him, and he pulled his chair back again. "But you were *already* involved in this circus."

"It's not a circus. It's a *fair*," he corrected.

"Whatever. How'd you get sucked into Mrs. K's pet project anyway?"

He shrugged. "With all the animals, it made sense for the clinic to be a sponsor, and it's important to participate and be a part of things and . . . um . . ." He trailed off almost sheepishly.

She didn't believe that at all and couldn't believe he thought she might. She just looked at him and shook her head.

"Fine." He sighed. "I have a hard time telling little old ladies no, okay? You happy now?"

That made her laugh, and it took the edge off, making her feel almost normal around him again. "Yep. That's kind of how I got into this. I'd hate to think I was the only weenie in town."

Tate frowned at the "weenie" comment, but he let it pass. "It's diabolical; that's what it is. I think this is why we're raised to respect our elders. It makes us easy pickings later, because we can't say no without being rude and bringing down the wrath of our ancestors on our heads."

It would have been funny if it hadn't been absolutely true. "And that's why I'm reluctantly running a children's fair complete with a face-painting booth and—" She squinted at Tate's list. He had the handwriting of a doctor, all right. "What are 'dours'?"

"That's 'clowns.'" He crossed it out and rewrote it a bit more legibly.

She repressed a shudder. Clowns creeped her out, but now probably wasn't a good time to mention it. "See? It really is a circus."

Tate's cup was nearly empty, and habit had her taking it for a refill before he could ask. On her way back, she grabbed a lemon bar from the pastry case to take with her to the table as a thank-you.

Setting it beside Tate's coffee, she said, "You are an angel and a saint to help me with this."

Tate looked at the lemon bar and then at her, his eyes narrowing suspiciously. "I'm helping you with *this*," he said emphatically, indicating the mess on the table. "*Just* this part. The getting-you-sorted-out part."

"You can't be serious." At his nod, she added a guilt-laden wheedle to her voice. "You can't abandon me in my hour of need."

"I'm not. I'm here in your hour of need. But only this *particular* hour of need. No way am I getting hip deep in this."

Doing her best to flutter her eyelashes and look pitiful, she said, "I'm still damseling *and* distressing, though."

Tate rolled his eyes at her sudden about-face. "You are not sucking me in. I will get you going in the right direction. I will sign your checks and back your plays, but the details are all you."

She tried to flutter again. "Tate . . ."

"You are not a sixty-something-year-old woman, so I *can* still tell you no." He grinned at her. "Flutter those eyelashes all you want, honey. It won't work on me."

"Fine." She pulled the lemon bar back to her side of the table. "But I'm blaming you if it all goes to hell."

"I have no problem with that," he countered. "But I do want that lemon bar."

"I don't think so," she said, picking it up as if about to take a bite. His eyebrows went up. This was suddenly fun.

"Even if I told you I'd decoded Mrs. K's notes and had all the answers you seek?"

She paused, the lemon bar inches from her mouth. "Do you?"

"Give me the lemon bar and find out."

The door opened and a small group walked in. She looked over and called out, "Hi! Be right with you," then turned back to stare Tate down. "*Do* you?"

He looked pointedly at the pastry in her hand. With a sigh, she set it down on the plate and slid it over to him. He picked it up immediately and took a bite, claiming it as his before she could reconsider. "Now go take care of your customers."

"You're terrible, Tate Harris."

"But I'll have this budget sorted out by the time you're done with them," he promised with a cheeky smile.

Damsels in distress can't be picky about how they get rescued, she thought, and went to help her customers.

Molly didn't exactly flounce away, but it was close—and kind of funny. He'd never sparred with her before like that, but it had been more fun than he'd anticipated and, more importantly, meant that last night's awfulness had been forgotten—or at least they would pretend it had never happened.

He still wanted to strangle this newfound need to meddle out of Helena, but Ryan would probably protest.

He had to give Molly props, though. She'd been a good sport about the whole thing, at least up until he'd doubled down on the fiasco with his apology. He might not have hurt her feelings, but he now knew exactly how she'd felt when she'd heard him snap at Helena. It was definitely a ding to the ego; that was for sure.

Especially since she'd been so very *earnest* in her declaration. That level of frankness wasn't just her trying to salvage her pride.

And, yeah, it stung.

He'd gone home and eaten the cookies Iona had made in her quest to win his hand, wondering—just a little— what about him had caused that level of distaste in Molly.

It wasn't as if he could ask, though, so he'd been left wondering.

And since she was being so friendly today, it made him wonder even more.

He watched as Molly seemed to be debating the qualities of two different kinds of coffee with her customers and wondered why Helena was so gung-ho on fixing Molly up with him. Pretty, smart, successful business owner, kind—all the fine qualities Helena was marketing were all right there on display. Her charms weren't some well-kept secret or anything. If Molly wanted to date, she shouldn't have any problem finding someone.

So why was she single, then?

He scrubbed a hand over his face. That wasn't his business, and why did he care? He was here to sort out Mrs. K's disaster of a record-keeping system, not ponder Molly's love life.

Just before he went back to the paperwork mess in front of him, he saw Molly smile at her customers. And while he'd seen her smile hundreds of times—the woman was always smiling, it seemed—this time he realized that it was always the exact same smile.

That made him pause.

Molly certainly wasn't afraid to tease or flirt—after all, she worked in the service industry; it was practically part of her job description—but it was always safely within the expected and socially approved boundaries. He thought about the conversations he'd had with her. At Latte Dah, she was professional, perky, and friendly. When she brought Nigel into the clinic, she was friendly, perky, and concerned. Around Helena, she was friendly, perky, and fun. Half of what was so strange about last night was that she *hadn't* been like that. It was what had led him to offer his services today—*not*, as Helena wanted to think, due to some desire to play Lancelot. *Sheesh*.

Right now her face was open and interested as she

talked to her customers—exactly the same as it usually was.

The more he thought about it, the more he realized that Molly acknowledged people, included people, and even listened to them, but she didn't actually *engage* with them, even though it seemed like she did. It had to be intentional, and she was so good at it that he doubted anyone ever noticed the difference.

But now he had noticed, and it seemed downright strange. In fact, her plea for help, her admitted confusion at the mess Mrs. Kennedy had left her in, and the frustration exposed by Helena's clumsy attempts at matchmaking probably meant he'd had more deeper and meaningful conversations with Molly in the last twenty-four hours than he'd had in the last two and a half years combined.

Helena considered Molly a good friend, and Helena had no patience at all for shallow or superficial people. It would stand to reason, then, that Molly had to regularly engage with *her* on some genuine level. Which meant Molly was actively choosing to keep her interactions with other people—including him—very superficial.

Of course, Molly might just be a naturally private person—a hard stance in a town this size—but, try as he might, he couldn't dredge up much "widely known knowledge" about Molly Richards beyond the basics. And he'd actually *spent* time in her company and had a common friend. That just crossed straight into weird.

Now he really was curious.

Molly pulled out one of the maps provided by the tourism board and pointed something out to the customers. That jarred him into remembering what he was supposed to be doing right now.

And it wasn't delving into the psyche of Molly Richards, as interesting as that might be.

He looked at the pile of papers in front of him. Half

the problem was that Mrs. Kennedy had never thrown anything away, so some of her notes and lists were years old. And since he doubted Molly had set foot in the Children's Fair before, she'd have no way of knowing that, making this overwhelming. All the information she really needed equaled maybe twenty of the two hundred or so pieces of paper Mrs. Kennedy had dumped on her.

Once he'd pointed her in the right direction, she'd be fine. If she could run Latte Dah, the Children's Fair shouldn't be much of a problem.

And while he didn't want to be dragged into the minutiae of planning, he did have an interest in its success—which was why he was here sorting things out for her. But as he'd learned the hard way, *showing* any interest in the success of an event was often interpreted as an offer to volunteer—if not run it single-handedly. That was something he simply did not have time for— even if he did have the temperament to deal with Mrs. Kennedy and her cabal of a bridge club.

He snorted quietly to himself. Everyone knew who really ran this town—and it wasn't Mayor Tanner and the council.

Two other customers had come in, keeping Molly busy behind the counter and giving him a few much needed extra minutes after his mental wanderings into Molly's life had put him behind. Hell, a good spreadsheet program was really all Molly needed. The budget was actually pretty simple—the point was to raise money, after all, and aside from some table and tent rentals and a little printing, there wasn't a lot of overhead as it was mostly people volunteering their time.

Volunteers were on a separate list, which he labeled in large letters across the top.

Pushing the other piles of paper into an untidy stack,

he carefully lined up the edges of the important ones and centered them in front of the chair where she'd been sitting earlier. Then he leaned back in his chair, crossed his arms over his chest, and smugly waited for her to look his way.

When she finally did look over, eyebrows raised in question, he smiled back at her as it registered on her face that he was done with the task. Then he picked up the lemon bar and finished it off.

A few minutes later, Molly finally came back to the table. "You're done? Really?"

"Of course. I told you I would be."

Her mouth twisted. "How very annoying."

That was not what he'd been expecting to hear. "Why is that annoying?"

"I spent *hours* going through all of this. You show up and *presto!* Either you're a genius or I really suck."

"I am a genius, of course." He waited for her to frown at him, and she did. "And you don't suck. The truth is," he said, dropping his voice to a confession-level whisper, "I've worked with Mrs. K on this long enough to not only know the basics of the event, but also how her mind works."

Molly didn't look mollified in the least.

"But honestly, all of your extensive sorting and organizing made this so much easier," he added.

"Of course," Molly said, with just enough sarcasm to assure him she didn't believe that at all. She sat and picked up the stack he'd left for her.

"You might want to contact everyone—the vendors, the volunteers, and all—just to get on top of everything, but the big picture is all there."

It took him about half an hour to walk her through that big picture—Molly had to get up at least twice to care for her customers—but he could tell she felt a little better about the event once he was done. "I'm sure it will be the best Children's Fair ever," he concluded.

Her eyes flew to his face. "Bite your tongue."

"Excuse me?"

"I don't want it to be the best. I just want it to be good enough."

"Good enough for what?"

"Good enough for it to be a success, but not so good they'll want me to do it next year."

"Smart girl." He could tell she was only half joking. She obviously took this responsibility seriously, if grudgingly.

"And what about all this other stuff?" She indicated the large pile of leftover paper.

"Stick it in a bag and hand it to Mrs. K when she gets back."

"I owe you big-time, Tate." He could almost see the tension leave her shoulders. Despite her words, she not only wanted to do it right, she *cared* about doing it right. "Thank you," she said, reaching over to gently squeeze his forearm. "Really."

Her hand was cool and smooth, and his muscle jumped at her touch, sending a jolt through him. He'd felt it last night, too, when he'd touched her, but he'd chalked that up to the stress and tension of the evening overall. Having it happen again was just . . . weird. He cleared his throat. "No problem."

Molly looked at her hand as if she'd never seen it before, then moved it to her lap with forced nonchalance. "You should probably leave now."

Not entirely sure what he'd done, he was lost for words now. But her tune and 'tude had certainly changed. "What?"

Her head tilted in the direction of a large wall clock. "Samantha's shift starts in about fifteen minutes. She

might be early for her first day—I know I would be—
and do you really want to be here when she arrives?"

And have Sam think he was checking up on her? *Hell
no.* "Good point. How much do I owe you?" he asked,
reaching for his wallet.

She waved him off. "It's on me. It's the very least I can
do in return for your help today."

Grabbing his jacket off the back of the chair, he
shoved his arms through the sleeves. "If you have any
other questions—"

An eyebrow went up. "Call Mrs. K?" she supplied.

That made him laugh. "Bye, Molly."

"Bye, Dr. Harris."

He was waylaid on his way out by Heather Jones
wanting to ask about the possibility of Prozac for her
dog—a dog that simply needed obedience classes and
a long, exhausting walk each day, although Heather
wouldn't believe him no matter how many times he told
her—and Sam was arriving just as Heather was walking
away.

She eyed him with extreme suspicion.

"Don't look at me like that. I'm not here to check up
on you."

"I want to believe you—"

"Then please do."

Her eyes narrowed. "But your past behaviors kind
of damn you outright."

Like it's a bad thing I want to look out for my sister.
He sighed. "I came to talk to Molly about Memorial Day
weekend activities. She's the one who set the meeting
place and time."

"Really." It was a statement, but a disbelieving one.

"Ask her yourself."

"I will. *Bye* now."

The emphasis on him leaving was impossible to miss.

"Good luck," he said over his shoulder, leaving her in the doorway to Latte Dah.

Odd as his conversation with Molly had been, it had one thing going for it that made him happy.

It proved there was at least one woman in Magnolia Beach who not only *asked* for his advice or help, but was willing to actually *take* it as well.

How refreshing.

Chapter 5

*A*ttitude was important. Everything else could be taught.

Three days later, Molly wanted to pat herself on the back for hiring Samantha Harris. Samantha still needed cheat sheets for recipes, and she was a little intimidated by the cappuccino machine, but she had a knack for creating rapport with customers and being attentive to their needs. The people she knew—more than half the clientele—teased and encouraged her and seemed to have great patience with her learning curve, but that rapport building meant the customers who didn't know her also had no problems with her lack of speed and occasional confusion, either. She had charm and wit and was cute as a button, too. She was going to do just fine at Latte Dah.

Plus, the girl could upsell like a master car salesman.

"Don't you want to take a cookie home to Anna? She's four now, right?"

"If you're going to the council meeting, you might want to get a large coffee instead of a small. Don't want to fall asleep in the middle of it!"

"We have this coffee mug with a puppy I swear looks exactly like your Muffin. She was such a great dog. You must miss her so much. Here, let me show you."

Samantha did it all with a great smile and genuine interest, and damn if they didn't all buy what she recommended.

Molly was updating the payroll with Samantha's information while Samantha frowned at the cappuccino machine again. "I promise it won't bite you," she said with a smile.

"I just don't want to break it."

"Well, I don't want you to break it, either, because it's an expensive machine, but at least show it who's boss, Samantha."

"You can just call me Sam."

"Which would you prefer?"

Sam looked up. "Excuse me?"

"I've heard you called both, but noticed you put Samantha on your name tag. I thought maybe you preferred that over Sam. I mean, my real name is Marlene, but my grandmother always called me Molly. It stuck and I like it, but I know not everyone likes their nicknames."

Sam thought it over for a minute. "I actually like Sam better, but I always start out with Samantha. Later on, when someone calls me from across the street, I know if they're a friend or an acquaintance."

"Very smart." She totally understood. Being Molly all the time instead of Marlene or Marley was a nice line between old and new, Fuller and Magnolia Beach, and one of the many perks of moving to a town where no one knew her before she was Molly.

Sam was studying her, head tilted to one side and eyebrows forming a little V over her nose. She'd seen the exact same look on Tate's face before when he was thinking hard, and at that moment she realized how much the siblings looked alike. She knew Tate and Sam had another sister, and Molly vaguely wondered whether the resemblance was strong there, too. She'd met Mrs.

Harris a couple of times around town, but it was clear Tate and Sam took after their late father.

She and her sisters were split—Jolie looked like their mother, Molly looked like their father, and Hannah was a perfect combination of both. Hannah had definitely gotten the better roll of the genetic dice there. Personality-wise, both her sisters were *just* like their mother, though, and if that was the price of beauty in the Richards family, Molly was just fine being the ugly sister.

But Sam's scrutiny was starting to make her a little nervous. "You don't look like a Marlene," Sam finally declared. "A Marley maybe, but not a Marlene."

While she agreed, she wasn't sure what Sam meant by that exactly. "Um, thank you?"

"You're a great Molly, though," she said with a smile. "Your grandmother gave you the perfect nickname."

"Thanks."

Sam wiped her hands on a towel, then walked over to the little counter area Molly used as an office during the day because her real office in the back was both claustrophobic and a disaster of Superfund proportions. "You know, to be honest, I don't really feel like a Sam *or* a Samantha," she said.

"What's your middle name?" It hadn't been on the paperwork.

"Diane." She wrinkled her nose. "I'm definitely not a Diane. I don't feel like I'm a Dee or a Di, either."

"What do you feel like, then?"

Sam thought for a minute. "A Chloe, maybe." She laughed. "But I don't see how I could pull that off. Even if I legally changed my name, it'd be too much trouble to get anyone around here to switch." She laughed. "I'd have to move somewhere else and start from scratch."

Don't knock it till you try it, honey. "Well, the slide from Marley to Molly isn't that far. Sam to Chloe is a leap."

Sam shrugged. "I guess I'm stuck with Sam, then."

"If it makes a difference, I think you make a great Sam."

"Thanks, Marley."

Her stomach clenched. "Don't call me that." As hard as she tried to keep her voice light and teasing, even she could hear the strain and the snap underneath. "It makes me think of Jacob Marley from *A Christmas Carol*," she said with a small laugh, trying to smooth it over. "I really don't want ghostly visitations screwing up a good night's sleep."

"Especially since you come in so early."

"Exactly."

Sam sighed and shrugged her shoulders. "So what can I do now?"

Honestly, there wasn't much for her to do right now. The few customers currently in the place were fine, and Sam had already straightened and wiped and swept. The girl either had endless energy or was trying to impress in these early days. Molly normally did paperwork during these lulls, but that wasn't something for Sam to help with—yet. Jane would sometimes knit or do a crossword puzzle when things got really slow, but somehow that felt like the wrong message to send in Sam's first week on the job.

God knew there were half a dozen things *she* could be doing, but Molly couldn't leave Sam alone just yet, simply because she might need help with a complicated order. She could show Sam how to do something like take apart and clean the machines, but while that would be helpful for Sam, it would only put Molly further behind today.

"I guess just make sure everything is stocked, check the milk pitchers—"

"I already did." Sam tapped the folder next to Molly marked "Children's Fair." "I could help you with that, if you need me to. Tate told me how Mrs. Kennedy kind of dumped it on you without warning."

"Thanks, but that wouldn't be fair to you. It's not in your job description."

Sam shrugged. "I don't mind. I've helped with it before. Not in the last few years, admittedly, because I wasn't here."

And that, Molly knew, was because she'd moved to Gulfport with her now ex-husband. It wasn't a topic Sam had broached with her, but it wasn't exactly a secret, either. She wasn't going to go there, though. It wasn't her business, and she didn't know Sam all that well, but she could still sympathize. At least Sam had realized her mistake quickly and had been able to get out before investing years into a rotten marriage. "Really?"

"Of course. I had to volunteer somewhere, and I like kids."

"I meant . . . you really wouldn't mind helping me with this?"

"Oh, sure. I've got to do something, 'cause I don't want to just stand around. I know you're not paying me to do that. And since I figure I'll need to be here the day of, at least I can say I did something to help."

This girl truly is a godsend. Molly handed her the phone. "I'm trying to touch base with everyone, just to make sure I've got them on the right list doing the right thing. For the vendors, I need to make sure the list of what we're supposed to be providing for them is correct, too."

"I can do that. No problem." Sam flipped open the folder.

Without that job hanging over her head, Molly found it much easier to concentrate on her task, getting payroll finished easily and paying bills. She was also half listening to Sam's side of the conversations—just enough to know that her carefully made lists weren't *too* wrong. *Yay me.*

Sam, it turned out, was a lefty like her brother, and

she had that same good posture she'd noticed the other day—no hunching over the papers as she worked. Both Harris siblings were tall and lanky, but both seemed blessed with the natural grace of athletes. Where Sam was built like a runner, with long legs made for jumping hurdles, Tate's build was definitely like a swimmer's, powerful but lean . . .

Good Lord. She had to stop these random Tate thoughts. Frankly, it was starting to freak her out. It didn't matter how much she'd rationalized it all in her mind. The simple fact was that she'd been just fine for *years*, and then one night, out of nowhere, Tate Harris had helped her into a warm, nice-smelling hoodie, and it flipped her switch. Suddenly she was pondering the breadth of Tate's shoulders as if she had some kind of reason or right to. And since she couldn't admire his physique without visualizing how it was achieved, she'd been picturing Tate swimming laps. In small trunks, the water sluicing over his back . . .

She gave herself a hard mental shake. Long-term celibacy was obviously not good for her mental health. Unless, of course, she *wanted* training montages and soft-core porn running through her mind at inopportune and highly inappropriate moments.

Like while you're training his little sister how to make espressos, maybe?

Yeah, very inappropriate.

And the images just wouldn't stop. Eventually they would—they *had* to—but until then . . . She shook her head and went back to the accounts payables in front of her, but the numbers didn't make any sense anymore. Her focus was shot now, and she knew it would be a little while before she was able to get it back.

"So is Tate driving you crazy?"

Molly jumped at the question, nearly knocking over her cup in the process. "Excuse me?"

Sam indicated the list she was working on. "That's Tate's scrawl. I'd recognize it anywhere. If he starts getting all control-freaky on you, just let me know."

Oh. That. "He's been nothing but helpful."

Sam snorted. "That's how he sucks you in."

"I don't quite understand."

"My brother wants to be Grand Master of the Universe, butting into everything and telling you how it should be done."

She recognized sibling irritation and exasperation when she heard it. "I'm sure he means well." *Unlike* my *sisters.*

Sam rolled her eyes. "Of course he *means* well. That doesn't make it less annoying, though."

Considering how Tate had already questioned her about Sam working here before she'd even started . . . "You're his baby sister. Isn't butting into your life what big brothers do?"

"Maybe. But he gets carried away sometimes with being 'helpful'"—she included the air quotes—"and crosses right over into 'won't leave you alone about it.' If he starts that crap with you, let me know and I'll get him to back down before he drives you screaming into the bay."

"I doubt that will happen. Tate got me sorted out only because I promised I wouldn't expect him to get more involved."

"He talks a good game, but once you let him in your business . . ." Sam sighed and shook her head. "Someone should have warned you that the boy's got serious control issues."

She'd never gotten that vibe from Tate, but she could see where Sam could confuse helpful concern with control—they were siblings, after all. But the slightly ominous "someone should have warned you" gave her pause. Tate was certainly active and involved in many things, but control-freaky? Surely Helena would have mentioned that before tossing her into the pot. That said, Tate and Helena bumped heads pretty often, each calling the other nosy and bossy. It was worrisome. She came from a family of control freaks and had married into a family of control freaks, and she knew this would not end well. "I'll keep that in mind," she said as the door chime went off and she turned around.

Speak of the devil. Helena waved as she entered and dropped her laptop at her favorite table close to the far wall. Helena liked to work in here; she said there was something very inspiring, yet relaxing, about the atmosphere.

Helena might feel differently after today, though.

Molly hadn't seen her in the last few days, although that might have been intentional on Helena's part. Helena had apologized again the day after that debacle via text, but Molly had been so busy getting the fair sorted out and training Sam that she hadn't had time to respond properly. She intercepted Helena before she got to the counter to order and steered her back toward the table, out of earshot of Sam. Helena's eyebrows went up. "What's up?"

"I thought I'd give you the chance to talk me out of poisoning your coffee."

At least Helena wasn't one to play dumb. "I'm sorry about the other night at Grannie's."

Molly waited. "Because . . ."

"I didn't mean for your feelings to get hurt."

That was missing the point entirely. "My feelings didn't get hurt." *Much.* "The only thing I felt was humiliated."

"That certainly wasn't my intention. And if it makes you feel better, Tate's chewed me over it quite thoroughly. I will not meddle like that again."

"Promise?"

"Cross my heart and swear to give up coffee if do."

Helena took her coffee almost as seriously as Molly did. "I'm going to hold you to that."

"Tate says he apologized, too. He really didn't mean it the way it sounded."

"He did apologize. Very sincerely. I'm not sure which one of us was more embarrassed over the whole thing."

"You're both overreacting, then."

So much for contrition. "Careful. You'd hate to get nothing but decaf here in the future."

Helena shook her head, horror on her face. "You wouldn't."

"Don't tempt me. It might keep you from having the energy to cause trouble."

"My intentions were good," she protested. "And I swear I really did think I'd seen some interest there before and was just trying to help it along."

Huh? "From Tate?"

"From you, actually."

Oh my God. That wasn't possible, but what was she doing that could be so misread?

Helena shrugged. "But I guess I was wrong. Or I was reading it wrong because I wanted it to be true. Maybe there's someone *else* you're interested in?" There was a hopeful, yet obviously prying, note in her voice.

"No." *I may have answered a little too quickly there.*

"At all? Why not? You've said yourself that the singles scene in Magnolia Beach is a little underwhelming, but there are a few decent guys around." Helena pulled out a chair and motioned for Molly to sit. "I've never pried before—"

Molly shook her head at the proffered chair and rested her hands on the back of it instead. This wasn't cozy-time girl talk, and she wasn't going to pretend it was. "And I appreciate that very much. It's one of the reasons I like having you as a friend."

"Okay, so . . ."

She couldn't tell Helena the truth, and she didn't want to lie. That rather left her at not saying anything at all. "Look, we are strong, intelligent women with lives and jobs and interests. Must we fall into the misogynistic stereotype of being consumed solely by the need to find a man?"

Helena's lips pressed together. "Well, if you're going to put it like that . . ." She sighed. "I will butt out."

"Thank you. Now, about manipulating Tate—and me, for that matter—"

"What?" Helena was all innocence.

"Your little dinner party?"

"Oh. That." Helena shrugged. "You needed help and wouldn't ask. Tate likes to fix things. Seems less like manipulation and more like helpfully creating a solution, if you ask me."

"Nice try. First of all, that's just wrong, and you know it. You should be ashamed of yourself." Helena, though, didn't look the least bit ashamed. "And secondly, Sam's just been telling me Tate's some kind of control freak once he's involved in something. What have you gotten me into?"

"You have to consider your source on that. Tate's just a typical oldest child—and a big brother to boot. He helped raise Sam and Ellie, so he sometimes crosses the line and gets nosy and bossy, and Sam just chafes against that."

That was slightly reassuring. But . . . "I've heard you say the same thing."

"Tate's like a brother to me. Same situation. Mostly, though, he really just wants to help. It's kind of a thing for him. If you ask me, it's because of his parents. There was a lot of chaos at his house growing up, and Tate has always been the one to smooth things out—especially for Sam. Think of it more as 'superhero coming to save the day' instead of 'control freak.'"

That struck a nerve unexpectedly. She didn't want to be saved. It was one thing to ask for some guidance, but she sure as hell didn't want "saving." Not now. She wasn't helpless. "I'm not sure that's better, you know."

"Of course it is."

Arguing with Helena was slightly less satisfying than arguing with a brick wall. She knew that Helena meant well, but . . . "If you ever want coffee again, you have to swear to stop meddling. Across the board," she added as Helena tried to interrupt.

Helena's lips pressed into a thin line.

Molly raised an eyebrow.

With a long-suffering sigh, Helena finally conceded. "Fine."

Victorious, yet magnanimous in that victory, Molly patted Helena's arm. "Good. Now you can have your coffee."

"Thank God." Helena threaded her arm through Molly's as they walked toward the counter. "I'd have agreed to pretty much anything you asked with the threat of a coffee embargo hanging over my head. But—" She paused before they got within Sam's earshot. "When you are ready to talk about it, I'm willing to listen."

The sweet sentiment should have warmed her. Instead, it felt like an icy rock in her chest. She merely nodded. "Sam? Do you want to get Helena's coffee?"

Sam jumped up immediately, grinning at Helena. "Sure. Give me something complicated. Challenge me."

"I'll be back in a second," Molly called over her shoulder as she went to the back, leaving Helena and Sam in an intense discussion. In her tiny, messy office, she closed the door and leaned against it.

She hated being secretive, but how could she explain

it all to Helena? Her marriage, her divorce, her family . . . it was all one big disaster area, and she couldn't explain any one of the situations without getting into *all* of them, and even just considering it made her head hurt and her stomach churn. Helena wouldn't judge her or anything—Molly knew that—but it was just embarrassing more than anything else. And she didn't want the pity—not even from Helena.

It was also frustrating, and a real beating on her ego, to relive the past—two more things she didn't need more of.

But she also wasn't going to let all that crap steal what pleasures she did have out of her life, either.

She just needed to get through this, and everything would go back to the way it was.

She hoped.

Tate knew that if he were a better person, he wouldn't mind so much. After all, his mother did carry him for nine months, suffer through twenty-six hours of back labor—he'd finally looked that up online to see what she'd been talking about, and yeah, it did sound like it sucked, but it wasn't like he'd done it intentionally—and feed, clothe, and house him for eighteen years. But he wasn't a better person, so spending his Saturday afternoon basically repaying his mother for that made him grumpy. Still, he wasn't a *bad* person, and he never could manage to flat-out hate his mother, either, so he'd do it and keep his bitching about it to himself.

It wasn't the physical labor he minded—some of this was his junk, too—and if there had been a way to do this without his mother's involvement, there wouldn't have been a problem. It was the emotional game playing, the intentional blindness, and the dishonesty of the whole thing that grated on him.

He tried to be understanding. Mom had been cowed

by his father, and where would she have gone if she had left him? At least she and her kids weren't homeless and starving. Maybe if she'd at least admitted that much out loud, he'd be *more* understanding, but Mom's denial was absolute. He could fight the battle and be frustrated or he could accept things for what they were.

Acceptance seemed the better choice.

But his mother had been toying with the idea again that she might move to Waycross to live with her sister, and she'd been leaning on Sam to start cleaning out sheds and garages in preparation for that possibility. And while it was more than likely *not* to happen, Sam was tired of the nagging.

And while Tate really didn't want to be here on a beautiful spring day cleaning out his father's man cave, here he was. His mother had refused to set foot in that shed since she'd found Frank Harris's body in it eight years ago. So the only alternative would be to leave Sam to deal with it all herself, and he certainly couldn't do that. Not again.

Intellectually, he knew he'd done the right thing by taking the opportunity and going to school, just as he knew he couldn't have taken Sam and Ellie with him, no matter how much he wanted to. But he couldn't forget the looks on their faces the day he actually left. While Sam and Ellie both claimed to understand and support that decision, there was simply no way to forget it. He'd been Sam's hero until that day, but now she wouldn't take a shred of help from him. He'd betrayed her, and he didn't know if she'd ever really forgive him for it.

"Any idea what this is?" Sam held up a triangular piece of metal that might have once been blue before left to rust.

He forced himself back to the task at hand. "Trash."

"I know, but what is it really?"

"Trash," he insisted.

Sam laughed and added it to the growing pile. "At least this is easy."

"I told you to throw a lit match in there. *That* would have been easy."

"There might be something of value in here. You never know."

He snorted. His family had never had much money—just enough to keep them respectable. There were no priceless heirlooms hiding out here. He pulled out a box marked "Old Clothes" and opened the lid. "Do you think this stuff is even worth donating?"

"Just set it aside. Terri might want the fabric for one of her crafts if the clothes are too dated to donate."

He moved it to the trash pile. He was not going to shuffle this crap around.

Sam caught him. "Hey, now."

"Trash, keep, recycle, donate." He pointed to each pile as he named them. "Pick a pile. There are only four choices and 'Cousin Terri might want it' isn't one of them."

"Fine. Just let me go through it first." She pulled a few things out. "Hello, 1987."

"I told you," he said when Sam closed it back up and shoved it over to the trash pile.

"It was worth a look, at least."

"Why?" He really just wanted to get this done as quickly as possible. Being out here was just picking at old wounds to see if they still hurt.

"Like I said. There might be something valuable in here. People have found original copies of the Declaration of Independence cleaning out old storage sheds and attics."

"I'm going to go on record now saying we aren't going to find something like that." Sam tossed a look at him over her shoulder as she disappeared back into the darkness. "Your best hope is that the junk man doesn't charge us a fortune to haul off all this crap," he called after her.

"Too bad we can't trade the bottles and cans in for cash." She appeared carrying another box that clinked as she walked, adding it to the recyclables pile. "We'd be rich."

Tate just shook his head. How the old man had managed to not die of alcohol poisoning long before his heart gave out had to have been some sort of medical miracle. In a way, he wondered whether this was why his mother "couldn't bear" to help with this project. Would she not be able to keep up her denial in the presence of solid proof? Or did she just really not want to have to face that truth?

"It's such a waste." Sam sighed.

Tate looked at her sharply, unsure what exactly she was referring to. The possibilities were endless, it seemed.

"Nothing quite like tossing out the remains of what could have been your college tuition, you know?"

Since Tate had enough student loan debt to send most people into heart palpitations—and only the string pulling of Doc Masters with the scholarship committee had kept that amount from becoming enough to give *him* palpitations—he knew exactly what she was talking about. "If you want to go to school, Sam—"

She waved him off. "One step at a time, bro. Believe it or not, I do have a plan."

"And that plan is . . . ?"

"Excellent and well thought out. Trust me."

He would have to. For now, at least.

God, just being here was messing with his head. He tried to shake it off.

Instead of pressing for the details of that excellent and supposedly well-thought-out plan, he wiped the sweat off his neck and pulled out the sawhorses that had supported the optimistically named "workbench" and tossed them into the trash pile.

It wasn't exactly a hot day, but they were both sweating

from the work and grimy from the years of dust. Sam had a long black smudge across her forehead and Tate's T-shirt was sticking to his skin. Looking at what they'd accomplished in just a few hours was impressive, but knowing how much was still left to do was disheartening.

Two boxes marked "Ellie" were set over to the side. Neither Tate nor Sam had opened them to even see what might be inside. The boxes caught his mother's eye as she came out with plastic cups of ice water for them. "Why don't you bring those into the house? I'll call Ellie and get her to come down and go through them next week."

Sam gave him a careful look and shook her head, forestalling anything he might say. "Sure thing."

"You're making a lot of progress," his mother said. "It's like a treasure hunt."

"Yeah," he said. "Sort of." *A sad, twisted one with nothing good to find.*

"I'm making lunch now, so I'll call you in when it's ready." Then she left, pointedly not sparing a glance at the collection of liquor bottles that outsized everything but the trash pile.

"Ellie's not going to come down here. When will Mom accept that?"

While their family dynamics might politely be called "complicated" and "requiring therapy," Ellie's husband had made his stand very clear very early on. There was no polite whitewashing of the truth by him: Frank Harris was a violent alcoholic who abused his family. Doug hated the father-in-law he'd never met—which was probably a good thing, as even the kind, even-keeled Doug might not be able to resist dealing out some justice on his wife's behalf. Doug might pity his mother-in-law, but he could not forgive her for not protecting her children and he didn't exactly encourage Ellie to visit the old homestead.

Tate liked Doug a lot for that.

"I know," Sam said. "But do you really want to get into that with her right now?" She shot a look at the house.

"At some point we're going to have to. That much denial can't be healthy."

"Can it wait until I have my own place again?"

Hell, they'd avoided it for twenty-something years now, so what was the real rush? He nodded.

"Good. I'll go through those boxes later and see what's in there. I'll call Ellie, and if she wants any of it, one of us can take it next time we go up."

"What will you tell Mom?"

"I don't have to tell her anything. She knows Doug doesn't like her, even if she doesn't know the truth why. She likes playing the poor, mistreated, and misunderstood mother-in-law."

"Our family is so messed up."

Sam laughed, but it was the hollow, humorless kind of laugh that spoke to resignation more than anything else. "There's no such thing as a functional family anyway. Every family is messed up in its own way." She slid Ellie's boxes off to one side with her foot. "At least *we're* not too screwed up from it."

"That's debatable."

"'We cannot let the hurts others inflict on us darken our own souls.'"

It was such an un-Sam-like statement that he nearly dropped the box he was carrying. "What the hell?"

"It's a quote from a book Molly loaned me. I'm finding it very helpful." There was a defensive edge to her voice, daring him to make fun of her.

"Molly's loaning you self-help books?"

"Yes. And I appreciate it, too. They make a lot of sense."

"I never thought you'd be the type to go for that new-agey drivel." He wouldn't have thought Molly would be, either. She seemed so happy and well balanced. Why on earth would she need self-help books? On the other hand, hadn't he just realized that Molly might not be exactly what she presented? Maybe the self-help books were part of that mystery.

"Molly said that book really helped her, so I'm inclined to think it's not drivel." She shrugged a shoulder. "Or at least I'm willing to give drivel a try."

Maybe Sam had some answers. "You and Molly must be getting pretty tight, then."

"I wouldn't say we're 'tight'—Molly's not the tell-you-everything type—but when things get slow, we talk." Sam looked at him and smiled. "I like her. I can see why she and Helena are such good friends."

"Oh?"

"Helena and Molly both run deeper than they appear. I mean, you *think* you know them, but when you try to put your finger on it, you realize you really don't."

He knew Helena better than anyone. But Molly? Sam was right about that.

"Say, did you know that Jane's pregnant?"

He was still examining this new information about Molly and her self-help needs, so it took him a second to catch up after Sam's non sequitur. "Jane Searcy?"

"Yeah. She's just starting to tell people."

"Tell her congratulations for me."

"I will, but I'm telling you because that's good news for me."

"Because . . ."

"*Because* Jane's going to cut down on her hours at Latte Dah, probably going to part-time once the baby arrives. That means more hours for me. Rachel and Holly can't pick up many extra hours because of their school schedules. I may even get a promotion."

"Did Molly tell you that?"

"No, Jane did."

"And you want a long-term career as a barista?"

"I like the job. The money's good and the people are nice. I can't complain about it."

"I'm glad."

She shot him a cheeky grin. "Glad I can't complain?"

"Well, yes. But more glad that you're getting it all sorted out." He knew that Sam had secretly hoped her marriage would turn out like Ellie's, keeping her away from all this. It took guts for her to come back and start over when that didn't pan out. He just wished Sam would let him clear the path a bit. It was the very least he owed her.

"We all make mistakes." She shrugged a shoulder. "I could be worse off than I am, you know. I have a place to live, I'm in no danger of starving, and I'm digging myself out of my mess. It's all good."

"I'm proud of you."

"Gee, thanks." She rolled her eyes, preparing to flounce away.

"That was honesty, not snarkiness," he assured her.

"Oh. Well, thank you." She gave him a small smile, then straightened her shoulders and looked back at the mess still awaiting them in the shed. "You know, your 'cleanse it with fire' idea is really starting to look good."

"I'm still standing by it."

Sam drummed her fingers against her thigh. "Do you know Dennis Handry?"

Only because Dennis did some dog walking and pet sitting and had put some flyers up at the clinic. "Not personally."

"He's trying to save up some money for a trip this summer."

"Okay . . ."

"He's a smart kid, easily able to tell trash from possible not-trash . . ."

"I like how you think, Samantha Harris." He stood and wiped his palms on his pants. "Put him to work and have him send the bill to me."

"Only if you let me pay half. Or at least a third—we should hit Ellie up, too. It's only fair."

Not if he could help it. "Whatever works." He'd worry about the fallout of that lie later, but for now Sam was following his lead, and he'd take that as a win. He didn't want to spend his free time out here in this dismal shed with all its bad memories. He felt lighter and cleaner already.

Sam smiled. Maybe she felt it, too. "Then let's go get cleaned up and eat."

"One second." There was something he needed to do.

Inside the shed, hanging off a shelf that held an old ashtray and a fifteen-year-old radio, was his father's belt. When he came outside carrying it, Sam scowled. "Why do you want that?"

"I don't."

He took it over to the grill and laid it on the rack. After dousing it in lighter fluid, he held up a match. "You want the honors?"

"Be my guest."

The lighter fluid burned with a blue flame, but the old leather didn't catch well, just smoldering and blackening instead.

Sam frowned, disappointed. "It's not going to burn."

"It doesn't have to." He'd made his point.

Sam squeezed his hand. "You're right."

They watched it for another minute, not saying anything. Then Sam tugged gently on his arm. "Let it go."

"I have."

He left it there, still smoldering, and went inside.

Chapter 6

The Frosty Freeze had to be responsible for most of the heart disease in the county, but that knowledge wasn't enough to temper the occasional craving for one of their bacon-chili-cheese hot dogs. Even Dr. Tanner and Dr. Richey, who should be the *leaders* in denouncing such a thing, could occasionally be seen at one of Frosty Freeze's weathered picnic tables indulging that craving. It made Molly feel a little less guilty when she also gave in.

"You're going to get chili on the checkbook." Tate grinned as he swung a leg over the bench on the opposite side of the table and sat. Even after a lot of stern chats with herself, something about that grin still did funny things to her. She took a deep breath and tried to focus.

"I'm being careful." She reached for yet another napkin to wipe her hands. To be safe, she ran a second one over her face. Bacon-chili-cheese dogs were delicious, but very messy. Then she handed over the checks to be signed. "Thanks for meeting me."

"No problem." He looked at the stack. "Well, this is all very official-looking."

She was rather proud of it. "I couldn't figure out how y'all had done this in the past, so I just created my own requisition form and paperwork. Mrs. K will be able to follow the paper trail easily."

Tate seemed to be fighting back a smile. She was trying to keep this all very businesslike, and he found it funny. *Lovely.* "I don't think the accounting has ever been quite so exact," he finally said.

"Well, I'm not going to be the one responsible for things not balancing out. This checkbook is a mess, by the way. I had to call the bank to get the account balance, and since I'm not on the account—"

Tate finally lost the fight and laughed at her. "Are you a CPA at heart?"

"I run a business—as do you, I might add. You should know better. Why haven't you made Mrs. K get all this organized?"

He snorted. "First of all, 'making' Mrs. K do anything is a laughable notion. And secondly, you forget that we trust people around here."

"That's a good way for money to go missing. Not that I'm accusing Mrs. K of anything shady," she quickly added. That was gossip she didn't want to start.

"Didn't think you were," he assured her, still obviously finding this amusing.

"So that's the table and tent rental invoice, and the others are supplies and such . . ." She watched, shocked, as Tate barely glanced over her carefully created paperwork before signing the checks with an illegible scrawl. She was rather surprised the checking account wasn't in worse shape. "Take all the time you need to look that over. Really, I don't mind." She was being snarky, but she couldn't help it.

"I trust you," Tate said with a smirk.

She didn't know whether she should be flattered or annoyed at this point. She was quite proud of her organizational work on this, and he found it funny? So much for Sam's insistence he was some kind of control freak.

"And there's my lunch. Perfect timing." He pushed

the papers back to her and smiled his thanks at the teenager who'd brought his food.

She was about to offer to walk him through the paperwork anyway, but then she caught sight of his lunch. "A
plain hot dog?" she asked. It looked so naked and strange
without all the toppings. Her own gluttony was obvious
by the trash next to her elbow, and she actually felt a little
ashamed. "I didn't know they even served them like
that."

"Only to special people."

"Oh, you're special, all right," she muttered.

Tate looked around, then leaned forward. "Don't tell
anyone," he whispered conspiratorially, "but I've never
really cared for the chili here."

"Isn't that illegal?" she whispered back.

"No. Merely blasphemous."

That made her laugh. "To say the least. And you call
yourself a pillar of the community."

He merely shrugged and took a big bite of the hot
dog. Molly was now in a bit of a predicament. She was
just fine as long as they had the business of the Children's Fair to discuss, but with that done, she lacked a
nice, neutral topic of discussion to bring up, and she was
afraid her awkwardness would show and raise questions.
It would be rude to get up and leave Tate to eat his lunch
alone, even though they hadn't planned to "do" lunch.
The Frosty Freeze was just a convenient place for them
to meet so that Tate could sign the checks. She'd come
early and eaten already, but it might be wrong to leave
now. He had given up whatever other lunch plans he had
in order to be here.

She could claim a pressing need to leave, but it felt
wrong to lie like that for no good reason.

And therein lay the problem: she had reasons, just not
good ones. She tried to look busy, flipping through the

checkbook and the papers as if looking for something specific as she hoped a good topic of conversation would present itself, but she kept *noticing* things, like the way his hair curled just the tiniest bit at the ends or how the tendons in his hands flexed into relief as he picked up his cup.

Good Lord. She'd known Tate for over two years and had never noticed *any* of this before. At least Tate seemed fine and unbothered. While that was a *good* thing, she reminded herself, it still made her feel worse because a one-sided attraction was just lame.

She should go. Tate might be one of those people who cherished alone time. Like her, he spent most of his day with people. He might *want* to have a few minutes to himself to eat his lunch in peace. Would Tate be too polite to ask her to leave, even if he wanted to? Was there a nice way for her to bring it up? Asking him if he wanted to be left alone *could* sound a lot like a politely worded "Mind if I stay?"

She was so caught up in her own internal argument that she was a couple of seconds late realizing that Tate had asked her something. And that she'd been staring at him.

Damn. "I'm sorry. What did you say?"

"You seem to be thinking real hard about something. Everything okay?"

"Just some planning." Mercifully, her brain kicked back in at that moment, and the Children's Fair was a safe topic. "I got a call from the Homestead Craft Center over in Bay Minette yesterday. They've offered to bring some of their people over to do demonstrations and crafts in return for a discount on vendor space."

"What kind of demonstrations?"

"Weaving, candle making, that kind of stuff. I think it would be interesting and educational. Different, too, from what's been done in the past. I just haven't figured out how to make money off it yet."

Tate laughed. "You have a fund-raiser's brain, that's for sure."

"That's the point of this, right? I'm thinking if we do it like the face painting—you know, asking for a dollar or two to try out the crafts—we could make some money that way."

"Sounds like you do have it figured out."

The matter-of-factness brought her up short. "Yeah, I guess I do. I think I just needed a second opinion. So, thanks." *Maybe I really can do this.* A little kernel of pride popped in her chest. "Mrs. K has called a few times just to 'check in.' I've been dodging her calls, but I think I'm ready to call her back now and bring her up-to-date."

"Want me to call her for you?"

"Nah. I can do it."

"Are you sure?"

"I'm positive. She shouldn't have left me in charge if she didn't want me to make decisions."

He looked at her carefully. "You're starting to enjoy this, aren't you?"

"A little," she confessed. She was starting to see the big picture now that she'd gotten the smaller parts under control, and her inner organizer had been awakened. Ms. Louise's encouragement to put her own stamp on it was almost as good as getting the okay from Mrs. Kennedy, even if she suspected Mrs. Kennedy's parting remarks about "everything being done" was actually code for "don't change anything." Maybe Tate's confidence wasn't misplaced, either. She met Tate's eyes across the table. "Don't tell anyone, though, okay?"

"Now we each have a secret to keep." He winked at her, and Molly felt a strange little glow in her belly. For a second there, everything seemed to get very still and quiet. Half of Tate's mouth curved up into a small smile. "So—"

"You both know there's no way to keep secrets in this town."

They both jumped at the voice, but it was only Helena, plopping onto the bench beside her. Eagerness on display, she dropped her voice and leaned in. "So what's the secret?"

Tate shook his head. "If we told you, it wouldn't be a secret, now would it?"

Helena clutched at imaginary pearls. "My two best friends are going to keep a secret from me?"

Molly nodded, just to irritate her, but she was secretly a little relieved at Helena's arrival. It had broken that odd moment of tension, even as she wondered what Tate had been going to say.

"Oh, and it's a good secret, too," Tate added sincerely. "Very juicy. Pity we can't share."

"I've got all kinds of dirt on you, Tate Harris," Helena said sternly. "I'd hate to have to share any of it."

Tate made a noise Molly could only describe as a scoff. "That might scare me if I didn't have an equal amount on you."

Helena waved a hand. "As if my dirty laundry hasn't been aired all over town already."

"Really? There still seems to be a question about how the police chief's cruiser ended up in Bayou La Batre."

"That's not nearly as mysterious as the origins of the fire in the equipment shed." Helena's smile was delightedly evil.

As amusing as this was—and as much as Molly might love to hear the truth behind those two bits of local legend—their bickering gave Molly the perfect excuse to leave. "I'm a bit superfluous in this mud wrestling bout, so I'll see y'all later." She gathered up her belongings.

Helena smacked Tate's arm. "Now see what you've done?"

"Jeez, Helena, stop hitting me." When she made a face at him, he added, "Because eventually I might have to hit you back."

"You wouldn't." She turned to Molly and put a hand on her arm. "You stay. I'll go. I interrupted y'all's lunch, after all."

"I think we were done anyway. Thanks for meeting me, Tate. I'll see you later, Helena."

She quickly crossed the street before either of them could say anything else.

There was still a very likely chance she'd screw this up, but the idea she might not was starting to gain ground. That was good.

She'd also made it through a meeting with Tate without too much one-sided unresolved sexual tension rearing its head.

That was *very* good.

Things were looking up.

"So, you and Molly having lunch together? I approve." Helena smiled smugly as she stole one of his fries.

"Really? It's been maybe three days since you promised to let it go and you're already back on that?"

"Four, actually," Helena said. "And anyway, I was just teasing. Molly threatened to poison my coffee if I brought it up again, so consider me officially and completely backed off."

On the one hand, that was great. On the other, though . . . Molly was giving his ego a bit of a beating. Maybe he was just imagining it, but every now and then he'd get a look from her that made him think her adamant denial the other night might not be quite adamant after all, but the look would disappear as quickly as it came, taking them right back to normal. He almost wanted to ask her why she wasn't interested—just for his own self-improvement, of course—but he was smart enough to check that impulse. And he certainly didn't want to encourage Helena in the slightest. He didn't have a threat with the same weight as Molly's coffee ultimatum. He was just going to have to figure this out himself. "We met so I could sign checks. You may have the career freedom to come and go as you please, but the rest of us have to squeeze meetings in where we can. Like at lunch."

"And you couldn't just drop by Latte Dah one of the other ten hours of the day it's open in order to do that?"

"First of all, Sam doesn't like it when I do that. She feels like I'm checking up on her. Secondly, since Molly got sandbagged by this without any warning, I'm trying to be flexible."

Helena glanced in the direction Molly had gone, making sure she was out of earshot before saying, "She's nervous about it."

"I know. I don't know *why*, but I know she is."

"No one wants to be the person who lets everyone down. I think she's a little too stressed over it, though."

"I think she's settling into the idea. She seemed okay today."

"That's good. I just worry about her."

That frown was about more than just Molly's stress over the Children's Fair. "Why?"

"Because she's my friend, and I want her to be happy. And I know she's got some issues, so . . ." She shrugged. "But who doesn't, right? We're not exactly the poster kids of good mental health ourselves."

He wondered whether Helena knew about Molly's self-help books. "Like bad issues?"

"I don't think so."

"You haven't asked?"

"No, nosy-pants, I haven't. I try not to interrogate my friends."

He lifted an eyebrow at her.

"Well, you're the exception," she admitted with a grin. "But you're the exception to everything. I've pieced together a few things, but she'll tell me what she wants me to know when she wants me to know it."

"Oh, if we all had friends like that."

"Hush. All I know is that she came here to start over. Whether it was family stuff or a bad relationship she left behind . . . I don't know. I don't think it was anything immoral or criminal, though."

"Why Magnolia Beach? Do you know?" he asked as casually as he could.

Helena nodded, chewing and swallowing another of his fries. "I did ask her that."

"Of course you did."

Helena ignored the snark. "She says she came down here on vacation once as a kid and loved it, so when the time came to pick a new town, this was the place."

"The tourism board must love that story."

"Probably. So why all the sudden interest in Molly?"

Funny how tone made all the difference. A different inflection or a different pitch and Tate would've balked at the question. But Helena sounded like Normal Helena, not Crazy Matchmaking Helena. "Working with her on the Children's Fair made me realize how little I actually know about her. I'd never really given her much thought."

"But now you are?"

As if he'd admit any such thing to her, previous normal tone or not. "Just curiosity. And she's giving Sam self-help books to read."

"Oh, that's good. I wish I'd thought of it. I think Sam will really benefit from them, especially if Molly's loaning the books I think she is."

"You read self-help books?" His jaw felt a little slack. Helena would probably be the *last* person on earth he'd expect to put any faith in self-help gobbledygook.

"Yeah. Why?" There was a challenge in her voice.

"You just seem . . ." There was that eyebrow of doom again. "I mean, you are . . ."

"I'm what?" Her tone was sweet, but he wasn't stupid enough to miss the obvious warning underneath.

"You're fine. In a not-crazy way."

"I could say that it's due to those books, you know. But I also spent a lot of time in therapy."

He nearly choked on his drink. "You went to therapy?"

"You didn't?" She seemed genuinely shocked.

"No. I'm not crazy."

"Neither am I, thank you very much. But therapy's a good thing for people like us."

"Like us?"

"People with screwed-up childhoods and the like. People with issues. It doesn't fix you, but it makes you less messed up, at least."

"You're saying I'm messed up?"

She didn't miss a beat. "Your dad was an abusive drunk, your mother enabled him instead of protecting y'all, you spent your adolescence running with kids who were walking cautionary tales, but at least they were more screwed up than you." She met his eyes evenly. "I stand by my statement."

"Wow." He didn't know how to respond to that. Especially since he had to admit she wasn't completely wrong, now that she'd spelled it out like that.

Knowing she'd made her point, Helena's smile was both kind and mocking. "All things considered, you're doing pretty well, but you could be better. I can recommend a couple of really good books."

"That's quite all right. I'll leave that to you and Molly and Sam."

She shrugged. "It's your loss. But do me a favor and don't ask Molly a bunch of questions. I know you mean well, but it's annoying."

"Excuse me?"

"It's one thing for you to do it to your sisters, or even to me, but not everyone will be as . . . accommodating."

"What do you mean by that?"

"Understanding is probably a better word."

"Of what?"

"Your buttinsky let-me-fix-it-ness."

Good Lord. "I don't—"

"You do."

"No, I—"

"*Yes*, you do," she said firmly. "Admit it, own it, make it your truth, my friend. You've got a bad case of White Knight Syndrome going on—"

"I do not."

Helena laughed at him. "Why do you think that all I had to do was toss Molly and the Children's Fair in your general direction for you to swoop in and help?"

"Since when is helping people bad?"

"It's not. Swooping in whether they like it or not due to a pathological need is the part therapy could have helped you with. You've always been like that, but it got worse while I was gone. Sam's calling you a control freak, so obviously you're riding her case a little hard. Don't do the same thing to Molly."

"Whatever," he mumbled.

Once again, Helena seemed satisfied that she'd made her point. He was willing to let her believe it—if only to end this ridiculous conversation. She patted him on the hand. "Unless Molly offers up the information, don't ask. Idle curiosity is no reason to butt into someone's life."

He felt a bit unfairly vilified, as if he were some busy-body looking for fencerow gossip. And jeez, when had being a nice guy and wanting to help out become a bad thing, worthy of pejorative terms? "This is your fault, you know."

"How?"

"I've known the woman since she moved to town and never gave her a second thought until *you* decided to mate us like pandas. If nothing else, I'm bound to be curious why you'd think we'd even suit each other."

"I like you both. You both like me. Therefore, you

must have something in common." She said it as if nothing could have been more obvious.

"I'm glad to know you gave it so much thought."

"Should I give it some more thought?" There was that hopeful, leading tone again.

"No. *No*," he repeated when Helena looked mulish. "My curiosity doesn't go that far—and neither should yours."

Helena sighed. "Fine. I need to run anyway. I'm really on my way to pick up Grannie's meds from the pharmacy." She scooted off the bench and patted his shoulder. "I'll see you later."

Helena had very kindly left him three of his fries to eat while he processed this new information. Mainly, he needed to come up with a better answer for why he was so curious about Molly all of a sudden.

Sure, Helena had forced the issue the other night, but it wasn't any worse than New Year's Eve, which had been pretty much forgotten. Maybe it was because Molly was everywhere now—employing his sister, running the Children's Fair—and he no longer had the buffer of Helena, Nigel, or high-octane coffee purchases to distract his attention.

Maybe it had just been too long since he'd been out with a woman.

Even that, though, didn't explain why *Molly* was now in focus. Or why he suddenly cared why she'd been so forthright about not wanting him to ask her out. *Yeah, that sting just isn't going away.*

He certainly liked Molly as a friend. Now he was trying to decide whether he liked her in other ways, too.

And while he really, honestly, truly did not want Helena thinking about his love life at all—much less entertain how much he and Molly might have in common—that didn't mean *he* wasn't going to.

Because now he was curious, that's all.

Chapter 7

Molly needed to get good and drunk. Unfortunately, she had to get up at five o'clock in the morning and function like a human being, so if she was going to wallow in the escapist bliss of box wine and not hate herself in the morning, she had to start drinking at what others would consider a far-too-early hour of the evening.

She was on her second glass and her attitude was improving already. Nigel helped, too, chasing the red dot of a laser pointer with such spastic determination that she had to giggle. It was both entertainment for her and exercise for him.

She'd turned off the ringer on her phone, but she heard it vibrate against the coffee table and leaned over just enough to see the screen.

Hannah.

Nope and hell no.

Hannah was the reason she needed to get knee-walking drunk in the first place, and another conversation with her today might just lead to alcohol poisoning. And there was nothing Hannah had to say that Molly wanted to hear anyway. She shouldn't have answered the phone the first time Hannah called, but somehow she just couldn't get past the juvenile naïveté that made her hope it might be different *this* time.

Because it never was.

If Hannah liked Mark so damn much, maybe *she* should marry him. And if all this was causing the family such embarrassment, why wouldn't they push back a little at some of the lies Mark was telling?

Because they believed Mark. Or at least they wanted to and pretended they did.

Even when she'd shown them the bruises.

And *that* was the part that drove her to fill her glass for the third time. Her family was so enamored with the Lane family, so desperate to be connected to them and reap the perks of that connection that they would happily force her back to Mark if they could only figure out how to do it without breaking multiple laws. She still had a few friends back in Fuller. She knew what was being said about her and the sympathy being lavished on both the Lane and Richards families because they had to put up with such an ungrateful, spiteful, and petty person like her. Her mother was a martyr and Mark was Prince Charming, and everyone was just praying Molly would repent and return home for the help she so desperately needed.

Yeah, right. If she ever actually *did* decide to return to the fold, their little melodrama would fall apart. So they were all just stuck here, in the middle of Act Three, because all the main characters were reading different scripts with completely different endings.

And she was exhausted by it.

Hate was a powerful emotion, but eventually even the strongest hate couldn't keep feeding the fight. She was simply worn down, worn out, and too tired of it all.

And there was not a damn thing she could do. She could cry from the frustration of it, but those tears had run out long ago. Any rage would be impotent and a waste of time and energy. Life was simply too short to waste on things she couldn't change, so she was trying to make the best of what she could.

Nigel, bored now with the laser pointer, jumped into her lap and swatted at her hand until she put the pointer down and scratched him under the chin instead. His loud purr rumbled against her thighs as he rolled to his back.

As she rubbed the soft hair on his belly, she gave herself one full minute to hate Mark David Lane with every fiber of her being, but she allowed only five seconds of self-recrimination for marrying him in the first place. She used the next couple of minutes as she always did any time she dealt with anyone in her family: breathing deeply and searching for calm acceptance and strength.

She never quite managed to find it, but at least she searched.

Her phone chimed to let her know that Hannah had left a voice mail that she had zero intention of listening to, ever. Her therapist had told her to limit contact with her family and to accept only on her terms, if she decided to accept at all. She'd been bad about setting that boundary in the past, but now . . . "I think the new terms should go into effect immediately. Right, Nigel?"

Nigel purred, so she took that as a yes.

Anything important she really needed to know—and she had yet to decide what that might actually be— would get to her through the few friends she had left.

Mark's numbers were simply blocked from her phone and all his e-mail was sorted directly to trash and deleted unread by the miracle of modern technology.

Anything *he* needed to tell her could go through her lawyer.

"Maybe I am spiteful and petty," she told Nigel. "But I'm happier this way."

She had the music she liked playing, a decent buzz going, and a kitty in her lap. Overall, life didn't suck.

So, of course, someone had to knock on her door.

Leaving her wineglass balanced on the arm of the couch, she scooped Nigel into her arms and took him with her to the door.

Tate Harris was the last person she expected to find on her porch, but there he was. She blinked, wondering whether she'd had more wine than she'd thought.

"Hi, Molly. Sorry to bother you, but—"

Nigel hissed and leapt from her arms, leaving a scratch on the back of her hand from his claws. The force of his leap caused her to sway in her slightly legless state, and she reached for the doorframe to steady herself.

Within seconds, she could hear ominous noises coming from under the couch. Molly was speechless. Granted, Nigel wasn't the most friendly of cats to begin with, and he actively disliked trips to the vet's office, but he wasn't usually like *this* at home, even when people came by. She rubbed the scratch on her hand. He'd drawn blood. "I don't know what's gotten into that cat."

Tate merely laughed. "Occupational hazard. Dude," he said in the direction of the couch, "you can only be neutered once, you know." He squatted then, and Molly saw the large box on the porch at his feet. "This was delivered to my house. It's your banners and stuff from the printer."

"Oh, thanks." She opened the door wider and Tate carried it in. She pointed at the small dining table and he left it there. "Sorry. I don't know why they sent it to you. I would have thought they'd know to send it to Mrs. K's house." Her lips were slightly numb and the words sounded strange, even to her own ears.

"I'd ordered some things for the clinic and they got delivered to my house, too. I think Mr. Patton's getting a little senile these days." He looked at her closely. "Are you okay? You seem a little . . . off."

She might have blushed. Or maybe she was just warm

in general. Either way, it was a little embarrassing to be called out like that. She just wasn't sure why, though. She was an adult, *and* she was in the privacy and safety of her own home. She had no reason to be embarrassed, and she refused to feel that way. She lifted her chin. "I've had several glasses of wine. And I'm going to have more."

One dark eyebrow arched up. "Bad day?"

"Yeah. Very much so."

He looked concerned. "Anything I can do?"

There wasn't anything anyone could do—which was the reason she was drinking. "Nope."

"Do you want to talk about it?"

"Not really. I don't want to be my own buzzkill." Belatedly remembering her manners, she got another glass from the cupboard and opened the fridge. "Would you like a drink?"

"Just some water, thanks."

She'd been reaching for the wine box, but the filter pitcher was right next to it. For a second, she thought Tate might be making some kind of statement about how much she'd had already, but then something else surfaced from her memory. Had she ever seen Tate drink? Helena certainly did—just not in the house, because Ms. Louise didn't allow it—but a quick review of the other places she'd been with both Tate and Helena came up empty. But there were stories that Helena had told her about the two of them when they were younger and alcohol had definitely been involved—and sometimes responsible for the results. She handed him the glass of water. "You don't drink anymore, do you?"

Tate shook his head.

She looked over at her glass, wondering whether it might be some kind of temptation for him. "Does it bother you when other people do?"

"Nope. I'm an excellent designated driver."

"I'll remember that." She'd never heard any talk of Tate having a drinking problem—and it would have definitely been discussed, especially since his father had been such a raging . . .

Oh.

"And that's exactly why," Tate said.

Molly jumped. Surely she wasn't drunk enough to be thinking out loud. Now she was blushing for real. "Um . . ."

"It's obvious what you're thinking," he explained. "My dad was a drunk. There's some science that says it might be a genetic thing, and that's not a risk I'm willing to take." He was very matter-of-fact about it, and she couldn't tell whether she'd offended him or not.

"I think that's a very wise position to take." Still, she felt the need to say, "I'm sorry I even brought it up."

He shrugged a shoulder. "It's refreshing, in a way. Most people just talk about it behind my back because it's more polite somehow than saying it to my face."

"Etiquette's tricky like that," she teased. "But I think they figure they're doing you a kindness. We all have family issues that we'd like to pretend don't really exist. By not mentioning yours to you, they're hoping you won't mention theirs to them, and everyone gets to live their little fantasy that it's not real. Or at least pretend that no one else knows the embarrassing and ugly truth."

"I'd never thought about it like that."

"Neither had I, actually," she admitted. "My brain hurts a little now."

Tate laughed. "Wine makes you philosophical, huh?"

"I guess so."

"Booze always just made me stupid. And reckless." He laughed. "I'm sure you've heard the stories."

The swaying of the room was beginning to make her a little ill, so she went to the couch and sat, motioning Tate to sit as well. "And here I thought it was Helena who'd made you do stupid and reckless things."

"Oh, they were always her ideas," he said, settling into the chair across from her. "The booze just made them sound like *good* ideas."

She laughed. "They always seem that way at the time. I now only drink with Nigel, because he rarely comes up with stupid ideas to talk me into."

Tate looked over to where Nigel's nose could just be seen peeking out from under the couch at the mention of his name. "Good kitty."

Nigel disappeared back into the shadow with a growl, and Tate shook his head. "So what kind of stupid ideas are we talking about?"

"What?"

"It seems a little unfair that you know *my* past sins, yet I don't know any of yours."

"You think I moved across the state only to share all my past shame now?"

"So there's shame as well as stupidity." He leaned forward, forearms on his knees. "This sounds interesting."

"Not really. Compared to you and Helena, I was a freaking saint."

He conceded the point with a smirk. "Most people are. That's not a very high bar." After a moment, he prodded, "Well . . . ?"

What could she say? "I wasn't exactly a conscientious student. For most of high school, I was more concerned about my popularity and having a good time than with my studies. I got into a lot of trouble."

An eyebrow went up. "Like 'call the sheriff' trouble?"

"No, nothing like that. My parents would have killed me. It was more in the 'mischief' category. Rolling the high school, throwing a smoke bomb into the visiting team's locker room, stuff like that."

"So you were a cheerleader?" She couldn't tell whether he was impressed or surprised.

"Junior varsity. Until I got kicked off the squad for drinking on the bus to an away game." Why had she just confessed that?

"So you were a party girl." *Okay, that is surprise on his face.* "I would not have guessed that."

"Only in the loosest possible definition of the word 'party.'" Tate looked confused. "My family is really conservative. Even by Alabama standards," she explained.

"Religious?"

"Crazy religious. They put the 'mental' in 'fundamental.' My father's a deacon in our church, so they were really strict. No drinking, no dancing, no Disney movies . . . I couldn't even hold hands with a boy without getting the stink eye."

"Drinking on the bus, then, would have been a pretty big deal."

"Yeah. But it was a bottle of cooking sherry I'd gotten from my grandmother's house."

"Yuck."

Her stomach rolled at the memory. "I felt like hell for days. I still have a taste for cheap wine, though," she added, nodding toward the box.

"What did your parents say?" Tate leaned back, relaxing into the chair as if he had no place to go. Strangely, she found she didn't mind the company. In fact, it was nice, and that was *very* strange, since she'd been in such an evil mood just a little while before.

She curled her feet up under her and leaned back. "Nothing I hadn't heard a dozen times before. Jolie and Hannah are perfect, you see, so I—" She stopped herself. This was not something she wanted to be talking about. *This is why I don't drink in public.* "Let's just say that I might have been a wild thing by some standards, but I was a long, *long* way from Helena-style antics."

"Well, there's only one Hell-on-Wheels," he said with a smile.

She was just drunk enough to have the nerve to ask *and* be able to deny it later if the question crossed a line: "Are you in love with Helena?"

Tate choked, but recovered quickly. "No. I used to have a pretty major crush on her, but that was a long time ago. Is that what you thought when you heard me tell Helena I didn't want to ask you out the other night?"

"Not really. Y'all are just really close, and I've heard people wonder about it. You haven't seemed interested in anyone since she got back."

Tate's lips twitched into a quick smile. "Oh, there's interest."

No wonder he'd reacted so strongly to Helena's attempt to match him up with her. "Really? Anyone I know?"

"Hell, I'm still trying to figure out if I know her."

That seemed unnecessarily cryptic. Or else she was just too wine soaked to make sense of it. "Well, you should probably tell Helena. At least she'd quit trying to set you up with me," she teased.

Tate seemed to find that amusing. Okay, she had to be a lot drunker than she thought, because she was completely clueless to *some*thing. And she didn't like being clueless. "I guess it's really none of my business, so I won't pry."

"Well, I'll let you know when I decide what I'm going to do about her."

Yeah, she was missing a thread here.

There was a moment of slightly uncomfortable silence; then Tate reached for his glass. "Who are Hannah and Jolie?" When she didn't answer immediately, he reminded her, "You pretty much know my life story. It seems fair to talk a little more about you."

She weighed the options and the possible repercussions and decided there wasn't anything to lose. "They're my sisters. Hannah is two years older, and Jolie is two years younger."

"Two sisters. That's something we have in common."

"Yes, but my sisters are sanctimonious, self-righteous bitches," she snapped.

Tate blinked. "Wow."

She cleared her throat, a little embarrassed at her outburst. "Sorry. I didn't realize how much I needed to say that out loud to someone other than Nigel."

"So you're not close, then."

That was an understatement. "No."

"And your parents?"

She hesitated, then settled on, "We don't really talk these days."

"Why?"

She could hear concern in his question, not just nosiness, but the topic still got her hackles up. "That's a really long story, and one I really am not comfortable discussing with you." There was a brief moment where she might have seen a bit of offense—or maybe disappointment—cross Tate's face, but she wasn't really in any condition to read or guess at subtleties. "Sorry. My family is kind of a touchy subject. And I've definitely had quite enough of them today already."

Tate nodded. "That explains the wine."

"Yeah."

He seemed poised to say something else, but the seconds ticked by in silence. She felt a little bad for shutting down the conversation like that. He obviously had questions, but at least he was taking her at her word when she said she didn't want to discuss it. Just as the silence started to turn awkward, he pushed to his feet. "I guess I'll leave you to it, then."

She was more disappointed than she wanted to be— and that surprised her—but she stood, too. "Thank you again for bringing the box by. I'm sorry it got misdelivered and you had to make the trip over."

"No problem. Good night, Molly. Hope your day gets better. And that your head doesn't hurt too bad in the morning." A gray paw reached out to swipe at his foot as he passed the couch on his way to the door, but it missed by a wide margin.

"Well, if it does, at least I know where I can get a good cup of coffee to fix it."

He laughed. "Indeed."

As soon as the door closed behind him, Nigel came out from under the couch looking very irritated. "You are one crazy cat." He twined himself around her ankles, purring, until she reached down to pick him up again. She sank onto the couch, but the urge to drink had passed now. Strangely enough, the visit with Tate had improved her mood. She was still irritated with Hannah, but the frustration had passed, and she was easing back into the better-off-without-them zone that kept her sane.

But something was bugging her, and it took her a few minutes to figure out what. Oddly, it was the fact Tate had stated an interest in some mystery woman. Not that it was any of her business, of course, but the fact that it was a secret had her wondering.

But it was good, really, that Tate had his eye on someone. Maybe all her weird feelings would go away if he started dating someone.

Damn it, now she wanted another drink.

There was no way Tate was going to tell sweet old Mrs. Lindlay that her dog was living on borrowed time and by every measurement available should actually be long dead. Of course, so should Mrs. Lindlay, actually, and Tate wasn't unconvinced the two of them weren't keeping each other alive by sheer willpower and stubbornness not to die before the other.

And while Cocoa, like her mistress, was arthritic and mostly deaf, she didn't seem to be in any pain or distress. Cocoa was just ancient, her muzzle nearly entirely gray. He gave the dog one more very gentle pat before zipping up the backpack that served as his bag and pushing to his feet. "Cocoa seems fine to me, Mrs. Lindlay. The anti-inflammatory medication seems to be working well for her."

"Oh, good. I get so worried about her poor little knees."

"She's just getting older and can't keep up with you like she used to. You need to take it easy on her."

Mrs. Lindlay laughed and patted his hand. "You're so sweet to come over here and check on us. Not many doctors make house calls anymore."

Including me. But Tate was also not going to make a ninety-something-year-old woman trek to the clinic. She rarely left her house these days. "It's my pleasure."

"Let me get my checkbook."

"I'll send you a bill." With luck, Mrs. Lindlay was getting forgetful enough not to notice when it didn't arrive. "Call me if you need anything. Don't get up," he added as she started to rise. "I'll let myself out."

On the sidewalk out front, he sent a quick text to Jack Lindlay letting him know he'd been by and that his grandmother's dog was probably immortal. Then he took the shortcut through the parking lot of Grace Baptist to get back to Front Street.

Seeing Molly come out of the church's front door didn't strike him as all that odd at first, but in light of her remarks about her family the night before, he'd assumed she'd left the flock. Even if she hadn't, what would be going on at the church right after lunch on a Thursday afternoon anyway? Too curious not to find out, he angled across the parking lot and caught up with Molly about the time she reached the sidewalk.

"How's the head today?"

She jumped. Obviously lost in thought, she hadn't noticed him approach, and she seemed surprised to see him there. "I was a bit fragile this morning, but a couple of cups of Rocket Fuel whipped me right into shape. Thanks again for dropping off that stuff. I'm sorry I was a bit tipsy."

"You seemed to need it, though." Since she'd shut him down so thoroughly the night before, he wanted to tread lightly, but he had to ask. Looking for the right mix of concern and levity, he casually said, "I take it there's no more news from your family today?"

Molly might have flushed a little—it was hard to tell in the bright sunlight. She either didn't remember or was regretting having let her guard down last night. "Nope. We're back to blessed silence."

"Is everything okay?" When Molly seemed confused at the question, he inclined his head back toward the church.

"Oh, *that*. Yeah. Today's my grandmother's birthday."

There was a sadness to her voice that told him the rest. "When did she pass?"

"Three years ago. Not long before I moved here."

"I'm sorry to hear that. I'm guessing you were close to her?"

"Thanks and yes. We were quite close. She always said we were the black sheep of the family, and I spent a lot of time at her house when I wasn't getting along with my sisters or my parents. I'm not the type to visit a grave, even if it wasn't all the way across the state, so I try to go to church for a few minutes on her birthday to remember her. She loved to sing in the choir." Molly smiled at the memory.

"I don't have very many memories of my grandparents," he confessed. "Ms. Louise kind of filled that role for me."

"Ms. Louise reminds me a lot of my nana, too. Helena's lucky to have her."

"She knows it. Even when they're driving each other crazy."

Molly laughed. "So what are you doing out and about?"

"Just running a couple of errands. It's a nice day to be out."

Molly nodded. "I think summer's officially here—even if the calendar doesn't agree. The humidity is certainly climbing." She ran a hand over her curls, smoothing them and tucking them back behind her ears.

They got quiet, and Molly started looking around awkwardly. The shift of the topic to the weather meant the three minutes of small talk required when running into someone had run its course. And since Latte Dah was in the opposite direction of the clinic, it was time for her to go on her way.

He was a little disappointed. After last night, he was feeling more comfortable with Molly, and his thoughts about her were definitely bending in new directions.

"Well," she said brightly, "it was good running into you. I'm sure I'll see you soon."

"Yeah, you, too. Bye."

He had so many questions about her, but his reasons for wanting the answers went beyond mere curiosity, and he wasn't afraid to admit that to himself.

At the corner, Molly turned and saw him still standing there. At first, he was a little ashamed to be seen lurking like that, but then she smiled and gave him a small wave.

And, somehow, that sealed it.

Chapter 8

When the phone woke him up, Tate's first thought was how bad his neck hurt. Thirty seemed to be the age where accidentally falling asleep on the couch while watching TV became a real thing—and also a real danger as he was simply too old to be comfortable sleeping on a couch anymore.

He rubbed his neck with one hand and reached for the phone. Squinting at it, he saw Molly's name on the screen, and smiled. Today's revelation had been spinning in his head all evening. Maybe Molly was having something similar . . .

Then he saw the time—close to two—and adrenaline kicked in.

Skipping any polite formalities, he answered with "What's wrong?"

"I'm sorry to wake you up, but I don't know what else to do. It's Nigel."

He could hear the panic in her voice and the threat of tears. If he hadn't already been on alert from a two a.m. call, that alone would have kicked him into gear. He went to the bedroom to get shoes. "What's he doing?"

"I think he's having a seizure or something. He's shaking and drooling—"

"Is he conscious?"

"Yeah. But he's really spacey and out of it."

He was trying to remember Nigel's history, but nothing helpful came to mind. "Is he bleeding? Vomiting?"

"He was vomiting earlier. A lot. Almost like he had food poisoning or something. But then he quit. I thought he was okay."

That gave him a clue. "Do you have any honey? Maybe corn syrup?"

"I think I do." He could tell she'd put him on speaker, and he could hear cupboard doors opening and closing in the background. Her voice got closer again. "Yes. I've got honey."

"Get a big tablespoon full of it and see if you can get him to eat it. If he won't, you'll have to use your finger to rub it on his gums." Even if hypoglycemia wasn't the problem, this wouldn't hurt Nigel before he got there.

"Okay." Molly still sounded on the verge of tears, but having something to do seemed to stem her panic, just as he'd hoped it would. As he pulled a clean shirt on over his head, he could hear her murmuring to Nigel, sweetly coaxing him to eat the honey. "He doesn't want it," she reported.

"It doesn't matter what he wants. Don't put a lot of liquid in his mouth, because we don't want him to choke, but he needs the sugar. Keep rubbing it on the insides of his cheeks and on his gums. Just watch your fingers if he starts to seize." Grabbing his bag and his emergency kit from the front closet, he found his car keys. "I'm on my way now."

"You're on your way?" She sounded both amazed and relieved at the same time.

"Of course. I'll be there in just a couple of minutes. Just keep feeding him honey and keep him calm."

All of Magnolia Beach was sound asleep, the houses dark except for the occasional night-light glowing in an upstairs window or a front porch light left on. Molly's house was only two blocks away—too close, really, not to walk, except that he'd brought his any-and-all-emergencies kit and that weighed a ton. And while he might have a pretty good idea what was wrong with Nigel, he'd rather be prepared. For now, though, he left it in the car and just took the smaller bag inside.

Mrs. Kennedy's house was completely dark, but the little guesthouse blazed like a lighthouse. The front door was slightly ajar, so he just knocked a warning as he let himself in.

Molly was on the floor, leaned against the couch, with Nigel curled on a towel beside her. Her face was drawn and colorless except for the dark circles under her eyes and a slight redness around her nose that told him she'd been crying. Her voice, though, was calm as she stroked Nigel with one hand as she dipped a finger into a small saucer of honey and slipped it into his mouth.

She looked up as he entered, relief evident all over her face. "I've been putting the honey on his gums, but there's no change," she said quietly.

"I didn't expect there to be just yet. That doesn't mean it's not working, though."

Nigel only gave a halfhearted growl as he knelt next to them. "Let's take a look at you."

Molly watched as he examined Nigel, but didn't say anything to him. He was used to being peppered with anxious questions, but Molly simply stroked the cat gently, calming him, as Tate poked him for a blood sample and checked his pulse.

Ten seconds later, he had his answer, and it proved his hunch correct. "He's hypoglycemic. That's when—"

"But Nigel's not diabetic," Molly interrupted him, showing a familiarity with the term that suggested she probably had at least one diabetic friend or family member. Frowning, she scooped up more honey and slipped her finger into Nigel's mouth.

"It's not a common thing, but there are some non-diabetes causes of hypoglycemia, and it's usually a sign of something else. You said he was vomiting after he ate?"

"Pretty violently."

"But he was bringing something up, not just bile?"

"Yeah, just regular vomit."

"Any chance he's gotten into something poisonous?"

"I don't think so."

"Did you change his food?"

Molly nodded. "It's a special diet blend I bought online."

"Probably an allergic reaction, then."

Her jaw dropped. "This is *allergies*?"

"Yes and no. My best guess is that he's allergic to that new food, which led to the vomiting, which allowed his insulin to spike, which led to the crash. I'll run some tests tomorrow—or later today, actually," he corrected, "to rule out anything more serious with his liver or pancreas, but right now that seems the most likely scenario."

"It was supposed to be all natural and—" She cursed rather colorfully. "I looked up online about putting him on a diet and got the new food it suggested. Instead, I nearly killed him."

"It's not your fault. And you did the right thing—stayed calm, called for help, and did exactly what I told you. You saved him."

"Will he be okay?" Her voice was quiet.

"Once we get his sugar levels stabilized, yes. Look, he's already stopped shaking."

"Oh, thank God." Molly closed her eyes and exhaled. "Now I'm shaking like a leaf, though."

"Take a minute or two. I've got this under control." Molly nodded and pushed to her feet. She was dressed in a long, baggy T-shirt from Bubba's Bait Shop and some kind of yoga leggings that clung to her like a second skin and stopped just below her knees. She went into the other room, presumably her bedroom, and he could hear her muttering to herself as she opened drawers and ran water.

He'd wait another ten minutes or so to do another glucose test, but he could tell Nigel was already starting to recover. He offered a bit more honey and Nigel licked it off his finger. The cat must be miserable, he thought, to not be growling at him.

"Wow, he *is* doing better." Molly came out of her room a few minutes later, zipping up a hoodie and carrying a pair of socks. She'd washed her face and tamed her hair. Leaning against the table, she put the socks on her feet, watching Nigel with a relieved look on her face.

"You intervened before he got too severe."

"I'm sorry I got you out of bed. I panicked."

"This was an emergency. I don't mind."

Molly gave him a weak smile. "I don't know how to thank you."

"What are friends for, right?"

"This goes above and beyond."

He shrugged. "Well, a cup of coffee would be nice."

She grinned. "That's my specialty. Regular or decaf?"

"Regular. I'm going to be here for a little while and I'll need the caffeine."

That stopped her in her tracks. "I thought you said he was going to be okay?"

"He will," he assured her, "but we've sent his blood sugar soaring with all this honey. I want to make sure it doesn't cause another crash."

"Coffee all around, then."

"Do you have any cat food that's not the new stuff? Canned, preferably."

Molly put a kettle on the stove and went to the pantry. Opening a can, she dumped the contents into a small dish and brought it over to Tate. "Do you think he'll actually eat after all that?"

"It would help if he did." He stayed with Nigel, coaxing him to take a few bites of food while Molly ground coffee beans and produced one of those French press things he'd never quite understood the point of. But then, he wasn't a coffee connoisseur; if it was hot and strong and caffeinated, he'd drink pretty much anything.

Molly produced not only coffee in urn-sized mugs, but biscotti as well, setting it all on the coffee table within easy reach. "Cream? Sugar? Whiskey?" she offered before she winced, then apologized. "Sorry. I forgot you don't drink."

"No need to apologize. I'm not recovering or anything. It's not like I have to fight to stay sober."

"Oh. Okay."

Since she obviously wasn't going to ask, he offered the explanation. "It's like avoiding veal for ethical reasons or bacon because of the nitrates. You know it's yummy, but you also know it's not right for you."

"So, black, then?"

He nodded, pleased she'd let it go so easily. "You could use a shot, though. It would calm your nerves a little."

"I'm actually okay now. I find your competence to be very soothing."

"Glad to hear it." And he was. More than he wanted to admit. He'd been focused on Nigel since he got here, but his focus was shifting a little now.

Molly sat down in her original spot and rubbed Nigel's head. "Oops, he's a little sticky. I guess my hands were shaking more than I realized."

"Well, when he starts grooming himself, it'll be one more sign he's feeling better." Molly leaned back and closed her eyes with a deep sigh, prompting him to say, "You've had a bitch of a week, haven't you?"

She opened one eye. "Yes, and I'm sorry you've had to witness so much of it. First a drunk Molly and now a weepy, freaked-out Molly."

"At least you don't get drunk and weepy at the same time," he teased. "*That* would be a little much to handle all at once."

"True. I try to limit my breakdowns to one emotion at a time. You missed my weekly Stressed Molly Children's Fair Breakdown yesterday . . ." She grew quiet as he took another blood sample.

"You can talk," he told her. "This doesn't require silence. What stressed you out?"

"The usual," she said offhandedly. "I'm really impressed."

"More like easily impressed. This is one of the easiest things in the world to do."

"No. You're an awesome vet, Tate. You're good with both animals *and* people."

The compliment was sincere, and, surprisingly, it meant a lot to him to hear her say it. "The people are harder, actually," he told her. "But they usually don't bite, so it's a bit of a toss-up, I guess." He showed her the reading on the meter. "*That's* a lovely number. Let's see if holds."

She held up crossed fingers. "I'm sorry I freaked out on you."

"Don't be. It's a scary thing to witness. And it was serious. If you'd waited, it could have killed him. He's lucky you were awake." That made him ask, "Why were you awake? Doesn't Latte Dah open in like three hours?"

"I'm a light sleeper and Nigel sleeps with me. I woke up when he started shaking."

"Luck, then."

"Yeah." She took a big gulp of coffee. "It's a good thing Sam wants more hours. She's going to get some today." Then her forehead wrinkled. "But you're going to be exhausted. I'm so sorry."

"Quit apologizing." He held a little food on his finger to tempt Nigel. "I'll go in and check on everybody and get some lab work ordered on this little dude, but I'll probably reschedule what I can and take a nice nap in my office." Molly started to say something, but he held up a hand. "Really. Don't apologize again. This isn't the first time I've pulled an all-nighter. It's just part of the job sometimes. And I got a couple of hours of sleep before you called."

"That doesn't make me appreciate it any less." She paused to press her head to Nigel's, who responded by rubbing his honey-covered fur against her chin. "I hate to sound like one of those crazy cat ladies or anything, but Nigel's my baby. I can't bear to think of something happening to him. Especially when it's my fault."

"First of all, quit blaming yourself. Nigel's not blaming you, and I'm not blaming you, so give yourself a break. Secondly, pets are like family. It's tough to see them ill or in pain."

"Nigel's my first," she confessed. "My sister is allergic, so we never had any growing up. Well, except for a few fish, but those aren't exactly cuddly. Nigel, though, just *owns* me, heart and soul. Loves me unconditionally. It's an amazing thing, and I hate that I had to wait this long to find out about it."

She said the words casually, but they hit him hard. Whatever she'd left behind when she came here . . . Well, it couldn't have been good. That knowledge clashed hard with the happy face Molly presented to the world, meaning she was either in deep denial or those self-help books were worth their weight in gold.

But the knowledge she'd been through something bad and come out okay gave him a new respect for Molly. She was more than just a pretty face, and way more than just "Molly-from-Latte-Dah."

The ideas he'd been merely toying with suddenly became full-fledged convictions, with plans and images and even a sound track. And while now wasn't the time to make a move, knowing he was going to—soon—

added an edge of anticipation and excitement to the situation.

Molly bounced between concerned pet parent and gracious hostess—cooing at Nigel and then plying him with coffee and biscotti. They talked easily of small, unimportant things—Sophie and Quinn's upcoming wedding, the bands playing during the Memorial Day weekend events, the possibility of him bringing another vet into the clinic to lighten his load, and her plans to eventually open a small coffee stand over near the beach to serve the tourists more easily. In a way, they were just killing time on the Nigel-watch, but it was nice, too. Comfortable.

Nigel was definitely on the mend, grooming himself and snuggling up to Molly for more love. When Tate went to test his glucose one last time, Nigel hissed and swatted at him, the "poke me one more time and I'll shred you, buddy" message abundantly clear as he stalked off in the direction of Molly's bedroom.

Molly laughed, then apologized. She looked tired now, with dark purple circles under her eyes from the lack of sleep, but the worry and strain had disappeared, and the color was back in her cheeks. "I'd say he's much better now."

"I agree." Tate stretched and started packing up. "I still want to run those tests on him, though. You can just drop him off at the clinic anytime after seven, and we'll call you when he's ready to be picked up."

"I will." She rubbed a hand over her face and pushed her hair back behind her ears. "Mercy, I'm exhausted. I'm so jacked up on caffeine, though, I don't think I could sleep even if I wanted to." She pushed to her feet and stretched, arching her back and groaning. Her shirt crawled a few inches up, showing off toned thighs—something he couldn't possibly ignore now, thanks to his newly arrived-at decision of the evening. She was compact and rounded in all the right places, something even the baggy layers of T-shirt and hoodie couldn't disguise.

Molly looked at the clock and shook her head. "I guess it doesn't matter anyway. My alarm's going to go off in forty-five minutes. I feel like I should offer to make you breakfast or something," she said with a laugh.

At least she hadn't noticed his stare. "Thanks, but no. If I go home now, I'll have time for a nap."

Her eyebrows went up. "Even after all that coffee? I feel like I've failed at my one job."

"I'll manage. Provided I can drag myself up off this floor."

Surprisingly, Molly extended a hand to him to help him up. Considering he topped her by a good six inches and probably at least thirty pounds, he found the offer a little amusing, but he took the proffered hand anyway.

Molly had a nice firm grip and soft, warm hands. When her first halfhearted tug accomplished exactly nothing, she used her other hand to grasp his wrist and planted her feet wider apart. "On three," she said. "One . . . two . . . thr—"

Nigel chose that moment to streak back through the room, right between Molly's legs, startling her and throwing her off balance.

In one slow-motion second, he realized that if she fell, Molly would hit the edge of the coffee table, probably with her head, and he gave her arm a sharp tug instead, pulling her forward and into his lap. Molly's knee landed painfully on his thigh, and her head bounced off his collarbone with a sharp crack. Still, it was better than the alternative, even as it knocked the breath out of him.

Molly sat up on her knees, hands pressed against her nose. "Ow! What did you do that for?"

"It was either that or stitch your head up after you cracked it open on the coffee table. I made a judgment call."

"I think my nose is broken."

Well, that was one way to make an impression on a lady. "Let me see."

Even through watery eyes, Molly managed to give him a "get real" look.

"Come on, I'm a doctor, remember."

"I'm not a poodle." The words were muffled behind her hands.

"I don't know," he teased. "With all that curly hair . . ."

Her eyes narrowed dangerously.

"MD, DVM . . . Beggars with possible broken noses can't be choosers."

With a sigh, Molly let her hands drop. As she was still kneeling between his thighs, her face was almost level with his.

Her nose was a little red, but there was no blood, no swelling. He gave the bridge a gentle squeeze, but it felt solid, and she didn't even wince when he did it. He wasn't an expert on human anatomy, but he couldn't see any obvious signs of a fracture. "I think you're fine. Maybe put some ice on it."

Molly froze then, her eyes widening. It took him a second to figure out why. Without even meaning to, he'd moved from examining her nose to pushing the hair back out of her face and tucking it behind her ears. His hand was still resting on the side of her head, his thumb gently stroking her hair.

Ah, hell.

Jerking away would make him look guilty or ashamed, but continuing on could make him look like a jerk. Or clueless. It was a bit of a catch-22. But Molly had the softest hair; all the curls rioting around his fingers tickled his skin, and he didn't want to let go. Those coffee-colored eyes were huge in her face—not in a bad way, just in a startled, "well, this is new" way. She was close enough that he could smell the peppermint of her lip balm and feel her breath as she exhaled.

He wasn't quite sure what he should do. He wasn't even one hundred percent sure what he *wanted* to do. This wasn't exactly how he'd pictured his move, but the deed was done and he didn't want to screw it up now. The longer Molly stayed there, not objecting to his touch but not moving otherwise, the more unsure he got.

Then Molly closed her eyes and her head moved ever so slightly against his hand. If he hadn't been so keenly focused on the feel of her, he'd have missed it entirely. Desire slammed into him, making his skin feel tight and hot, his brain taking that movement as permission.

But a second later, it was over, and he was left grasping the air where Molly used to be.

Molly was blinking and clearing her throat, feeling the bridge of her nose and clamoring gracelessly to her feet, muttering the whole time. A flush climbed up her neck to her cheeks, clashing with the purple shadows under her eyes.

He could almost convince himself that it hadn't happened.

But it had happened.

And it changed *everything*.

Molly decided she was way too old to be pulling all-nighters. She felt like death on toast, and while her body craved sleep, she could not shut her brain down long enough to actually *fall* asleep for longer than a few minutes, even though the lack of sleep and the vivid, jarring dreams made her thoughts foggy and disjointed at best.

She was simply no good for anything today. She'd made it through the morning at Latte Dah, leaving Sam in charge once things had slowed down, and had come home with every intention of a long, hard nap, but that just wasn't happening.

Lying on the bed and staring at the ceiling was starting to annoy her. She'd splurged on the duvet and linens, making her bed into the perfect nest, but she couldn't seem to get comfortable.

She was worried about Nigel, of course, but it wasn't a panic. By the time she'd dropped him off at the clinic this morning, he was so fully recovered, even she began to wonder whether she'd imagined the night before. If there had been some terrible underlying cause for last night's crash, she'd know soon enough, and she knew better than to borrow trouble by running worst-case scenarios through her head.

But that didn't keep her from trying to tell herself that she was *totally* and *completely* worried about Nigel, and that was the *only* thing keeping her awake and edgy.

Unfortunately, she was a terrible liar.

No, the thing that had thrown the monkey wrench into her mental gears was that moment last night when Tate had stroked her hair and looked at her as if . . . well, as if he'd *wanted* her. It was one thing for her to play with the idea from *her* side—there was no real harm in it, other than the mild strain of frustration.

It was a whole different thing to think that Tate might be also playing with the same idea.

Men had flirted with her ever since she moved here. Mostly it was light and harmless and fun, just enough to buoy her ego when she felt unattractive and unlovable. But she kept everyone kindly and safely in the Friend Zone, and it hadn't been a problem.

But now Tate, who'd never given her so much as a flirty glance before, was shaking her equilibrium like an earthquake. Because what happened last night hadn't been flirty and it certainly hadn't been light. There'd been that moment of . . . *damn.* A shiver went through her again, same as it did every time she thought of it.

This was a whole new kind of frustration. Earthquake Tate had shaken something loose inside her, and the frustration had a new, sharp, and scary edge.

She was imagining things she had no business imagining. Her mind had taken that moment and run wild with it, giving Tate a starring role in some pretty graphic fantasies every time she closed her eyes. Every nerve she had was on edge, yet she was unable to make a move either way.

It wasn't just frustrating. It was infuriating. And it was hell.

Plus, there was the complication of Helena. Even if she could act on any of these ideas, disaster lurked. Helena and Tate had a bond Molly had to respect even if she didn't fully understand it. And while Helena might have played with the idea of matchmaking between her friends, Molly doubted Helena had thought the possibilities all the way through—especially what would happen if it went bad. Even if Molly had been free to act, Tate would still be a hazard area for that very reason. She and Helena were close, but probably not close enough for Molly to hurt Tate without repercussions.

But if Tate did make a move, how would Helena react if Molly rejected him?

She flopped over onto her belly and pulled a pillow over her head.

Of course the most hair-pulling part of it all was that even if she could decide what she wanted to do, there was only one option actually available to her.

Nothing.

And she hated doing nothing. Hated the feeling that there was nothing she *could* do.

Since she couldn't sleep and it was too early to drink, Molly went and took a long, hot shower. She felt better, awake if not rested, and a careful application of concealer over the bags under her eyes made her look awake and somewhat human—at least from a distance.

At least banging her nose last night hadn't blacked her eyes. *That* would have just been too much.

She called Sam as she tied her shoes. "I'm about to head that way. Do you need anything? Do I need to go by the bank for change?"

"I was hoping you'd call before you came, because I didn't want to call and wake you up. First, no, I don't need anything, and everything is under control. Second, Jane is on her way in. She says you should take the rest of the day off, and she'll help me close."

"That's sweet, but—"

"And Tate called. I told him that you'd gone home, but he didn't want to call and wake you. He said if you called to tell you that Nigel's fine, and all the tests came back normal. You can call him for the details, but he didn't want you to worry."

"That is a relief." It meant that giving Nigel that new food *had* been the catalyst, and though it was her fault, at least he didn't have some horrible disease. "But Jane doesn't need to—"

"It's fine," Sam insisted. "We've got it worked out. Take the rest of the day off and relax."

She hesitated. It wasn't that she was a workaholic who couldn't leave her business alone—she had a great, trustworthy staff completely capable of running Latte Dah in her absence. But taking the rest of the day off didn't sound that appealing. She'd already discovered that she couldn't be left alone with her thoughts today. Relaxing didn't seem likely.

But she *could* go get Nigel and spend the rest of the evening working at home with him on her lap. Maybe bring home some barbeque for dinner and just wait until she was exhausted enough to fall asleep regardless of how much her brain wanted to spin. "That actually sounds like a good idea. Tell Jane I said thanks, and y'all call me if you need anything."

"Will do. Enjoy your evening. I'm glad Nigel's okay."

"You and me both. See you tomorrow."

Her next call was to the clinic. "Hi, Jenny. It's Molly Richards. I hear I can come get Nigel?"

"You can. He aced all of his tests. He wasn't happy about taking them . . ."

"He's a grumpy one, I know. I hope no one got shredded in the process."

"Don't worry. We know how to handle a grumpy kitty." She laughed. "He's ready to go whenever you get here."

"I'm on my way now." She went to the bedroom and got the hoodie Tate had loaned her weeks ago. She'd had ample opportunity to return it before now, but it had simply slipped her mind. But considering her current state of confusion regarding Tate, she was going to need to keep a distance from him in the near future—at least until she got her head sorted out—and returning that hoodie now seemed to be a step toward creating that distance.

Limiting contact was the wisest choice. At least for now.

She probably wouldn't even have to see him today since she was just picking Nigel up, and she could leave the hoodie with Jenny at the desk, drawing a line in the sand—at least maybe for her subconscious.

While the nights might still feel springish, the days were warming up nicely, inching into the mid-eighties with bright blue skies and lots of sunshine. Just being in that sunshine helped improve Molly's mind and attitude, even making her feel a bit more energetic.

Tate's clinic was on the far north side of Magnolia Beach—which in reality wasn't all *that* far—but it wasn't a walk Molly wanted to make while carrying Nigel in his carrier, either. So while it was exactly the kind of beautiful day that begged for a walk, she drove. Maybe later she could go down to the Shore for a little while. Or she could go for a long, exhausting run to burn off some frustration and maybe tire her enough to actually sleep.

The waiting room was emptier than usual, with only one sweet-looking mutt panting happily at the end of its leash. The lady at the other end of that leash smiled at Molly.

Half-caf soy vanilla latte, extra sweet. She couldn't remember the woman's name, though, so she just smiled in return and went straight to the counter.

Jenny already had Nigel's paperwork ready to go, and she called someone in the back to get Nigel ready. "Since he doesn't like his carrier, I didn't want to get him loaded until you got here."

"That's sweet, but Nigel can deal." She handed over a credit card for Jenny to run and glanced over the bill. Not as bad as she'd braced herself for, but maybe it was a good thing Nigel liked the cheap cat food better. But the fact it wasn't as bad as she'd feared had her examining the charges carefully.

Nothing was listed for Tate's house call.

"Are you sure this is correct?" she asked.

Jenny came over to check the bill. "I entered it all myself, straight off Nigel's chart." She dropped her voice. "If it's a problem, you know we can set you up a payment plan."

"No, that's not it. I was actually expecting to pay more."

"Well, it's a happy surprise, then." Jenny handed her the receipt to sign. "Tate wants to talk to you for a second before you leave. We'll bring Nigel back to you in his office."

Molly nodded. She needed to talk to Tate now, that was for sure. Jenny pointed her down the hall, where Molly could see Tate sitting behind a desk.

"You look exhausted," Tate said in way of greeting. "Have you not slept?"

"A catnap or two. I've been worried about Nigel."

"All of his tests came back negative. Liver, pancreas— I tested for all the usual causes of hypoglycemia and found nothing. So that's good."

"So it was the food."

"Since it's never happened before, yes, it's probably the food. And while I could attempt to isolate exactly what caused the reaction, why don't you just stick with the food you know he likes and don't give him that new brand again. And if you do decide to try new foods in the future, watch for vomiting and bring him in immediately if he starts, so we can monitor him." He smirked. "I suggest you only introduce new foods in the mornings if you want a good night's sleep."

She nodded. "Now, speaking of a good night's sleep . . ." She paused as a tech came in carrying Nigel's carrier. She could hear Nigel growling in displeasure, so she stuck her fingers through the gate and stroked him.

Once the tech left, Tate prompted her. "What about sleep?"

"I didn't see a charge for your house call."

"Don't worry about it."

"But I do. You gave up your night to come take care of my cat."

He shrugged as his ears turned slightly pink. "That's what friends do."

"I would never take advantage of my friends like that."

"I don't want to charge you for it." When she started to protest, he held up a hand. "I don't even know how to charge you for it."

"Huh?"

"I don't normally do house calls, and when I have to, it's through the emergency vet service, and they do that billing."

Somehow she didn't quite believe that was the truth, but it was rude to call someone a liar to his face. "Well, you have to let me pay you something."

Tate thought it over. "Fine."

Molly reached into her purse, but Tate stopped her by lifting a hand. "You can buy me a late lunch." Looking at the clock, he corrected himself. "Or an early dinner."

"What?"

"I'm *starving*. I took a nap today instead of eating lunch when I normally would. Jenny managed to reschedule the rest of my afternoon appointments, so I'm free once I finish with Peaches and Julia."

Julia—that's her name. That tidbit processed faster than Tate's request for lunch—probably because Tate's request was so completely unexpected that her brain wasn't fully recognizing it.

"So," he continued, "all I want to do now is take a shower and get something to eat. And yes, I could just grab something on the way home, but I eat alone more often than not and would appreciate the company—if for no other reason than it will keep me from falling asleep in my dinner."

He had that sweet, self-deprecating smile on his face again. Molly was charmed, even if she really didn't want to be, and it made the request impossible to ignore because it was so simple. After all, she ate alone a lot, too, and she hated it.

"It's the curse of being single, isn't it? Eating alone, I mean."

Tate nodded.

She was responsible for the fact Tate had been up half the night and had to skip lunch so he could sleep. She owed him a lot more than a meal.

And since she'd just insisted that he charge her for the house call, she couldn't refuse to pay what he asked— especially since it was so reasonable, both in monetary cost and human courtesy.

Good Lord, she'd just talked herself into it, all common sense be damned.

"I've got to take Nigel home and get him settled, and you said you wanted a shower. Do you want to go somewhere or should I bring something to your place?" He raised an eyebrow in question. "Kind of like a food house call."

He nodded. "That actually sounds great."

"Gary's Barbeque okay?"

"Yes, very much."

"How long do you need to finish up here and shower and such?"

"Forty-five minutes, give or take?"

"Great. I'll see you then." She grabbed the handle of Nigel's carrier and left before she could weasel her way back out of it.

As she put Nigel in the car and fastened the seat belt around his carrier, she noticed Tate's hoodie on the floor.

So much for that limiting-contact idea.

Chapter 9

Two and a half hours later, she was seated at Tate's kitchen table licking rib sauce off her fingers. She'd given up trying to be dainty or even remotely ladylike one rib in, and now she was just trying to keep the majority of the sauce off her face and shirt.

Tate's house was a mirror image of Mrs. Kennedy's— one of the three floor plans the developers offered after Hurricane Betsy destroyed much of Magnolia Beach in the 1960s. But where Mrs. Kennedy's house was firmly dated and decorated in that same decade, Tate's house had been completely rehabbed and redone in earthy tones and clean lines. It suited him—it was comfortable and modern and very livable. She wasn't exactly sure what she'd been expecting, but she'd been pleasantly surprised, nonetheless.

Tate was surprising her as well. He'd answered the door barefoot and wearing baggy cargo shorts, his shoulders and chest nicely outlined by an *almost*-too-tight T-shirt. His hair had still been a little damp from his shower, and he smelled of warm, wet skin and soap. She'd nearly dropped the food off and left, figuring she could come up with some kind of excuse.

But then Tate turned on the charm at a level she'd

never witnessed from him before, and even though she tried to resist, she was being won over by it. By him.

He was funny and easy to talk to, too.

And while part of her wanted to question what she was doing here, with him, the rest of her didn't care. She knew this wasn't a date, but it was fun to pretend, just for a little while. It had just been so long since she'd done anything remotely like a date, and she was having a good time.

As for Tate, she had no idea what was going through his head, what he might think this was, but he was certainly staying on the safe side with his charm. It was so platonic and friendly, in fact, that if it hadn't been for that *moment* last night, she wouldn't have given it a second thought.

Of course, she was also operating on approximately two hours of sleep, so this could all just be a hallucination. It was all the more reason to not try to read anything into this other than exactly what it was. A meal. Between friends.

Because they were actually friends now, not just two of Helena's friends. That much she knew, and she wasn't unhappy about it.

As long as she didn't overthink it, at least.

"Next thing I know, this cat has climbed me like a tree, blood is going everywhere, and one of the other students starts puking his guts . . . Sorry," he interrupted himself, shaking his head. "I forget that most people don't have conversations involving bodily fluids at the dinner table."

"It's okay. You weren't graphic enough to turn my stomach. I guess you kinda have to have a strong stomach to be a vet. Or any kind of doctor."

"It's not necessarily a strong stomach. It's just accepting that stuff comes out of bodies and dealing with it." He shrugged. "Sometimes you still gag, but you deal."

That made her laugh. "I think that would be a great mantra."

"What?"

"You know, a Zen life mantra thing. 'Sometimes you gag, but you still have to deal.' That's life in a nutshell."

"Very true. It's a picturesque, if slightly gross, sentiment, but true nonetheless."

She eyeballed another rib, debating whether she had room. "So if bodily fluids don't gross you out, is there anything that does?"

"Bugs," he answered without hesitation. "Killing bugs, specifically. They make that crunching sound, and that's just gross." A little shudder shook his shoulders.

She dropped her napkin onto her plate dramatically. "And with that, I'm done with my dinner."

Tate looked a little abashed. "You asked."

"I was done anyway," she assured him.

"Your turn." He leaned back in his chair, seemingly completely at ease. "Tell me interesting tales from the coffee shop."

"There are fewer of those than you might think. Coffee and pastries lack drama." She laughed. "Mainly because they don't fight, bite, or bleed."

"True. But you deal with people. They're far more dangerous."

"Only before they're fully caffeinated." He laughed, which made her smile. It felt good. "You have to deal with people all day long, too."

"Yes, but I also get to pet the kitties and the puppies all day long. There's nothing better than that for stress relief."

She loved how he unashamedly expressed his love for the critters he treated. "Do you ever get tired of them?"

"The animals?" He looked surprised at her question. "No."

Leaning back, she crossed her arms over her chest. "Then why don't you have a pet?"

"Well, I work long hours—sometimes even through the middle of the night," he reminded her, "so they'd be left alone a lot. A cat might be okay with that, but not a dog. And since I often foster cats *and* dogs until they get homes, there could be interspecies fighting. Maybe one day, though."

"I'm not sure I should trust a vet without a pet," she teased.

"I'll remember that the next time you call me at two o'clock in the morning." Tate winked at her as he went to the fridge to get the tea pitcher. After refilling her glass, he started to tidy up the table. "Thank you for dinner, by the way."

"And thank you for answering the phone at two o'clock in the morning." Clearing the table seemed like her hint that it was time to leave, even if he had just refilled her glass. Tate had to be exhausted, and since this early dinner had extended into actual dinnertime, he was probably ready to call it a night.

But then Tate sat back down, casually leaning back in his chair again, those long legs stretched out under the table. *Okay, we're not done.* "How are things with the Children's Fair?" he asked. "You all set?"

"I think so. I keep going over everything, thinking I must have forgotten something pretty important somewhere, but everything seems to be ready to go. It helps, of course, that so many of the people have been involved with this for years and know exactly what they're doing."

"I told you." There was just a hint of smugness in his voice.

"Yes, you did. Bask in it. If it all goes well, and we make the money goal, you can chant all the 'I told you so's you want."

"There won't be any need for that. The fact that I'll

know, and you'll know, and I'll know that you know I know—that's all the gloating I'll need."

"Well, aren't you the gentleman."

Tate leveled a look at her over the rim of his glass. "I wouldn't say that."

Okay, there was *definitely* something in his tone that time, and it raised the temperature in the room about ten degrees. And that smile . . . *Damn*. There was no way she was imagining it, but that didn't mean she knew how to process it, either.

It doesn't matter, though, she reminded herself, *because . . .*

That thought screeched to a halt when Tate's fingers stroked gently down her arm. "You look exhausted," he said. "Maybe you should call it a night."

The disconnect confused her. A touch at the same time he was putting an end to the evening? Was this a test of some sort? If she said she wasn't tired, was she agreeing to something? Or was she misconstruing a friendly, compassionate touch? Was he just genuinely worried about her?

She was enjoying herself and didn't necessarily *want* to leave, and Tate's face wasn't giving her any clues, so . . .

Either way, going home was probably her best bet. Maybe once she had a good night's sleep behind her, she'd be able to make sense of it. "Yeah, you're right." She pushed her chair back from the table and stood. "I also want to check on Nigel."

Tate stood, too, and once again she felt very *aware* of him. His size. His smell. She'd gotten so comfortable over the last couple of hours that she'd forgotten, but that touch . . . The situation had changed, and so had her focus. "I promise you," he said, "Nigel's fine. But I know you want to check on him all the same."

Mercy, his *eyes*.

Yeah, she needed to go. *Now*.

She nearly tripped over her feet on her way to the door. "Thanks again for last night."

He followed her. "Thanks again for tonight."

Grabbing her bag with one hand, she reached for the door with the other, landing on the knob at the same moment Tate's hand did. Stepping back quickly, she trod on his foot, stumbling sideways into him.

Sweet Mary, mother of God. She could feel her cheeks burning.

Chuckling, Tate held her by the shoulders, steadying her on her feet. "Do you think you can get home on your own?"

"Yes. I'm sure of it. I'm obviously just really tired."

"Well, I'm sorry that I kept you up even longer, but I appreciate dinner and the company."

"It was the least I could do." *That sounded rude.* "And I enjoyed it, too."

Tate was still holding her, but loosely, so even the tiniest step back would have broken the contact. But his hands were large and warm and felt nice, even if this whole situation was causing her insides to churn in conflicting and confusing ways.

Then she made the mistake of looking up to meet his eyes. So blue and so kind and so . . . *Oh.* That heat was new. It paralyzed her, and everything slipped into slow motion.

Tate was going to kiss her. That one thought ran through her brain on repeat, and although one small rational part of her knew it was a bad idea, the rest of her wanted him to. *Badly.*

She was still surprised when he did. His lips were warm and gentle, offering just enough pressure to promise, but not demand. She wanted to melt into it, into *him*, and though she knew she shouldn't, she kissed him back, rising up onto her tiptoes to extend the moment.

His fingers tightened around her shoulders, and she

let her tongue sneak out for one quick, fleeting taste of him, right before her brain kicked back in, causing her to rock back onto her heels and put some distance between them. Tate's mouth followed hers, sucking gently on her bottom lip for one second longer—just enough to stoke the embers in her belly into a glow—before letting her go.

Damn.

But it was the shy half smile Tate gave her that slayed her, mixing sweet, gooey feelings with hot, long-repressed need. It was too much. "Good night, Tate."

"Good night, Molly. Sleep well."

The fact that it was still light outside made the "Good night. Sleep well" a little ridiculous-sounding, but the daylight burned off the magic and made what had just happened seem even more surreal.

And it sucked.

She wanted to barge right back in and kiss Tate until she couldn't breathe, get up close and familiar with the planes and angles of his chest, learn the taste of his skin . . .

But she couldn't. No matter how much she wanted to.

She had too much to lose, and good Lord, she had no idea how she could possibly explain it all to Tate. No matter what the people back home in Fuller thought, she did still know the difference between right and wrong, and this was pretty much the textbook definition of "wrong."

It just felt really right.

Surely she'd earned that kiss. She *deserved* an amazing kiss from an incredible guy. She could give herself a little while to just enjoy the moment and worry about the possible repercussions later.

It wasn't as if she could let it go any further, so she might as well enjoy what she could.

She'd focus on that. Just for a little while.

Tate had kissed her.
And she'd liked it.
A lot.

It had been three days since Tate kissed Molly. He hadn't really planned to do it quite like that, but the opportunity had presented itself and he didn't regret it.

Well, maybe it hadn't been his smoothest move ever, but Molly hadn't slapped him, either.

And as far as kisses went, that one had been pretty damn nice. It had been a sweet, nearly G-rated kiss, the kind you felt in the heart, but the effect on him had been more NC-17 and he'd felt it all over.

It had taken more control than he'd have said he possessed to let her walk out of there. Hell, if she only knew just how hard it had been and how much he'd wanted to lock the door instead, she'd be filing a restraining order on him just to be safe.

So as much as it was killing him, he'd let the last few days pass without bringing up that kiss, trying to give her time to process it without being all stalkerish. He'd seen her a couple of times, but only in passing. She'd called him twice, but both calls were quick and focused entirely on the Children's Fair, which was now less than a week away.

Since everyone in town was really busy getting ready for the weekend events, he didn't really take her distance *too* personally. Plus, Helena's warning that Molly had "issues" and probably a bad relationship behind her meant he was trekking into possibly dangerous territory without a map. It would behoove him to be cautious. Hell, she'd been saddled with a huge project and had dealt with a serious health scare with a pet. That alone was enough to be dealing with at the moment. She didn't need a lot of pressure from some guy right now just because he'd made a pass.

But those three days had been a trial to his patience, and on day four he had none left. He wanted to see her, maybe even take her to dinner—and definitely kiss her again—so he went to Latte Dah after work.

A large group seemed to be having a meeting of some sort in one corner, and a smaller group of teenagers had squared off in the other, disturbing the general tranquility that normally reigned in Latte Dah. Sam was behind the counter, working the cappuccino machine like a pro. At first, he thought Molly wasn't there, but then he saw her, over at one of the smaller tables with Helena, both of them frowning and gesticulating as they spoke.

Helena's presence here gave him pause. He had to assume Molly hadn't said anything to her about that kiss, simply because he would know if Helena knew. There was no way she'd let that pass without comment.

But he couldn't really talk to Molly—much less ask her out—if Helena was listening in.

On the other hand, if Molly was feeling awkward about that kiss, Helena might give them a bit of a buffer, letting her ease into the idea. And regardless of anything else, he'd at least get to talk to her for a few minutes, allowing him to get a reading on the situation.

"I would not go over there if I were you," Sam warned from behind him as he headed in their direction.

He turned to look at his sister. "Why?"

"Because they are taking turns ranting and freaking out."

Sighing, he sat at the counter. "Memorial Day stuff?" Sam nodded.

"I do not understand them. They're capable, competent adults organizing a couple of community events. No one's asked them to build a rocket or perform brain surgery, but to listen to them, you'd think dozens of innocent lives hung in the balance."

"Don't be such an ignorant ass."

"I beg your pardon, Samantha Harris?"

"You're being very dense. Do you honestly think that if Helena screws up that bake sale or raffle people will just shrug and say, 'Oh, well, no lives lost'? No, they're going to bring up every stupid, dumbass thing she ever did in her life in order to 'prove' that no one should have let her be in charge of anything in the first place. This is trial by fire for her."

True. He hadn't thought of it that way, and he of all people really should have. "So what's Molly's excuse?"

"This is her first time really being a part of this, much less being in charge. She is definitely feeling the pressure to prove herself and not let people down. And not only does she have to do it right, she's got a fund-raising goal to meet as well."

"I talked to her the other night, and she seemed fine."

"I'm sure she is, overall. But even if she weren't, she wouldn't tell you."

That stung. "Why not?"

"Because they need sympathy, not justice, right now."

"I can give sympathy."

Sam gave him a pitying "how can you be so stupid?" look. "You are incapable of straight sympathy. You'll tell her she'll do fine, there's nothing to worry about—"

"Well, it's all true."

"And then you'll start trying to sort out the problem and fix it."

"And that wouldn't be helpful because . . . ?"

"Because that's not what either of them wants to hear right now. Let them freak out if they need to. They're under pressure."

"All the more reason for me to go over there and see if I can do anything to calm her—them—down."

"No. There's nothing over there for you to do. And they're not in the mood to listen to other people anyway.

I teasingly threatened to switch them both to decaf, and Helena looked like she was about to put my head on a platter."

He watched them for a minute. "They are taking turns talking, but they're not looking at each other. Is that some girl-sympathy thing I don't understand?"

Sam was reveling in her superiority. "No. They're talking *at* each other, not *to*. It's venting," she explained in a tone that clearly called him dumber than a bag of hammers.

He let it pass, simply because he couldn't take his eyes off Molly and Helena. It was the strangest thing he'd ever seen—and with two sisters, he'd seen a hell of a lot of strange girl stuff. He could wish they'd just believe him when he told them everything would be fine—and that the world wouldn't end even if it wasn't—but Helena rarely listened to him and Molly wasn't proving to be much better. "How long have they been at it?"

"About an hour." She lowered her voice. "I did switch them to half-caf on the last refill. I'm afraid they'll stress themselves into a stroke." Sam smiled as she refilled a coffee for another customer. "And by the way"—she turned back to him—"did something happen between you and Molly?"

He stiffened involuntarily, but Sam didn't seem to notice. He tried to sound casual. "I don't think so. Why?"

"When she started in on her weekly freak-out today, I told her to call you."

"And?"

"She got all flustered and knocked over her coffee. Then she started swearing."

The fluster could be promising, but the swearing . . . "Er, um . . ."

"I figured she wasn't going to tell *me* if my brother had been being a dick, and I'm not going to say anything to you except knock it off if you are. I like Molly."

"I like Molly, too."

He'd meant it in the most offhanded, "I'm merely echoing your statement" kind of way, but Sam's head snapped around and her eyes narrowed at him. "You do?"

Damn, sisters are dangerous creatures. "Yes. We're friends."

He could tell by her look that Sam didn't wasn't buying that wholesale. Still, she said, "You might want to be careful. Helena's trying to set you and Molly up. Someone might get the wrong idea."

Sam was good, but she wasn't *that* good. She was fishing, but he didn't have to take the bait. "I'm aware of that. As is Molly, too. Don't worry."

She smiled and leaned across the counter. "Not that I'd object, you know."

"Hush." *Great. Just great.*

"I could even put in a good word for you with Molly, if you were leaning that way. Very casually, of course."

"I'll take a tall black coffee—to go." Any ideas he might have had about talking to Molly now were completely off the table. Not with Helena and now Sam ready to butt in at any moment with meddling and matchmaking. He did not need commentary—helpful or heckling— from the peanut gallery.

"You're no fun."

"And you're not fixing my coffee," he reminded her. "Some barista you are."

Giving him that pitying look again, Sam did finally make him a to-go cup of coffee, but she waved away his money. "No charge."

"Giving away freebies to the customers is a good way to lose your job."

Sam pulled back, clearly insulted. "I would never do that."

"Well, I'm not letting you buy my coffee."

"I'm not. Molly is," she clarified. "Per her edict last

week. You drink free here because you saved her cat's life."

"I can't let her do that."

"It's not like you drink the good stuff anyway. Barbarian." She sniffed with disdain.

"You don't even drink coffee. If anyone's a barbarian, it's you."

"But at least I know the difference between good stuff and merely cheap stuff."

"What happened to the customer always being right?"

She laughed. "It's your prerogative to drink whatever you like. But it's my prerogative to judge you for it."

"Whatever." He slipped a five into the tip jar.

Sam shook her head at him. "Molly splits those tips among the staff at the end of the shift. You're paying me, not her."

That was fine by him. Sam needed the money, too. He'd have to take up the free-coffee issue with Molly another time. But all things considered, it might be best for him to avoid dealings with all three of these women—particularly in a group. As much as he'd like to have a minute with Molly, she didn't seem to be in the mood. Helena—aside from also being in an evil mood, too—would only embarrass everyone if she figured out his thoughts, and Sam was just way too perceptive at times.

He knew when to make a tactical retreat, so he took his coffee and left.

Honestly, he knew that just because *he'd* decided he was interested in Molly in an entirely new way, he couldn't assume Molly was also in the same place. *Yet.* After all, just a couple of weeks ago, she'd heard him proclaim quite forcefully that he was *not* interested in her. It was a rather dramatic turnaround in his attitude, at least on the surface, and it could be a little confusing for her.

Of course, she'd also told him that she wasn't interested

in him, either, but that was before. It could have been the truth or a bit of face-saving bravado under the circumstances, but she'd had *some* kind of shift in her thoughts since then. When he'd kissed her, she'd kissed him back—however briefly.

All the more reason to make his interest clear and see what she said.

Safely out of sight of the coffee shop, he tossed the coffee he'd ordered only to distract his sister into a nearby trash can. Then he went to the gym to distract himself.

He was on his way home when Molly called. "Sam said you stopped by today wanting to talk to me."

"Yeah." He'd wanted to do this face-to-face. It would be easier if he could see her reactions. Then he realized it had been quite a while since he'd actually cold-called a woman to ask her out, and he wasn't entirely sure how to do it anymore.

"Tate?"

He'd lost his chance at small talk with that delay, and now he couldn't even get a reading from the pleasantries. He forged ahead. "I'd like to take you to dinner." He thought he might have heard her sigh, but that didn't make much sense. "Maybe tomorrow night?"

"I appreciate the invitation, but I can't."

"Oh. Another night, then?"

Okay, he definitely heard a sigh this time. "I'm going to be honest with you."

Neither her words nor her tone boded well. "Please do."

"I think it's best that we just stay friends. I realize I may have misled you or made you think otherwise, and I'm very sorry about that. I know you won't believe this, but it's not you. It really is me. I've got some . . . personal stuff going on, and I can't. But thank you anyway. I'm flattered."

He'd never been shot down quite so completely yet politely at the same time. He could tell she was choosing her words carefully, and he could also tell there was a hell of a lot hiding behind those carefully chosen words. He wished he could ask what, because "it's me, not you" always meant "it's you," and there was no way that didn't sting. "Okay, then. I guess I'll see you later."

"Bye, Tate."

If he weren't so confused, his ego might be smarting more than it was. He knew she wasn't seeing anyone—and if she were, she would have just said so and ended it there. And he knew Molly was attracted to him—he'd caught her appraising his assets before—and there was that kiss.

Maybe Sam was right; maybe he had done something to piss Molly off. The most obvious would be kissing her, but since she'd seemed an active participant at the time, could she be mad about it now?

He had no reason to believe she was lying to him, but he didn't think she was being completely honest, either.

Molly was turning out to be far more complicated than he'd thought.

Chapter 10

The days passed in a complete blur, and before Molly was ready, it was Saturday morning and she had twenty-two tents, over a hundred people, and an ark's worth of animals set up in the park. The sky was perfectly blue and cloudless, promising a warm, sunny day. It wasn't quite nine o'clock yet, but people were already out and about, and there was a crowd of wild-eyed and hyper children milling outside her gate waiting for this year's Children's Fair to officially open. She was a little afraid she might get trampled when it finally did.

A couple of the adults she could see were carrying Latte Dah to-go cups, and it made her smile. She knew the line there would be out the door. It always was first thing in the morning whenever there was something like this going on downtown. Business would be steady all day, too. It was killing her not to be there, even though she knew Jane and Sam would have it under control. Rachel and Holly, the two high schoolers, had both picked up extra shifts, too. She had to believe Latte Dah was in good hands or else she'd lose her mind.

She could use a cup of coffee herself right now, if for no other reason the smell would be nice. She'd placed the animals as far away as she could, but the breeze still wafted an unpleasant aroma into all the areas. She could only hope that once the fire department lit their big grill and started cooking that that smell might overpower the other.

A chicken ran past her legs, hotly pursued by Robbie Hannigan, who was helping his father with the petting zoo. She just stepped back out of the way. After the Tent Catastrophe of six a.m., the Great Goat Fiasco of six forty-five, and the Clown Brawl of seven fifteen, one lone chicken on the loose was not nearly enough to shake her composure now.

There were tents with people spinning and weaving, tents where kids could make corn husk dolls, and tents where kids could get their faces painted. There was a small stage where jugglers and puppeteers and a one-man band would perform. There were midway-style games and cakewalks and a bouncy castle. It was as much wholesome family fun as could possibly be crammed into a park.

It was way too early to be too self-congratulatory, but she was pretty pleased with herself, all things considered. Barring a hurricane or fire—and the fire department was already here anyway—this was happening.

Ready or not.

She'd seen Helena in passing, setting up a bake sale booth for Ms. Louise's church, but she hadn't had time to stop and speak. A little later, Ryan had come through in his official capacity as mayor, checking to see whether she needed anything and congratulating her on a job well done. In fact, everyone she saw was full of praise— which was hard to believe, but still very nice to hear.

She was frazzled and nervous and in desperate need of a drink already, but she just might pull this off. And she couldn't believe how good that made her feel.

Just outside the gates to the park, she could see the red cross flag being raised above the first aid tent. Next to that was the smaller animal first aid and pet adoption information tent run by Tate's clinic. She'd seen him earlier when he'd come in to talk to Cliff Hannigan as the animals were being unloaded out of their trailers, but he hadn't said much to her other than "good morning."

She hadn't had much time to think recently, which had kept her from brooding, even if it hadn't been enough to push the whole Tate situation completely out of mind.

His attention, that kiss . . . all kinds of long-dormant feelings were suddenly and uncomfortably active. And it was hard to ignore those feelings even though she knew she had to. Hell, she hadn't been so giddy that she'd been asked out by a boy since high school, and for one fleeting moment it had been grand. Turning him down had sucked, though—doubly so because she'd heard the disappointment and confusion in his voice. Which was understandable, considering she'd kissed him back the other night. He must have been assuming she'd say yes.

And if life were fair, or even normal, she would have. She'd wanted to.

Damn it, she'd let it go too far and now she'd created a problem.

John Ragland, the new youth pastor at Grace Baptist and a volunteer clown today—although not one who'd been involved in the brawl—nearly tripped over his floppy red shoes as he caught up to her. "The crowd out there is getting restless."

She looked around and then checked her list to make sure everything was marked off. "I guess we're ready. Would you like to do the honors?"

He grinned. Even knowing it was just John behind the face paint, Molly was still a little creeped out. Clowns gave her the willies. "I'd be happy to. But are you sure you don't want to do it?"

The chicken ran past her again, squawking loudly.

She sighed and stepped out of Robbie's way. "No, you go ahead. I think I'll see if I can help with the escaped poultry."

Now there's a sentence I never thought I'd hear myself say.

By the time the chicken was safely back in its pen, the fair was in full swing. She knew that people came in from all over the county for the weekend's events, but she was normally stationed inside Latte Dah and therefore didn't know how thick the crowds actually were. In hindsight, that was probably a good thing. If she'd truly known how big this was, she'd have been far more panicked about it and probably would've had a nervous breakdown.

"Excuse me, are you Molly?"

She turned to see a dark-haired woman carrying a cup from Latte Dah. "Yes, I am. Can I help you?"

The woman extended the cup toward her. "This is for you. And Sam says to tell you everything is just fine."

The aroma alone was enough to brighten her spirits. "I appreciate you delivering the message—and the coffee. Sam is an angel." *And a mind reader.*

The woman snorted, then caught herself. "Sorry. It's just that I don't think of Sam as an angel. I'm Ellie, Sam's sister."

Ellie, the sister who rarely came to town and didn't stay long when she did. Based on what she'd picked up from Sam, the Harris siblings were close, so Ellie's issue was more likely with her mother. "Oh, I've heard so much about you. It's nice to finally meet you."

"I don't come to visit very often, but I thought my kids might enjoy the fair, so we came down for the day."

Ellie didn't favor Tate or Sam beyond the dark hair. Tate and Sam were both tall, with athletic builds, and Ellie was petite and curvy. "I hope y'all have fun."

"I hear you got this job when Mrs. Kennedy dumped it on you."

"I wouldn't say 'dumped' . . ." *At least not publicly.* She needed to be diplomatic.

Ellie smiled and shook her head. "I know Mrs. K. I can only imagine how you ended up with it. But I will say that everything is great. Lots of choices, well organized. Good job."

"Thank you."

"I will also tell you that everything really is fine over at Latte Dah. The line is huge, but it's moving quickly."

"That's a relief." Now both Harris sisters were topping her list of favorite people today.

"And Tate was right. It's some of the best coffee I've ever had."

She tried to keep a simple smile on her face. "That's very kind of him to say. And *you* are saying all the things I need to hear right now."

"It's all the truth." She smiled, and then Molly really saw the family resemblance. "I've heard both Tate and Sam talk about you, so it's nice to finally meet you."

She had to wonder what Tate had said about her—and when he'd said it—but there was no way to ask, and now she was a little uncomfortable. She really couldn't let thoughts of Tate throw her off her game today. "And you, too," she repeated. "Thanks for the coffee delivery. That was very kind of you. I'll let you get back to your family now."

Ellie put a hand on her arm. "One last thing. I'm friends with Marie Kennedy, and she says that you're not to worry, because her mother has every intention of taking this back."

"Oh, you *are* saying everything I want to hear." She was proud of herself for pulling this off, but she also didn't want to get sucked in permanently.

"Then I kind of feel bad about telling you . . ."

"What?" A little bolt of panic shot through her.

Ellie's mouth twisted. "I overhead Mrs. Wilson talking to Tate about what a great job you're doing. She sees you moving into other leadership roles next year."

Ugh. "Well, thank you for the heads-up."

"My pleasure. I hope it all continues to run smoothly."

Amazingly, to Molly at least, it did. There were a couple of small things here and there, a few lost children who needed comforting until their parents could be found, a few people sent to the first aid tent, but no fires, no massive blood loss, no explosions, no more escaped livestock . . . She considered it a success.

By eight o'clock, everyone was packing up, and she was sitting in the back of the information tent counting the cash with the bank president and his wife while Deputy James stood guard.

"Good job," Jessie Hollis said as Duncan wrote out the receipt. "That's about four or five hundred dollars more than last year."

"Really?" She'd hoped to get close, but she never dreamed she'd surpass previous totals. There were still a couple of bills to pay, but there were still some checks to come in, too, so . . .

She'd done it. It wasn't a complete disaster. She had this sudden urge to call home and gloat, but she quickly tamped it down.

Instead she gloated quietly to herself.

"We'll walk this over to the bank," Duncan said, "and it'll be officially deposited in the account Tuesday morning when we open."

"I appreciate it." She stood and stretched. "And just in time," she added, since the guys from the rental place were standing by to strike the tent. She moved out of their way and waved good-bye as the Duncans and the deputy left.

It was over. She was done.

Jane had closed Latte Dah over an hour ago, and Sam had stopped by with the assurance that everything was fine, and she didn't need to go to the shop for anything. Sam offered to save her a seat at the concert, and while Molly was tempted, she was also bone tired.

And she had a business to open in the morning.

Right outside the park, the food trucks were serving barbeque and boiled shrimp, and the firemen still had their burgers for sale. Oddly, she wasn't hungry. She did, however, get a beer and carry it down to the Shore.

With the concert about to begin, the Shore was pretty deserted, with only a few couples here and there, mostly teenagers. She walked a little ways along the boardwalk, away from the people, then sat down, dangling her feet over the edge and looking out over Heron Bay.

It was gorgeous, perfect weather, cool after a day in the sun, and the breeze felt good on her face. Fuller was on the river, and she'd grown up a lake and river girl, but once she moved down here she'd realized she was a beach girl at heart. Even if she wanted to, how could she live anywhere else after living here?

She was happy and proud of herself for a job well done, but there was also a heavy feeling in her stomach, a discontent that really seemed out of place.

This was home. She was settled, with friends and a business, and she loved it here. But the truth was, she was still in limbo, unable to really move on. And while days, weeks even, would go by without her thinking of Mark or her family, the knowledge that she wasn't finished with that part of her life was always in the back of her mind, keeping her from feeling truly settled here.

And the last few weeks had really driven that home for her.

She wanted to blame Helena, or even Tate, for awakening that discontent, but she knew it would have happened eventually. At first, she'd kept busy just trying to survive—trying to adjust to life in a new place on her own for the first time and building her business. She hadn't had time for anything or anyone.

And she'd still been healing.

But then everything had clicked into place, and the last eight or nine months should have seen the triumphant rising of the New Molly from the ashes of the old. She was a fully integrated member of this community—she was liked and had been trusted with a big responsibility without anyone worrying she wouldn't succeed.

Except that she wasn't really a fully integrated member of society because she wasn't really *that* Molly yet. She couldn't be.

But she wanted to be.

The fact she wasn't made her want to bang her head against something hard.

She settled for taking a big gulp of her beer.

The music from the concert provided ambiance to her pity party, and she leaned back on her hands to stare at the sky. Normally she liked being alone, but tonight she felt lonely. Closing her eyes, she turned her face to the breeze to help clear her head.

She heard footsteps behind her, and didn't think anything of it until they slowed and stopped. She opened her eyes and wasn't really all that surprised to see Tate. And while it only complicated things more to admit it, she was happy to see him. "Hey."

"I wanted to see how it went today," he explained. "I went by your tent, but you were already gone. Susan Jones told me she saw you headed down this way, and when I saw a lone shadow down here I thought I'd see if it was you." He squatted next to her, his face creased in concern. "You don't look very celebratory, though. From what I heard, it all went great."

"Oh, it did," she assured him, deliberately forcing her eyes up, away from the calf and thigh muscles on display from that squat. That just had her staring into his eyes, though, which wasn't much better. She swallowed hard and decided watching the water was a much safer idea. "I survived farm animals, small children, *and* clowns. And it looks like we beat last year's total by a couple hundred dollars, too. It's definitely celebration-worthy." She shrugged to explain her lack of enthusiasm. "I'm just too worn out to actually do it."

"At least it's only a one-day event."

"Thank goodness for that. I don't know if I could do another day."

Tate sat and dangled his legs off the boardwalk, mirroring her posture as he leaned back on his hands as well. "Are you not a fan of our local talent?"

"The concert?" He nodded. "They're great, but I have to be up early to open the shop."

"You don't normally open on Sundays."

"No, but I'd be crazy to stay closed when there's that much going on in the streets outside my door. I'm only going to be open until the parade starts, though, and I'll close on Monday instead since most folks will be at cookouts or at the Beach anyway."

"Sounds reasonable."

"I try."

They sat quietly for a moment. Then Tate sighed. "I'm wondering if I owe you an apology."

"For what?" she answered automatically, then instantly regretted it.

He didn't look at her, but he didn't hesitate, either. "Kissing you the other night."

Boy, he was blunt. She had to respect that, even if she wished he wouldn't be. She didn't want to talk about that right now. Or ever, really. "You don't owe me an apology."

"It seems like you've been avoiding me since then—"

"I've been busy."

"I know. But I just don't want you to feel uncomfortable about it. Around me."

"You're a good man, Tate. And I know that usually when people say it's them and not you they mean the exact opposite, but it *is* me. I'm not really there yet." She sighed. "It's a long story."

"Obviously."

Tate didn't leave, but he didn't say anything else, either, even though it was obvious he was curious and hopeful she'd elaborate. The silence stretched out until Molly couldn't handle it any longer. "I finally got to meet Ellie today."

"She told me. And she said to tell you that the boys really enjoyed the fair."

She nodded her thanks. "You and your sisters are really close, aren't you?"

"Yeah, we are."

She could hear the genuine affection for his sisters in his voice. And even when Sam grumbled about him, there was love in her voice, too. Part of her knew that it shouldn't be a big deal, that siblings were supposed to get along and act like a family, but it made her feel even more like an oddity in the world. Her family was great on paper, but crap in real life. "That's nice. You're the oldest, right?"

He nodded. "There's four years between me and Ellie, and almost seven between me and Sam."

Since Sam had just turned twenty-four a few weeks ago, that meant Tate was thirty-one, and she was the same age as Ellie—who was happily married with two adorable children. And based on the approximate ages of those children, Ellie had gotten married at about the same age she had, albeit with better results. "Usually with an age difference like that, it's hard for siblings to be close."

"Well, we had a pretty messed-up childhood, so it

tends to draw you together. For sanity's sake, if nothing else."

His matter-of-factness just floored her. "You're pretty open about it."

"There's really no use trying to whitewash it or pretend it didn't happen. Everyone knows, even if they don't talk about it. It's no secret. My father drank, and when he drank, he beat on us."

She winced. "Was it hard? Knowing that everyone knew, I mean?"

He thought that over for a minute. "Maybe," he finally said. "I was a teenager before I realized that wasn't how all families were, and by then it was just the way things were and unlikely to change."

"But if everyone knew, why didn't someone do something about it?"

"The state came out a couple of times, but there was never enough evidence for them to do anything. My mother still insists he was just 'strict,' and since corporal punishment isn't illegal, it can be difficult for folks to decide where the line between discipline and abuse is."

"So no one believed you?" She knew how bad it was as an adult not to be believed. But for a child? *Jesus.*

"Sometimes it's really hard to know what goes on behind closed doors. And my father held down a job, kept his family fed and clothed, went to church every Sunday . . ."

She knew that picture of "nice, normal family" all too well. But hearing Tate talk kind of made her problems seem overrated. Mark had hit her, but it was nothing like what the Harrises had had to deal with.

"Honestly, it's probably harder now," he said. "Everyone knowing, I mean."

That got her attention. "How?"

"I can tell folks wonder if I'm going to be like him.

If I had a couple of drinks at the bar on a Friday night, folks questioned my sobriety. If I got mad, they worried I had his temper. I couldn't even fight with a girlfriend without folks checking her for bruises the next day. It made me start to worry about it. How much of it could be genetic, you know?"

"DNA is not destiny. It's all about the choices you make."

"I know."

There was something almost grim in his voice—regret, maybe, or even disappointment, but since he hadn't pushed for an elaboration earlier, she would return the kindness. "Then why stay here if people were treating you like that? Why not go somewhere else and just start over?"

Tate gave her a knowing look.

Damn it. I might as well just tell him my whole frickin' life story.

He shrugged. "My sisters, mostly. I want to stay close to them. And I decided not to let my past define me. Everybody's got a sob story. We may have had a messed-up childhood, but Ellie, Sam, and I are doing okay overall. And that's what matters."

She couldn't help but notice he hadn't included his mother in his list of reasons. That was very telling. "You are doing quite well. All of you. You should be proud."

"Success is the best revenge and all that."

"True." For the most part, she was happy and successful, and that had to bug the crap out of Mark—if he even knew. "But sometimes it's hard to remember that." She looked down at her hands, realizing a second too late how very telling that statement was, too. *Damn. Just stop talking already.* But Tate was just too easy to talk to.

"Hey," Tate said softly. Molly looked up and knew

he'd understood everything she hadn't said. "Whatever it is, I'm here to tell you that you're doing okay, too. You should be proud of yourself. Trust me on that much."

"Thanks." That meant a lot. More than it probably should and more than she wanted to admit.

"You're welcome." Tate smiled and patted her gently on the back. It was a completely normal and friendly gesture, totally appropriate under the circumstances, meant to offer comfort and support, both of which Molly discovered she desperately needed. Without thinking, she leaned sideways against him, and his arm extended around her into a half hug, cuddling her sideways across his chest.

Tate was warm and he smelled good, and even knowing that she shouldn't, that this was tantamount to leading him on, Molly couldn't quite bring herself to pull out of the embrace. She could feel the solid wall of his chest and the even thump of his heartbeat against her back. Their thighs ran side by side to the edge of the boardwalk, and she could feel the tickle of the hairs on his calves against hers as their feet swung gently off the edge of the boardwalk out of sight.

This was nice, but . . .

With a sigh, she tried to pull away and sit up, but she had to brace her hand on his thigh to do so. The muscle tightened under her palm, and she lifted her head to find Tate's face just inches from hers.

She couldn't help herself, making the move before she even thought about it. Tate met her halfway, his mouth slanting over hers. There was no hesitation this time, and her hand wrapped around his neck, threading through his hair and holding him in place.

Tate responded immediately, his arms closing around her, pulling her into his lap as his tongue slid in to stroke against hers like a hot, wicked promise.

This was a kiss. Completely different from the careful, almost hesitant one last week.

It was hungry and honest, bordering on carnal, and a real shock coming from sweet, kind, understanding Tate Harris. All that tingly desire bubbling in her blood the past couple of weeks paled in comparison to the pure, unexpected *want* that slammed into her with a force that scared her a little.

Mercy.

Her blood roared in her ears and pulsed hot against her skin, making her acutely aware of each stroke of his hands—down her back, across her waist, up to her neck, then down to her hips to pull her snugly against him. Tate *wanted* her. She could feel it, taste it, and it was both intoxicating and empowering.

She broke the kiss, gulping for air, and Tate's lips moved to her jaw and her neck, sending shivers over her skin before he found her mouth again, kissing her hard and deep before slowly gentling, finally resting his forehead against hers as they both fought for breath.

"Damn," she whispered appreciatively, and she heard him chuckle slightly in response. Then sanity started to return. *Damn.* She carefully loosened her grip on his shoulders. She couldn't slide back without falling off the boardwalk, so she settled for using her knees to raise herself a few crucial inches off his lap and away from the evidence that he'd enjoyed that kiss as much as she had. She felt Tate sigh as he put his hands on her waist to help her off his lap and back onto the boardwalk beside him.

I can't believe I just did that. Her face felt like flames were licking it, but her whole body was thrumming. She was massively aroused and totally ashamed of herself. "Tate, I'm sorry. I shouldn't have done that—"

"It's okay." He ran a hand through his hair and gave

his head a little shake as if to clear it. "You're not there yet. I know." He pushed to his feet and extended a hand to pull her to hers. She couldn't meet his eyes and stood there staring at her feet until Tate put a finger under her chin to lift her face. "But do me a favor, all right?"

Anything. "What?" Her voice sounded as shaky as her legs.

He leaned close. "When you do get there, let me know." With a small smile that tripped her heart, he turned and left.

Chapter 11

The Sunday events were usually Tate's favorites of the weekend—the dog talent show was always good for a laugh—but today he was a little scattered, unable to focus properly on anything. At least a thousand times already—regardless of how inappropriate or inopportune the moment might be—his mind kept wandering back to Molly and that kiss.

And since summer had arrived in full force today, "hot and bothered" had taken on an entirely new meaning. He was sweaty and sticky from the heat and humidity and grumpy after a restless night caused by the aftereffects of that kiss. It felt as if the hormones of a sixteen-year-old were in control of all his higher brain functions. Just the sight of a Latte Dah to-go cup was enough to crank his engine.

As the day progressed, though, sightings of those to-go cups became few and far between. Molly had said she'd close Latte Dah when the parade started, but he hadn't seen her at any of the other activities afterward. Had she just gone home? She had to be tired after a long day yesterday and an early start today. Or maybe she was avoiding him.

Stephen Leary was trying to make the family's poodle dance a cha-cha without great success, but that just made Tate think about how he'd teased Molly about her curls and how they'd felt tangled between his fingers. That led his thoughts to last night and how perfectly she'd fit in his lap, against his chest, how soft her skin was, and how she'd curved into his hands in all the right places. And her mouth, dear God, her *mouth* . . .

But Molly wasn't "there" yet. That was fair enough. There was definitely something bad in her past, something she wasn't quite finished dealing with yet. He understood that and tried to keep that in the forefront of his mind.

He was definitely there, though, pitching his tent and flying the flag, which made this a little frustrating, to say the least, but he could give her some time. She was obviously *getting* there. Hell, she'd kissed him like she was starving; he'd actually *felt* the hunger.

He'd just have to be patient. Give her a little time and some space. She was still very guarded and needed to come to trust him a little first.

The sound of applause brought him back to the dog show rather forcefully, and he joined in politely, even though he had no idea how the cha-cha had turned out.

But that was the last act, and after the ribbons were awarded, the day's events were pretty much done. He was completely done, though, and there was nothing else he *had* to do for the rest of the weekend.

He was loading up his stuff when Quinn came by. Sophie was hanging on to his arm, her nose pink from the sun and a goofy grin on her face. They were obviously deliriously happy together, and it added a poignant pang to the lust already simmering under his skin. "You want to grab something to eat before the concert?" Quinn asked.

Tate shook his head and picked at the damp fabric of his shirt. "I want a shower. I probably smell worse than the horses after the parade. I'll catch up with y'all later, though."

"We'll save you a seat at the concert," Sophie said, waving good-bye as she pulled Quinn toward the food area.

It was a short walk home, and once he was out of the business district the streets were mostly empty, save the occasional family with young children calling it a day and heading home. As he passed the corner of Molly's street, he snuck a peek toward her house. Her car was out front, but that didn't actually mean anything other than that she hadn't left town this afternoon. It certainly didn't mean she was home, and just because he hadn't seen her today, it didn't mean she wasn't downtown, but that she just wasn't near him.

Cool air hit him the moment he opened his door, and he dropped the stuff he was carrying to embrace it. *Thank you, inventors of air-conditioning.* It only took a moment for his shirt to turn clammy against his skin, so he stripped it off as he headed to the fridge for a bottle of water. There wasn't much in the fridge in the way of food, but he was too hot to be hungry anyway. He'd grab something from one of the vendors later on his way to the concert.

First stop, though, was a shower.

This was exactly what his plans for the weekend had always been, but that was before he'd kissed Molly, and now he was a little dissatisfied with the plan. Part of him wanted to call her, see if she wanted to join him and Sophie and Quinn at the concert, but that was pretty much the opposite of giving her space. Needless to say, it also reeked of neediness on his part.

But after that kiss, neediness had taken on a new meaning.

Sighing, he reached over and cranked the water all the way over to cold. It didn't really help.

When he was clean, dry, and dressed—if still a little chilled—he thought he heard his doorbell, which was more than strange. Who would be looking for him here?

He entertained several possibilities on his way down the stairs, but Molly was still the *last* person he'd expected to find on his porch.

His response was instantaneous: heat rushing to his skin, pulse kicking into overdrive, blood rushing south. Then he noticed she looked like a very flustered angel, in a knee-length cotton skirt and a snug white-and-gold V-neck T-shirt that showed her chest was as flushed as her cheeks. Her curls were loose, framing her face like a halo, and she tucked the stray strands back behind her ears nervously.

That gesture tempered the rush, but only a little. "Hey."

"Hi." Her smile was shaky.

"Is everything okay?"

"Everything's fine. Am I interrupting? I'm sorry I didn't call first. I can come back some other time if you're busy." Her words were tumbling over each other, and she was looking pretty much everywhere except at him. "You know, never mind. I'm going to go—"

He caught her by the elbow. "Just wait. You're not interrupting anything. Why don't you come on inside?" He still had no idea why she was here—and quite frankly, his body didn't much care—but the part of his brain that was still working had him moving cautiously.

She jumped a little when he closed the door behind her.

"Would you like something to drink?"

She shook her head, still not making eye contact.

"Well, then would you like to sit down?"

She shook her head again. "How are you?"

"I'm good. And you?" he asked carefully, perching on the arm of the couch. He was a little afraid that any sudden moves might cause her to bolt like a deer.

"I'm a bit nervous."

He bit back a smile. "I hadn't noticed. Want to tell me why?"

"Because this is awkward." Molly tried to smile again, but it faltered. "When you kissed me the other night . . . Well, it's been a really long time since anybody has kissed me."

He didn't know how to respond, or even whether he should. "I think that's a shame."

He got a weak smile in response. *Progress.* "And the last time anyone seriously asked me out . . . I was in high school. Before I got married."

The word brought him up short, but it made sense. A bad marriage could have done a number on her head and would explain why she wasn't "there" yet. So maybe he wasn't the problem after all.

"So I'm definitely rusty at everything, and after the disaster of my marriage, I'm not entirely sure about anything . . ." She looked up at him quickly, then dropped her eyes back down to her hands. The corner of her mouth turned up. "But it was a really *good* kiss."

God, she was killing him. He dug his fingers into the fabric of the couch to keep them from reaching for her. His throat was tight, but he managed to say, "I thought so, too."

"And you wanted me to let you know when I was 'there.'"

He realized he was holding his breath.

She licked her lips and cleared her throat. "Well, I'm not quite all the way 'there' yet."

He waited.

Molly took a deep breath. Then she lifted her eyes and met his evenly. "But I'm *here.*"

Christ. The possibilities implied in that sentence lit him up like a bottle rocket. But those possibilities were all across the spectrum, and while he was on board no matter what that "here" might entail, the ambiguity kept him frozen in place. She still looked ready to bolt. At the same time, though, her hands had stilled, as if saying the words had committed her to whatever "here" was. He realized the ball was in his court, and she was waiting for him to make his play.

He held out a hand to her.

She took it, curling her fingers around his and giving it a squeeze, letting him guide her forward until she stood between his thighs. A curl had sprung loose again, and he pushed it back into place, letting his thumb stroke over the soft skin of her cheek. "So, would you like to go to dinner?"

"Maybe another time." And then she kissed him.

All that nervous energy in her seemed to disappear, and her mouth was hot and sure when it found his. It broke the thin thread of his control, causing him to groan as he pulled her against him from hip to chest. She answered him with a sigh, arching into his body, twining her arms around his neck.

Molly tasted like wine, making him wonder whether she'd needed to seek a little liquid courage to come over. She was kissing him with a passion that had him feeling drunk, but he didn't want Molly making this decision anything other than clearheaded. As much as his body screamed at him that it didn't matter what got her here, only that she was here now, it did matter. It nearly killed him, but he pulled back and waited until she opened her eyes. There was a glaze across them, but it seemed like it was more from desire than alcohol. Still . . .

"Do I want to know how many glasses of wine it took to get you here?"

She blinked, momentarily confused, but then her tongue slipped out to taste her lips. Then she smiled. "Just one. To calm my nerves." Taking a step back, she reached for the hem of her shirt and pulled it up and off in one quick move. "I'm fully aware of what I'm doing," she said as she walked back into his arms.

Molly was soft and warm and wonderful. She sighed into his mouth as he cupped a breast in his hand, then shivered when his thumb raked over her nipple, and her hands fisted in the fabric of his shirt.

Those fists moved to his hair as he kissed his way down her neck and used his tongue to trace the skin that swelled above her bra before sucking her through the fabric.

He'd thought that kiss last night was incredible and insane, but this was something else entirely. Freed from whatever had been holding her back, she was a fantasy come to life in his arms. He tasted her neck again, nibbling his way to her shoulder, easing the straps of her bra off her shoulders and releasing the clasp so it joined her shirt on the floor. Molly responded by pulling his shirt up, forcing him to release her as she pulled it over his head and tossed it aside.

She ran her fingers over his chest, around his nipples, tracing the line from sternum to navel. He was being inspected, appreciated, and damn if it wasn't sexy as hell.

His balance on the arm of the couch was too precarious for this, but as he stood, his chest slid over Molly's and the sensation was enough to make him wobble. Molly sucked her breath in sharply, and he knew she'd had the same reaction.

It made him smile.

Hands in her hair, he tilted her face up to his and kissed her hard. When she was breathless, he pressed his forehead to hers and fought to catch his own breath.

"Do you want me to carry you up the stairs?"

It took a moment for the words to penetrate the fog, and another moment for Molly to recognize the words as English and give them any meaning at all. Kissing

Tate had turned her mind to mush. Last night had been only a sample of what he was capable of.

That small taste had haunted her, turning her dreams into erotic X-rated movies, throwing her off her stride all day when a memory would pop up—in full sensory detail.

She'd served a hell of a lot of coffee this morning, but she remembered nothing of it. She'd watched the marching band and the cheerleaders line up for the parade in front of Latte Dah and then walk away, and the symbolism of her life and good times passing her by smacked her in the face almost painfully.

She didn't have to live like this. Either everything would work out or it wouldn't, but if she wasn't helping or hindering anything by inaction, then action couldn't help or hinder, either.

Either way, she knew she was tired of spending her life *waiting*.

Then the next thing she knew, she was on Tate's front porch.

But Tate was now waiting for an answer to his question—the bigger one lurking underneath the question he'd actually asked. She recognized this as her chance to back out and go home, or even just back up to an evening of heavy petting on the couch.

It was tempting. It would be safer. Easier. Less scary.

No. She wanted this. She wanted *Tate*. He'd lit a fire inside her with that kiss, showing her what she'd been missing—and not just recently. She'd *never* been kissed like that. Like he couldn't get enough of her.

And *damn*, he was just so perfect. She'd known he'd have a good chest, but it was broad and defined, hard in all the right places, the crisp, dark hair narrowing to a thin line before it disappeared into the waistband of his shorts.

He was breathing hard, but then so was she, and those

blue eyes burned hot. His hair was mussed and sticking up everywhere from where she'd played with it, gentling the angles of his face.

And he was still waiting for her answer.

"Lead the way."

He kissed her instead, both hungry and sweet at the same time, and it thrilled her all the way to her toes. It went on for a long time, making it hard for her to find her breath.

Following him up the stairs gave her a lovely view of his back—equally as nice as his front—which she'd never really looked at before. She'd felt his thighs under hers last night, felt them squeezing her tonight, so she had an idea what the rest of him was like, and knew she was not going to be disappointed there, either.

Once in Tate's room, with the bed *right there*, her bravado finally started to falter. Above and beyond anything else she needed to worry about, there was one part of this she hadn't thought all the way through: she'd slept with only two men in her entire life, and none at all in three years. After the way she'd just thrown herself at him, Tate might be expecting porn-star-level skills.

But then Tate was behind her, his hands on her shoulders, stroking down her arms and across her belly as he kissed the side of her neck. She could feel the heat of his skin against her back, and she leaned into him and quit worrying. Hooking her thumbs in the waistband of her skirt, she slid it over her hips. Shimmying out of her panties, she let both of them drop to the floor.

Tate's teeth grazed her shoulder and his hand immediately angled south. She grabbed his thighs for support as her knees went weak and she lost her breath completely.

Mercy.

She had no idea how she ended up in the bed. Her head was still spinning, and she wasn't entirely sure she hadn't blacked out. The sound of Tate's shorts hitting the floor only barely registered, as did the shifting of the mattress as he joined her there, rolling her beneath him and settling between her thighs.

But the toe-curling, mind-melting kiss definitely registered, as did the feel of him sliding inside her. *Lord, have mercy.* Tate groaned her name against her hair and she arched against him, gripping his biceps to anchor herself as he braced on his elbows and started to move.

Tate's eyes never left her face, but her self-conscious embarrassment at that scrutiny quickly evaporated as the pleasure built inside her. She was so close to the edge, and she locked her legs around his waist, wanting him to take her over. His hands fisted in her hair and his forehead dropped to hers as he began to move faster, thrusting into her until she saw stars.

It didn't take long for the tremors to start, and she held on to him as she shook, only vaguely aware of Tate collapsing on top of her a few moments later.

His heart was slamming against her chest, and she could barely breathe, but the solid weight of him on top of her was incredible. Air didn't seem to be a good enough reason to move.

But Tate did move, pulling her with him as he rolled, reversing their positions. The cool air felt good against her sweaty skin, and she lay there, boneless, her legs tangled in his.

The directionless languorous movements of his hands lulled her, keeping her in that dreamy space where she didn't have to think.

But, of course, it couldn't last.

"When you said you weren't 'there' yet, but you were 'here,' what exactly did you mean?"

She angled her head to look at him. "It's a little late to be asking that, don't you think?"

Tate laughed, causing her whole body to shake. "I got the gist of it, I think."

"True."

But Tate seemed to want an answer. He was playing with her hair now, pulling the curls out long and letting them spring back into shape. This didn't exactly seem like the right time for confessions, regardless of what movies might imply about those afterglow moments. She was honest enough to know that it was mostly her own selfishness in not wanting to spoil her mood that held her tongue. She didn't want to think about it, either, but it was a little late for that now. So how to answer him without lying to him?

You're lying to him either way, her conscience reminded her. A lie of omission was still a lie. She couldn't meet his eyes, so she watched her fingers as they drew circles on his chest.

"It's complicated," she finally said. "I've got a lot of stuff I still have to work out. A lot of stuff I still need to *figure* out. I'm not sure how long that's going to take to get there. And until I get there, I can't offer much to someone else."

She felt him nod against the top of her head as if he understood.

Ugh. She was disgusted with herself. That was the most evasive truth ever, and the guilt sat heavy on her chest. Tate didn't deserve that kind of weasely answer, but she was simply too chicken to tell him the full truth. She liked him, but she certainly didn't like herself much right now.

She'd used him. Oh, he'd been a willing participant, but that didn't change that fact.

Sitting up, she pushed her hair out of her face and slid to the edge of the bed. "I'm sorry."

His eyebrows knitted together. "For what?"

"For kissing you last night. For coming here tonight. I should have told you all of that up front."

Tate rolled to his side, propping his head on his hand. *Why does he have to look all sexy and adorable?* "You did. You told me you weren't there yet."

"But—"

In a sneaky fast move, Tate caught her around the waist and pulled her back down onto the bed, easily rolling her underneath him and caging her with his arms. "So we'll just hang out here, okay?"

It was the smile that accompanied the words that sealed it for her. "Okay."

Then he kissed her again, and she couldn't think at all.

It was bliss.

Tate was a little disappointed to wake up and find that Molly was gone, but the light flooding his bedroom told him how late it was, so he couldn't be all that surprised.

Downstairs, he drank juice straight out of the jug and checked his phone. There were a ton of texts from people wanting to know why he hadn't shown up for the concert last night, and he laughed. He'd forgotten all about it once Molly had arrived. And while he was a fan and enjoyed a good show as much as the next person, his evening had been far, far better.

But he couldn't exactly tell his friends what he'd been doing instead, now could he?

He wasn't entirely sure what Molly had been trying to tell him last night to explain her sudden change of mind, but he knew there was a hell of a lot she *hadn't* told him, either. Which was fair enough. Everyone had issues and came with baggage.

At the same time, he was selfish enough not to worry too much about it right now. That self-knowledge didn't exactly paint him in the most flattering light, but he couldn't be unhappy that Molly had decided to come to him last night, whatever reasons had driven her.

He could hear his neighbors on both sides gearing

up for their Memorial Day cookouts. The Ferguson kids were screaming as if they were being murdered, but a glance out the window showed water hoses and squirt guns as the weapons of choice. As he watched, their cat, Sadie, jumped the fence into his yard seeking refuge as a stream of water headed her way.

He had a couple of options for today—invitations to various backyard parties, a gathering down at the Shore. He could—and probably *should*, even though he knew he wouldn't—put in an appearance at the events at the War Memorial.

But he found himself wondering what Molly had planned for today. Scrolling through the texts on his phone again, he made sure there wasn't a message from her, and then he checked his e-mail, too. He was acting like a teenager with a crush, but he refused to feel bad about it.

He could just call her and ask, of course.

After a shower, though, he decided to just walk the two blocks to her house and see. It was on his way to Jack's house anyway, so if she was busy or out, he'd just go on from there and wait for her to call.

While a lot of downtown businesses were closed today, anything that catered mainly to the tourists would still be open for business, and the beach area would be busy. There was plenty to do for those who wanted to go find it.

But this side of town was almost all locals, and it had a definite lazy feel today. And with the sun shining, it was a perfect day to be outside, maybe find a hammock in the shade and do nothing.

He waved to Mr. Fillory across the street as he climbed the two steps onto Molly's porch. Before he could knock, though, he heard a loud bang from the back, followed by a loud, colorful curse.

Heading around the side of the house, he could hear muttering. "Molly?"

Hands on her hips, Molly seemed to be yelling at her porch. Wearing a snug blue tank top and cutoffs that were a little too short for his heart health, with her hair pulled back from her face and covered in a blue-and-white bandanna, she looked a little like a modern Rosie the Riveter.

When she saw him, she set the screwdriver she was holding on the step and picked up a water bottle. After a long drink, she gestured to the screen door. It was raw wood, not yet painted to match the rest of the porch, and clearly brand new. "I put the damn thing on backward and upside down."

She was frowning, so he smothered a laugh. It was crooked, too, but considering her current mood, he felt it was best to not mention that. "Want some help getting it down?"

She sighed. "Please."

He moved Molly's step stool aside and unscrewed the hinges from the doorframe.

"I wasn't trying to sneak out this morning," she offered matter-of-factly. "I had to come home to feed Nigel, and you were sleeping so soundly I didn't want to wake you."

"Well, I'd had a long night."

She smiled awkwardly. "I'm not used to sleeping past seven or so. Even if I don't have to get up to open the shop, Nigel will play alarm clock. And I had a pretty long to-do list waiting for me anyway."

It was a conversational move back to neutral, less sexual territory. *Okay.* "Isn't one of the joys of renting that your landlady takes care of stuff like this?"

"The door only broke last week, and since Nigel likes to come out onto the porch—and hang on the door, which is what finally broke it beyond repair—I didn't want to wait. They told me at the store that this was a

very easy job I could do myself, so I thought I'd try."
She rolled her eyes.

"You were close," he said, trying to be diplomatic.
"Here, can you hold it while I screw these in?" It only
took a minute and the door was back on. He opened and
closed it to test it. "There you go."

"Thanks. I've got a kitty that's dying to come outside." She pointed, and he could see Nigel sitting in the
window, looking forlorn. "So what brings you by?"

"I came to see you," he answered honestly.

It wasn't that confusing a statement, so Molly's long
pause was a little awkward. Finally, she said, "Don't
you have something else to do?"

Well, then. He'd seriously misread the situation.
"Sorry I bothered you. I'll go."

"Oh, no," Molly said quickly. "That came out wrong.
I'm just a little surprised that you don't have other plans
already."

"Oh." He did not want to admit his relief at her explanation. "I have places I *can* go. I just wanted to see you
instead." Then he realized the flaw in his plan, the part
he'd moved past a bit too quickly. "But you probably
have places to go today . . ."

"I actually planned to stay here today, conquer my
to-do list."

"That's not much of a day off."

"I don't get very many."

"All the more reason to enjoy it."

"Don't tempt me, Tate Harris. I'm trying to be good."

Nothing ventured . . . He moved to stand in front of
her and let his hand rest lightly on her hip. "And here
I thought you were pretty damn good already."

Her cheeks turned slightly pink. "You're a bad influence."

"I try." He let his hand slide up over her waist, her

ribs, and her shoulder to trace gently over her collarbone. He'd discovered how sensitive it was last night, and he was rewarded as her nipples hardened against her shirt. She closed her eyes and swayed slightly on her feet, angling her head to the side to let him stroke the soft skin of her neck. "Hanging a door is a big project, and you should reward yourself for the accomplishment."

The corners of her mouth turned up, but her eyes stayed closed, even as he tugged at the knot securing the bandanna around her head, sending it fluttering to the ground and releasing her curls into his hands. "But you hung the door," she reminded him.

He kissed her forehead, her temple, the top of her ear. "Then maybe you could reward me," he whispered.

Her hands landed lightly on his hips, seemingly to steady herself, and he let his lips trail down her neck to her shoulder. Molly's fingers tightened.

She smelled like oranges with just a faint hint of coffee clinging underneath, and he inhaled deeply, exhaling over her skin and watching the gooseflesh rise. Molly shivered and leaned into him, pulling his hips toward her as her mouth found his for a long, sweet kiss.

He was the one who ended up breathless, and the want was a real and painful thing. Her hand cupped his cheek, and he turned to kiss the palm.

"I really do have a long to-do list."

Her thumb was stroking over his lips, forestalling any response he might make.

"But it is my day off, you know."

He was already boosting her up, cupping her hips with one arm as the other hand reached for the door.

Today was a perfect day to be *indoors*, after all.

Chapter 12

Molly wasn't even sure she believed in hell anymore, which was very convenient since she was sitting in a handbasket—metaphorically, at least.

In reality, she was nestled in her bed with Tate's chest as her pillow. Her head rose and fell gently with each of his slow, even breaths. At least it was a *nice* handbasket.

Poor boy. He certainly earned a nap today. Hell, she was still all tingly and sated, but there was a weariness underneath. Neither of them had gotten much sleep last night. She'd probably gotten even less than Tate, but that was her own fault, and for much the same reason she couldn't sleep now. She felt she'd made an important choice yesterday. She'd chosen to be happy. To grab what she could and make the best of it. She'd been making the best of a bad situation for a long time, but this was a different approach. The intent before was merely to survive. This time, she was looking to thrive.

Unfortunately, that Pollyanna approach was shadowed by nearly crippling guilt that she was desperately trying to keep at bay. It wasn't that Tate was pressing her for anything really, and other than that one detail, she didn't have anything to hide.

That one detail, though, was enough. She should just

tell him, get it out there and deal with it, but she couldn't. Not that she was ashamed—which honestly, she was, a little—but she didn't want that nastiness touching her shiny new life.

Not knowing how Tate might react to the news was also enough to make her hold her tongue. Talk about screwing stuff up right out of the gate.

So the guilt was there, welling up every now and then to choke her. But the happiness was there, too.

It was really hard to hold both the emotions in her mind at the same time. It gave her a headache just trying.

"Those look like some really deep thoughts."

She jumped and opened her eyes to find Tate staring down at her, his forehead wrinkled in concern.

I have to tell him. Just say it.

This wasn't how she'd wanted to have this conversation. And she certainly didn't want to have this conversation naked.

"Yeah, they are." She sat up and pulled the afghan from the foot of the bed around her shoulders. Then she took a deep breath, fortifying herself.

Then she realized that she might not *need* to have this conversation. They'd had sex, but that alone didn't create a relationship with Tate that required her to tell him all her innermost thoughts or anything. She didn't even know whether this was going to go anywhere, so why was she twisting herself into knots over it? This was *her* struggle, *her* problem, and in a way dragging Tate into it wasn't only unnecessary, but also unfair to him.

This was about *her*, not him. She was overthinking this.

She'd be stirring up a lot of crap and angst over what might not turn out to be anything more than just a fling.

There'd be a time to tell him, and she'd know when that was. She just had to get out of the mind-set she'd been in for so long—the one where the guilt and blame and everything else was always hers to carry. Hell, she'd talked about this in therapy, but it hadn't made sense until just now.

She didn't owe people explanations about her life or her choices.

Just like that, a huge weight lifted off her shoulders. She felt like a brand-new woman.

Which, in a way, she was.

"Molly? You okay?"

Tate looked wary and confused, and she realized she'd left him hanging there during her epiphany. "I'm hungry."

His eyebrows went up. "Those deep thoughts were about food?"

"Yeah. There's none in my kitchen. I wasn't expecting company today."

Tate laughed and rolled onto his back. "Boy, you take food seriously."

"Almost as seriously as I do coffee."

"Well then, I guess I better feed you." He groaned as he pushed up to a seated position. "Provided I'm able to move."

"You just had a nap. You should be raring to go," she teased.

Tate took the challenge, stalking her across the bed, only just missing her as she rolled off it and to her feet. Defeated, he collapsed face-first onto her duvet and groaned.

Her clothes were at the foot of the bed—the shirt was inside out, but they'd been in a hurry—and she slipped into them quickly. Then she tossed his pants at him. "I'm going to go feed Nigel. Get dressed."

Tate's grumbling followed her out of the room.

Nigel was on the back of the sofa, glaring balefully at her bedroom door. "Don't be grumpy," she said, stopping to nuzzle her forehead against his. "You're still my main man."

As if he understood and was mollified by her words, Nigel threw a smug glance in the direction of the bedroom and followed her into the kitchen. When Tate appeared a few minutes later, Nigel merely sniffed at him before returning to his dinner.

Tate sighed. "Your cat hates me."

"My cat hates everyone. But yeah, he probably hates you the most. You were sleeping in his spot."

"Jeez, I save his life and he begrudges me a nap in your bed."

"I thought I saved his life?" she teased.

"With my help." Tate wrapped his arms around her and she relaxed back against his chest as he nuzzled the side of her neck.

This moment was perfect. Bliss. She deserved it and, more importantly, she'd *earned* it. She wanted to just savor it for a minute.

But then he abruptly let her go. "I'm about to get very distracted," he explained, "so if you really want to eat, we'd better go find food now."

Everything seemed different. Somehow brighter and clearer than it had been yesterday, as silly as it might seem to believe.

It was a perfect evening, and Tate held her hand as they went back downtown in search of food. They bought a bucket of boiled shrimp and took it to the park for an impromptu and slightly messy picnic. Tate told her the-rest-of-the-story stories about some well-known Tate and Helena shenanigans—including a hysterical incident involving the late Mr. Cutter's goats that Molly was going to have a very hard time *not* mentioning to Helena the next time she saw her.

And the whole time, Tate kept smiling at her, kept *looking* at her as if she were some kind of amazing creature, and actually listening with interest when she spoke.

It was awesome. The best date she'd ever had.

And Molly could honestly say that when Tate kissed her later that night, she saw fireworks.

She was "there."

Tuesday morning was a little slow, but that was to be expected. The whole town had a celebration hangover. Since Molly was feeling a little bit of that herself, she wasn't complaining. Her nose and shoulders were sunburned from Saturday, she was sore in several muscles she'd forgotten she had from Sunday's and Monday's adventures, and she hadn't gotten to bed until late last night.

Well, she'd gotten to *a* bed early enough, just not *her* bed and not to sleep.

When she thought about the weekend, it had that movie montage feel, complete with cheesy sound track. And it made her smile at the oddest moments, something that had not gone unnoticed by her customers.

And there was nothing she could say when they asked why she was in such a good mood.

She was dusting the pictures on the wall when the chime over the door rang. Looking up, she saw Helena. Other than a couple of quick waves as they passed each other on Saturday and Sunday, it'd been nearly a week since they'd seen each other, much less had time to talk.

Helena usually came in at least once or twice a week now for a chat and a chance to work undisturbed at her favorite table, but Helena was missing her laptop case today. That plus the wrinkle between Helena's eyebrows meant something was definitely not good.

Tossing the feather duster behind the counter, she met Helena halfway. "Hey. What's up?"

Helena grabbed her elbow and moved her toward the back. "I need to talk to you." She kept her voice low, even though the only customer in the place was all the way by the front window and wearing headphones.

Molly was worried, but before she could say anything, Helena added, "You and Tate?"

How does she know already? Surely not from Tate. He didn't seem the type to go bragging, not even to Helena, even if he'd had time to do it.

"Please." Helena rolled her eyes as if Molly had actually said something. "More than a dozen people saw you two kissing at the fireworks show last night. I had four e-mails about it before midnight."

Damn it. They'd been in the shadows, all the way in the back of the crowd, and everyone *should* have had their eyes on the sky. They hadn't been hiding, but she'd thought they'd at least been discreet. Or unnoticed.

There's no such thing as a secret in a small town.

"So everyone knows?" Since she was still coming to grips with it all herself, she wasn't sure she wanted the news to spread far and wide just yet. She wanted to enjoy it quietly and privately first.

"Pretty much. Or if they don't know already, they will soon enough. I mean, this isn't 'rock the foundations of Magnolia Beach' big, but it's still pretty damn interesting. And why did I find out secondhand? How long has this been going on?"

"It's new," she assured Helena, who still didn't seem appeased. Molly was almost afraid to ask, "What are people saying?"

Helena understood. "Nothing bad, I promise," she said, patting Molly's arm and flashing a big smile. "I mean, we're talking about you and Tate. What's not to love about it? Any cattiness will come from the broken-hearts crowd, and that will be easily identifiable as sour grapes."

The broken-hearts crowd. Tate was pretty eligible and would fetch top price at a bachelor auction—not that Magnolia Beach would ever hold such an event. She'd been through a bit of that cattiness before, though, back when she'd started dating Mark. It was petty crap, but it wasn't fun, either. "Hmm."

Helena snapped her fingers. "Focus, please. I still want to know why I didn't already know about this."

"Like I said, it's new." She wasn't sure what she should or shouldn't say. She was excited, sure, but now she was smack-dab in the middle of dangerous territory. Helena was her friend—possibly her best friend—but this was *Tate*, and, BFF or not, Helena's inner Mama Bear was not to be taken lightly. How could she have forgotten that very important fact?

Because Tate's tongue is a thing of wicked beauty and magic.

"I knew you two would be great together." Helena was practically preening. "*So* . . . tell me all about it."

"Have you talked to Tate?" Molly didn't know whether they should have an official story or not. It certainly hadn't occurred to her to think of one. Hell, who'd have thought the news would spread *this* quickly? How much did Tate and Helena share? How much should *she* share, considering Helena knew both of them? Damn, they'd jumped from "not interested" to "mind-blowing sex" pretty quickly, which she didn't think Helena would judge her a slut over . . . but all bets were off when it came to Tate.

"I called him this morning, but he didn't answer. Jenny said he was in surgery." She waved a hand dismissively. "When? How? *Details*."

Molly stood, stalling as she tried to think fast. "Do you want some coffee?"

Helena's eyebrows pulled together. "Sure, I guess, but . . ." Following Molly behind the counter, Helena stopped her before she could pour. "Am I missing something? I'm the only one who seems giddy here."

Once again, Molly was overthinking, worrying out of habit instead of remembering that things were different now. *She* was different now. She needed to get used to that. But right now she needed to temper Helena's excitement before she got too carried away. "I just think you need to hold back on the giddy."

"Why? Did something happen? I mean, you were kissing, and I know Tate's a good kisser—"

Molly bobbled the cup, but caught it in the nick of time.

"Only once. A long time ago. Very brief," Helena explained quickly. "You like him, though, right?"

"It's Tate. What's not to like?" That was vague, but true.

"And he likes you."

She couldn't stop the smile. "I think so."

"I *know* so. So what's with the dithering?"

"It's all *very* new. Like Saturday night new." There was no point mentioning the night with Nigel or the next night at his place after dinner. "Give it some time, maybe, before we start analyzing anything?"

Helena laughed. "I'm not saying y'all have to get married right away—"

Molly dropped the cup and it shattered on the floor. Coffee splashed everywhere, barely missing Helena's feet. "Damn." Kneeling, she started to pick up the pieces.

Helena knelt to help, too, not seeming to make a connection between her words and Molly's reaction, thank goodness. "Well, I think it's great, and y'all make an adorable couple. I will try to keep my giddiness under control." Her lips twitched. "For now." She stood and tossed the cup pieces she was holding into the trash and passed Molly a towel. "But just remember whose idea this was. Don't be surprised when I gloat later."

Molly managed a smile, but she was still reeling a little. Helena was already on the other side of the counter, picking up her stuff. "What about your coffee?"

"I'm good, actually. I really just came for the intel," she admitted. "Gotta run."

Off to interrogate Tate, probably. She wondered if she should text him a warning.

Nah. He'd been handling Helena far longer than she had. He could fend for himself. And anyway, if Tate was caught off guard and said something interesting, Helena would be back here PDQ to follow up—that much she was sure of.

While she was ready to date, she wasn't sure she was ready to date *publicly*, in a small town, for everyone to witness—and offer their opinions, too. She'd certainly gone from zero to sixty, and though she didn't really regret it, she could wish she'd moved a little more cautiously—or at least circumspectly. Nothing like jumping right into the deep end.

The bell over the door jingled again, and she looked up to see Sam on her way in, a huge knowing smile already wreathing her face. Sure, news traveled fast, but jeez, had there been an announcement in *The Clarion* today or something?

So much for enjoying this quietly by herself for a little while.

It didn't take long for Molly and Tate to officially become an "item." *Everyone* seemed to know within days. People brought it up as Molly made their coffee, telling her what a lovely couple they made. When they went to dinner, little old ladies smiled knowingly and approvingly. Folks wanted details, and some people disturbingly wanted more intimate details than she wanted to provide, but no one seemed to have any qualms about asking her whatever questions came to mind.

She'd forgotten what dating in a small town could be like. She'd gotten so used to her privacy, it hadn't really occurred to her how seeing Tate would put her personal life on everyone's radar. It was a little shocking, very disquieting, and rather hard to adjust to.

Of course, when she'd started dating Mark, everyone knew about it, too. They thought that Mark would be a good influence on her, and since the Lanes were pretty much *the* family in Fuller, her mother had been over the moon with the connection to that family and encouraged it greatly. And since neither of their families really approved of casual dating, things were expected to get serious quickly and people were planning their wedding after their third date. Overnight, her past sins had been forgiven—if not completely forgotten.

Hell, it was pretty much the first time her mother had been pleased with her. Hannah, who'd been used to being the favorite and perfect child, had been pea green with envy and wonderfully pissed as Molly had been elevated to the princess of the family.

That much about her marriage still made her smile.

But this was different. This wasn't Fuller, Tate wasn't Mark, and she wasn't the same naive little girl she'd been back then. And while Mrs. Riley had patted her cheek at the Shop-N-Save and told her what pretty babies she and Tate would have, she wasn't feeling any real pressure.

But it was new and nice and Molly was enjoying the experience. It had been a really long time since someone had seen *her*, not just Molly-from-Latte-Dah. She'd been hiding in plain sight—even from herself, it seemed—but now she really felt as if she was living again.

And it wasn't just Tate. It was nice to rediscover that side of herself, but this new feeling was internal, and Tate was just one manifestation of it. Not that she could explain that to anyone, and not that anyone was noticing much of a change in her anyway, simply because her inside had finally caught up to her outside.

The days sped by in the endorphin-riddled, post-orgasmic chemical rush of a new relationship, and she was being hit with both the added excitement of personal empowerment and the ongoing banality of everyday life.

It was exhausting.

And it didn't help that she wasn't getting as much sleep these days, either. That five a.m. alarm was killing her.

But it was still amazing.

On Saturday, though—two weeks to the day that Tate had kissed her for the second time—Molly hit the wall. No amount of coffee was going to keep her alert at this point, and she didn't want to risk falling asleep tonight while she was out with Tate. Jane laughed knowingly when Molly asked her to stay and close so that she could go home for a nap, but she didn't care.

Nigel was more than happy to snuggle up next to her in bed, and Molly was asleep seconds after her head hit the pillow.

Nigel's outraged yowl woke her up. The room was shadowy, and she had that napped-too-hard hangover disorienting her. Then she saw the dark figure in her doorway, and the adrenaline rush as she sat up nearly made her yowl as well. A second later, though, the figure morphed into Tate, and she leaned back against the headboard, pressing her hand against her chest to stave off the heart attack. "You scared the life out of me, Tate."

"I called. I knocked. I was afraid you were dead." He sat on the side of the bed, but Nigel held his ground, refusing to move from his spot this time. "I thought you said you were a light sleeper. And you should really lock your door during tourist season."

"Tourists don't wander this far out. And I am a light sleeper."

Tate merely raised an eyebrow.

"Usually," she amended. She scrubbed her hands over her face, trying to wake up. She took a big drink from the glass of water on the nightstand. It had been sitting there so long it was now room temperature, but it cut through the moss in her mouth. "What time is it?"

"Seven forty-five."

A four-hour nap. And she had been supposed to meet him at six thirty. "I'm so sorry. I'll go get dressed super fast." She flipped the edge of the duvet back, but Tate caught her hand.

"Are you feeling okay?" Concern written all over his face, he pressed his wrist against her forehead. "You don't feel feverish."

"I'm fine, Dr. Harris. I was just tired and my nap got out of hand."

He nodded. "I wondered how you were functioning on so little sleep. I guess I should probably apologize for keeping you up so late at night."

"Not necessary. I wasn't exactly kicking you out of my bed—or leaping out of yours."

"Well, I said I should. I didn't say I was going to." He grinned at her. "I try not to lie to people."

"Let me go wash my face and change—"

"Why don't we just skip it?"

"But we can still make it, if I hurry."

"You're obviously exhausted."

Now she felt really bad. "Then go without me."

"Nah. Are you hungry?"

"A little."

"Why don't I run get some takeout, and we'll just hang here tonight so you can get to bed at a decent hour."

"But you wanted to go see Grayson sing."

Tate shook his head. "It's no big deal. It's not like he doesn't sing somewhere around here every couple of weeks. It won't hurt his feelings if I skip a show. And"—he leaned forward, trapping her between his chest and the pillow—"I'd rather spend the time with you than Gray any day. You're prettier, for one thing."

She tugged on his shirt, pulling him closer. Nigel huffed and jumped off the bed, out of the way. "Well, I'm actually feeling quite refreshed after my nap. If you don't want to go out, then I'm very happy to stay in. And I don't have to get up in the morning, either." In her best come-hither voice, she asked, "What would you like to do?"

Tate's smile was very telling—until it turned into a frown as his phone went off. "I'm on call tonight," he said in apology as he fished it out of his pocket. "I've got to see who it is at least." Then he rolled his eyes. "What I'd *like* is for my mother to move to Georgia."

"Do you need to answer that?"

"No. Sam's already texted me about it. I'm not getting into the middle." He sent the call to voice mail and set the phone on the nightstand next to her glass with a sigh. "And I'm driving her to Ellie's tomorrow to see the boys, so I'm sure I'll hear all about it then." He slid his body over hers and settled his hips between her legs. "Now, where were we?"

In a way, she had to admire the way Tate could keep his life clearly compartmentalized, even when compartments threatened to bleed into each other. It was something she was still working on, but when Tate kissed her, it seemed so easy, too.

Focus on the now.

She threaded her fingers through his hair and pulled his head down to hers.

"So is Mom really going to move to Waycross this time?" Ellie didn't look up from the peanut butter and jelly sandwiches she was making for the boys, but Tate knew the question was far from casual.

"Probably not," he said, but then softened the truth with, "But she could surprise us."

Mom was currently in the living room watching Kyle and Justin play a video game with the level of interest only a grandmother could fake. Ellie might not come home very often or spend much time with Mom herself, but she didn't deny Mom access to the boys, either. It was a compromise.

"But you're still cleaning out the house and stuff?"

"It needs to be done, regardless. Once Sam gets on her feet and moves out, I'm hoping Mom will be willing to sell and move somewhere smaller and less falling-down. I'm tired of trekking out there to fix stuff."

"Then don't. You're just enabling her."

"I should let her climb on the roof? Just hope she doesn't fall and hurt herself?"

"It's better that you fall and hurt yourself? You're not a roofer. Or a carpenter or plumber or handyman of any sort. Let her hire someone to do that crap."

"And what would the neighbors say?"

"Who cares?"

"I do. I have to. Sons are supposed to take care of their mothers. I'd have every little old lady in Magnolia Beach shaming me in the streets if I didn't."

"But if you fall and break your neck, who'll take care of your patients? You have your own responsibilities and things to do, which you can't do if you're out at Mom's mowing her grass or if you die in a roofing accident." She held up the jar of peanut butter. "You want one?"

He nodded. "Let's not get too dramatic."

"Then let me remind you that if you hurt yourself, you'll have to move back into Mom's so that *she* can care for you. How does that sound?"

That was a horrible thought. "Promise me you'll shoot me instead?"

Ellie sighed. "I'll call Aunt Elaine, maybe see if she can convince Mom to actually move this time."

"It'd be good for her."

"And you and Sam, too." Ellie cut the crusts off his

sandwich, then cut diagonally to make little triangles before handing him his sandwich on a Thomas the Tank Engine plate. He felt five years old. He couldn't help but notice, though, that the boys had superheroes on *their* plates.

"How's Sam doing?" he asked, then took a bite.

Ellie's eyebrows went up. "You're asking me? You live there. I don't."

"Sam talks to you. She doesn't talk to me."

"Sam would talk—if you'd learn to listen."

"I listen. Sam's the one who doesn't listen."

"No," Ellie corrected. "Sam doesn't do what you tell her to do. That doesn't mean she's not listening." She shook her head. "You've got to let her find her own way. She's a big girl. Wait until she asks for help."

"She won't ask."

"Then maybe she doesn't feel she needs help yet." Ellie was the only person on earth who could sound both reasonable and exasperated at the same time.

"So you both keep saying."

"Well, now who's not listening, huh?" Her smile was mocking.

"Whatever."

Ellie patted his shoulder. "You mean well, and it's sweet. That's what's important. Even if it is annoying. Kyle! Justin!" The boys came running, and she handed off the sandwiches. "Go to the table to eat," she called after them, but the food was already half gone before the words were out of her mouth, and the boys were back at their game in seconds. "I swear, I should just toss the food in their general direction like I'm chumming for sharks," she muttered.

Both the boys took after Doug—no Harris DNA showing up there, which might not be a bad thing, when he thought about it. And Ellie was a great mom, devoted to her kids. Not everything had to get passed down the generations, and that was enough to make him hopeful for the future.

DNA was not destiny.

"Look," Ellie said. "Sam chose to go home. I offered to let her move in here, and Doug had a line on a job for her and everything. She turned me down."

"So she's crazy as well as stubborn."

"No, she's proud and determined. Going home took guts." She shook her head. "I don't know how either of you do it. God knows I couldn't."

"The only reason to go home would be so your family and friends could help you back onto your feet. It's driving me crazy."

"Well, it's not really about you. Let Sam make her own choices, just like we made ours. All we can do is be there, ready to catch her if she falls."

That was easier said than done.

Ellie wiped her hands on a towel and refilled his glass, obviously done with that conversation. He was almost happy about that until she spoke. "So, you and the coffee girl, huh?"

News travels fast. "Her name is Molly."

"I know. I also know she's about my age, super sweet, smart, kind, a fan of seventies funk music, and an avid reader of historical novels."

He hadn't known about the books. "She also likes cats."

"Nigel, right?"

"You're very well informed for someone who's met her all of once."

"I talk to Sam, remember? She's thrilled, by the way."

"Well, she and Molly spend a lot of time together at the coffee shop. They're friends."

Ellie leaned against the counter and grinned. "She's pretty, too."

"I agree."

"You like her?"

"Yes."

"And she likes you?"

"It seems like it. And I certainly hope so."

"Yay. Sam was worried you'd start pining for Helena again once she came back to town."

He sighed. "She knows we're just friends."

"I know that, but Sam has always been awed by Helena. I think she wanted you two to get together and was pining for that to happen a bit herself. I tried to tell her—"

"So she doesn't listen to you, either. Good. I'm not alone."

Ellie snapped the towel at his leg. "You don't hold the patent on concern for your siblings, you know. We get to worry about you, too."

"Neither of you need to worry about me."

"Then you don't need to worry about us," she challenged. "We just want you to be happy."

"And I need to have a woman in my life to be happy? If this conversation were reversed, you know, you'd be screaming about sexism."

"Don't try to change the subject. You will not make me feel even a little bit bad about this. So tell me about her."

"I thought Sam took care of that."

"She did, but I want to hear what you have to say. Aside from the usual pretty, smart, sweet . . ."

He shrugged. "She's all that."

"And . . ."

He wasn't sure how to describe it. "There's something about her. I can't put my finger on it, but she's amazing."

"But you've known her for a while, right?"

"Yeah, she's been in town for a few years. And she's friends with Helena, so I've spent more time with her in the last few months."

"But you're just getting together now? What tipped it over?"

He'd asked himself that same question a hundred times. "I'm not entirely sure. She just went from 'person I know' to 'person I'd like to know better.' Sometimes you just don't see what's in front of you. And then, one day, you do."

Ellie's hand fluttered to her chest. "That's almost romantic, Tate."

"Gee, thanks."

"No, I'm serious. I didn't know you had it in you. But I'm glad to see you do."

"Are you saying I'm not romantic?"

"You're a good man. Very kind and very sweet. You're also very pragmatic and like things with clearly defined edges. So, no, I didn't think you were the romantic type."

Maybe I should send Molly some flowers or something.

"Is this serious?" she asked.

He nearly choked. "You're jumping way ahead, don't you think?"

"Planning ahead is not the same thing as jumping ahead," Ellie answered primly.

"Well, let's not plan ahead, either. This is still very new."

"Two weeks, but you've known her for years. New, yes, but not too new. It's a good time to bring her to dinner, I think."

"Patience, Ellie. You'll scare her off."

"From what Sam tells me, Molly is made of tougher stuff than that. Oh, don't roll your eyes at me," she snapped, catching him doing exactly that, "I want to get to know my brother's new girlfriend. Crazier ideas do exist."

"You've just never been like this before."

Ellie sighed. "I went to school with Tamara and Jennie. I knew those relationships weren't going anywhere from the start."

"You could have told me," he muttered.

She ignored him, continuing, "And Kara . . . I could tell by the way you talked about her that it was doomed from the get-go. Molly is different."

"You've met her *once*. And secondhand information from Sam is hardly evidence of anything."

"But I've known *you* my whole life." She grinned. "You're smitten."

"Smitten? I think I just lost half my testosterone."

"Nah. There's nothing wrong with being smitten. Especially in the early days. I think it's sweet. Enjoy it."

"I plan to."

"And you'll plan a dinner or something soon so I can meet your Molly properly?"

My Molly. He kind of liked the sound of that.

"We'll see how it goes."

Chapter 13

"Do you have anything to snack on?" Molly was curled up alongside him on the couch, her head resting on his chest.

Tate smiled to himself and stroked the curve of her hip underneath the big shirt she wore. It was all she was wearing, actually, and he liked that. "Worked up an appetite?"

Sitting up, she pushed her hair back from her face. With a cheeky grin, she leaned over and gave him a kiss. "More like knowing I need to keep my strength up." She cocked her head to the side. "Or are we done for the night?"

He tangled his hands in her hair and pulled her back down for a kiss. "You might need a little something to get you through." Then he thought about the contents of his kitchen. "There's not much, though, I'm afraid. Maybe a couple of cookies?"

"That'll work. Don't get up," she said as he started to lever himself up. "I'll get them."

"Blue container on the counter," he called after her. The T-shirt only just covered the curve of her butt, displaying a long, lovely length of thigh as she walked.

She came back carrying the container, one cookie with a bite missing already in her hand. Sitting next to his feet at the other end of the couch, she chewed and swallowed. "Oh my God, this is so *good*. It might just be the best thing I've ever had in my mouth."

"Really?" He wagged his eyebrows at her, earning him a frown.

"Seriously, where'd you get these?"

"Iona made them."

"Do you think she'd let me sell them in Latte Dah?" Taking another bite, she closed her eyes and chewed, a blissful look on her face. *Damn.* That was the same look she got when she . . .

He forced himself back to the conversation. "She might. You certainly won't be finding them here any longer."

"Why not?"

He sighed and stacked his hands behind his head. "Because of you."

"Me?" Her eyebrows pulled together in confusion. "What did I do?"

"Me." At her look, he laughed. "It's Iona . . . Well, she . . ."

"Oh." Understanding dawned on Molly's face. "These are 'please love me' cookies."

That's one way to think about it. "'The way to a man's heart is through his stomach' and all that." He sighed. Tomorrow was Iona's regular day to come, and since there was no way Iona didn't know about Molly by now, his chances of delicious pot roast and fresh cookies were slim to none. "I won't be surprised if Iona goes on strike. When she gets even a little bit jealous, my quality of life goes downhill. The fact I'm actually *seeing* you, though, might push her into quitting outright."

Molly's mouth twitched. "Does she have actual reasons to be jealous?"

"You mean, have I given her reason to think I'm interested? No."

"Iona's a lovely young woman—and a hell of a cook, obviously. You could do worse."

"She wants to get married, though. The sooner the better. In fact, she might have monogrammed towels already."

Molly coughed. "Oh." She set the container over on the coffee table, and the neckline of the T-shirt gaped, giving him a view of her cleavage. "Well, that means she probably won't want to do business with me, either. That might be for the best, though. I'd end up eating more of these than I sold."

"Yeah, well, I'm going to starve to death and my house will be condemned within a week."

"You could learn to cook and clean for yourself, you know." Molly seemed completely unsympathetic to his plight. "You're not helpless."

"I don't want to spend what free time I have cooking and cleaning." He knew he sounded spoiled and probably petulant, but it was true.

"I can't say I blame you."

"You don't think I'm lazy?"

"Life's too short. There are so many things that suck but still *have* to be done, whether you like it or not. If you don't *have* to personally deal with something, why waste that time when you could be doing something you do like?"

"That's a great philosophy, but not likely to help me with Iona."

She shrugged. "You're on your own there. Sorry."

He pushed up onto his elbow. "If you could off-load one thing out of your life and have someone else deal with it, what would it be?"

Molly thought for a moment. "Realistically speaking? Or anything at all?"

This could be interesting. "Whatever."

"Running. If I could figure out a way for someone else

to run and yet I'd still reap the benefit, I'd *totally* out-source that."

That surprised him. "Running is worse than cooking or cleaning?"

"I don't particularly like doing that, either, but . . . I don't know."

"What?" He nudged her with his knee.

"I couldn't have someone in my house like that. I'd feel . . . 'invaded' is not the right word. Maybe exposed? It's like letting someone read your diary—only they know all your real dirt and bad habits."

"Somehow I don't doubt that if I kept a diary, Iona would have found it and read it."

"That doesn't bother you?"

"I've got nothing to hide."

"Nothing at all?"

"Nope. I'm an open book. Ask me anything."

Her eyes narrowed, and he suddenly feared he was about to have to confess to all kinds of things that should be covered under some sort of statute of limitations. "I don't believe you," she said after a very long minute. "Everyone has parts of themselves and their lives they want to keep private."

"I grew up in a small town with two nosy sisters. I don't know what the word 'privacy' means."

"I *also* grew up in a small town with two nosy sisters," she reminded him. "That's all the more reason to want to have parts of your life that *aren't* public knowledge."

He sat up and moved down to her end of the couch. "So what are your secrets?"

"What makes you think I have secrets?" she challenged.

"You just said—"

She shook her head. "I said 'private.' There's a difference. Not wanting everyone to know all your business isn't the same as keeping secrets."

"Tell me something private, then."

Molly seemed to be weighing the options. "I tried to paint Nigel's toenails once. It didn't go well."

He scooted another inch closer. "No. More private than that."

"I sleep with a night-light. I don't like the dark."

"That's a little better." He leaned in and kissed her right where her jaw met her ear. "Come on now, you can trust me to keep your secrets. Tell me something no one else knows."

At that moment, he felt the change, as if she'd flipped a switch, distancing herself from him and the conversation. *Damn.* He pulled back and saw that her eyes were shuttered and withdrawn. He'd gone too far. They'd gotten so comfortable recently that he'd forgotten that there were parts of her cordoned off as no-go zones. It bugged him that she still wasn't ready to trust him with those secrets, but he didn't want to back her into a corner, either. Quickly, he tried to backpedal. "Never mind. I'm just teasing you."

Then she smiled, but it was that smile she always gave everyone, not the genuine kind he'd seen and come to love. Oh yeah, he'd stepped in something. She stretched and glanced over at the clock, and he knew what was coming next. "It's getting late. I need to get home."

Damn it. He put a hand on her leg to keep her in place. "I'm sorry. I wasn't trying to pry. You don't have to tell me anything you don't want to."

"I know. And I'm not trying to be all 'Lady of Mystery,' either. There are just some things I don't want to talk about."

"And I won't ask again. If you want to tell me, you can, but—"

She nodded. "Thanks." Patting his hand, she scooted off the couch, adding, "But I really do need to go home and get to bed. It's later than I thought, and Monday mornings are always busy. People need their fix to start the week."

He watched her as she went upstairs to get her clothes without comment, not wanting to dig the hole he was in any deeper. *Helena tried to warn me.* But this was more than just idle curiosity on his part. The pieces of the puzzle he had were starting to worry him—not about her, but *for* her.

The self-help books, the desire for privacy, the facade she presented to most people, the estrangement from her family—he didn't need to be a therapist to know that all equaled something bad that Molly wanted to forget. Whatever it was, though, she wasn't letting it destroy her. She wanted to be happy.

And if he wanted to keep her, he'd have to back off. He just wished she trusted him enough to tell him. To let him help. It was so frustrating to know there was something but be unable to do anything about it.

When she came back down a minute later, the shuttered look was gone and the color was back in her cheeks. He caught her hand as she passed by to get her keys. "Hey—"

She put a finger against his lips. "We're good. Really."

"You're sure?"

"Yeah." She rose up on her toes to give him a quick kiss. "I'll see you later."

He didn't want her to leave. "I'll walk you home."

Molly rolled her eyes. "It's two blocks. I could be home in the time it takes you to get your clothes on."

He cupped her face between his hands and kissed her, wanting that kiss to help him make sense of his own thoughts.

The one thing he did know, though, was that he was going to have to play it her way. And that meant backing off and letting it go. He had to earn her trust, and that was the only way to really do it.

It wasn't easy, though.

Today was a good day.

There was nothing Molly loved more than a full house at Latte Dah. Every business owner liked to see business booming and money going into the till, but having a crowd at Latte Dah was like having a big family gathering where she got to play the matriarch.

The point of a coffee shop wasn't coffee, after all; people could make perfectly decent coffee at home. People came here for community and companionship and conversations, and she got to be right smack-dab in the middle of it all.

The adult Bible study group from Grace Baptist was in the front corner, and the talk had long moved from the holy to the earthy—grandchildren, taxes, where to catch the best fish. There was a group of young moms, their babies napping in strollers, two moony-eyed teenagers who, based solely on the slightly awkward body language, had to be on a first or second date, and four members of the historical society with their heads together in serious conversation. A few sunburned tourists and folks on laptops were mixed in and sharing tables, and Molly just wanted to give everyone a big group hug.

This was why she'd opened a coffee shop. Not for her love of coffee—which *was* genuine and true—and not because Magnolia Beach didn't have one before she'd opened hers. She loved the *idea* of a coffee shop, and Latte Dah had surpassed even her dreams for its acceptance among the locals.

Jane, who'd started wearing her apron strings tied beneath her tiny baby bulge to show it off, was behind the counter while Molly made a sweep through the room grabbing dirty cups and visiting briefly with customers.

Quinn Haslett was already here in his official capacity as editor/photographer/reporter for *The Clarion*, nursing a cup of coffee and chatting with the director of the women's shelter as they waited for everyone else to arrive. The big cardboard checks, one for the county animal rescue and one for the women's shelter, sat close by, already bearing her and Tate's signatures in black marker.

Duncan and Jessie had been right. After all was said and done, the funds raised from the Children's Fair had exceeded last year's amount by over five hundred dollars, and both charities would be getting sizable donations.

She'd done it. It had nearly killed her, but she'd done it. And the amazing part was no one seemed surprised that she *had*. She'd always been the screwup, the one who couldn't be trusted to properly organize a kegger in a brewery, and yet she'd done this. She'd exceeded expectations, and it wasn't because the bar had been set ridiculously low. It was the most incredible realization that these people didn't underestimate her—and something that she hadn't consciously understood until today.

And she wasn't ashamed to admit she was reveling in it.

Tate finally swept in, greeting her with a chaste kiss on the cheek before introducing her to the small dark-haired man he had in tow—the director of the animal rescue. "I gotta do this fast," he said under his breath. "I'm swamped today."

"Then let's do it."

Clapping his hands a couple of times, Tate got everyone's attention, silencing the low rumble that had filled Latte Dah. "For those of you who don't know me, I'm Tate Harris, your local friendly veterinarian. It's my privilege to help sponsor the Children's Fair each Memorial Day. The Children's Fair is a tradition in Magnolia

Beach that families look forward to every year, and the money raised goes to excellent causes that truly deserve our support. Eula Kennedy has always been the driving force behind this event, but unfortunately she was unable to provide her usual excellent leadership this year. The person she tapped to serve in her stead, though, did an amazing job, and we are thankful for her hard work. On behalf of all the families who had a great time, I'd like to thank this year's chair, Molly Richards."

There was a heartening round of applause as she stepped forward. She wasn't terribly comfortable speaking in front of people, but this was exciting, and that overcame her initial panic. "Thank you. It was my pleasure. I'm deeply grateful to everyone who donated their time and talents to making this event great. We couldn't have done it without them. I'd like to welcome Camille James from the Haven Family Shelter and Carl Martin from the Mobile County Animal Rescue and present you both with these checks to support the work you do for the people and animals of our community."

There was another round of applause as she smiled for the camera and shook hands. She motioned the guests forward to make their speeches, but she caught movement out of the corner of her eye and something about it pulled her attention. It was just a man standing slightly off to the side by himself. Why he was twinging her Spidey-senses, she didn't know, but he was. She moved a bit to try to get a better look at him. She could only see him from the back, but there was something familiar about the shape of his shoulders and the way he held his head . . .

Then he turned slightly and she saw his profile. Her heart jumped into her throat, and she froze.

No. Sweet baby Jesus, this was *not* possible.

She closed her eyes, certain she was mistaken, but when she opened them, the horror was real.

It was Mark. And he was *here*.

She hadn't laid eyes on him in nearly three years—not since the day she'd left Fuller and he'd shown up to try to stop her. He looked pretty much the same—a little heavier, though, with the Lane family paunchiness already starting to take root.

Mark looked up and caught her eye. Then he casually looked around the crowded room and smiled.

That smile curdled in her stomach. He couldn't have planned this moment better, and Molly knew he was going to work it for all he could.

And there was not one goddamned thing she could do to stop him.

"Molly? You okay? You're really pale." Tate's voice was concerned, and his hand was on her back in support, but she couldn't turn to look at him. She'd missed the opportunity to tell him, and now it was going to bite her in the ass. She'd gotten so caught up in her New Molly life that she'd forgotten—or at least not wanted to think about—the truth and the disaster waiting to befall her.

Well, it looked like her wait was over.

Narrowing her eyes at Mark, she tried to visually threaten him into not making a scene, but that slick smile only broadened.

Following her stare, Tate asked, "Who's that?"

She didn't have an answer to give him, but it didn't matter anyway. Mark was already right in front of her, leaning down to give her a kiss.

She jerked away, and Mark's lips grazed her cheek. Beside her, she could feel Tate stiffen in shock and confusion and possibly umbrage, but she could only deal with one disaster at a time. The feel of Mark's lips finally jerked her out of her frozen shock. "What the hell are you doing here?"

"I came to see you, sweetie. What else? It looks like a big day. You should have told me." Turning his attention to Tate, Mark stuck out his hand. "Mark Lane. Molly's husband."

He'd intentionally raised his voice, and the shocked silence that followed in the wake of his words felt like her death knell.

Oh God. She wanted to die. No, she wanted to kill Mark and *then* die.

"Her husband?" Tate parroted as his hand fell away from her back. The hand he'd automatically extended to Mark also dropped to his side. "Molly?"

A million questions hid behind that word, but she didn't have the ability to address any of them right now. She couldn't even bring herself to look at Tate, as she was simply too afraid to see confusion and condemnation on his face. Mark just looked smugly pleased with himself. "You son of a bitch."

Her words seemed to break the silence that had been so complete only seconds before as people tried to make conversation and seem normal while eavesdropping at the same time.

So this is what it sounds like when the world crashes down around you.

"Don't be like that, Marley—Molly," he corrected. "I know it's been a while and you're mad, but we can work this out."

There were too many people staring at her in varying degrees of disappointment and censure—and just moments after they'd all been watching her with pride and pleasure. She wanted to cry. She wanted to hit something—starting with Mark's smug face.

It was his smug face that pushed her into action. She turned to Tate, and the look on his face slammed into her stomach. "I'll explain later, okay?"

"What's there to explain?" Mark interjected. "I've come to visit my wife."

"Shut up," she snapped. Then, straining for some level of calm in her voice, she addressed the general crowd with a weak smile. "If y'all will excuse us." Grabbing Mark by the arm, she dragged him through the kitchen and out the back door into the alley.

Once the door was safely closed behind them, she whirled on him. "I *cannot* believe you. I knew you were an ass, but I can't believe you would make a scene like that."

"Embarrassed? Good. You should be. I was rather surprised to get here and find out no one had heard of Marley Lane. It took me forever to get any answers. Imagine my surprise when I found out you'd taken a lover—and that no one cared because no one knew you were married."

How long had he been in Magnolia Beach? Must be just today because she'd have heard about it otherwise—especially since he'd been asking about her. *Oh God. He's been asking about me.* Probably all over town, telling everyone he was her husband. Who all had he talked to? She was ruined. There were some lines that just couldn't be crossed without penalty, and adultery was one of them—no matter how progressive someone might be. And Magnolia Beach wasn't exactly a hot spot of progressive sexuality.

"Since I don't *want* to be married to you—a fact you are very well aware of, so don't look so damn shocked—you can hardly blame me for not sharing that piece of information with the rest of the world." She fought to keep her voice under control. She didn't want him to see the worry or the hurt. Only the anger.

"Like it or not, we *are* married."

"In a fair and just world where your daddy didn't have the judge in his pocket, we wouldn't be."

"Marriage is forever, Mary Marlene Lane. You took

vows in a church, in front of God. 'Till death do us part.' You remember that, don't you?"

"I also remember the part about 'love, honor, and cherish.' You broke your vows first."

His shoulders bowed up. Mark wasn't used to back talk. "You're my wife."

"Much to my dismay." She saw Mark's hand twitch. "Try it, and I'll be a widow instead of a divorcée," she warned. A look of surprise crossed Mark's face, but she could tell he believed her words. And they'd shocked him.

The rush of satisfaction and girl power was immediate and new. "I assume it's too much to hope that you're here with divorce papers for me to sign, so what do you want?"

"I don't need a reason to visit my wife." God, he was petulant.

"Actually, yes, you do."

"Well, maybe I came to *remind* you that you are my wife."

"You cannot be serious. I. Want. A. Divorce." She was nearly shouting now, but she couldn't help it. "I do not want to be married to you. I don't even *like* you."

"Our families, our *church*, don't believe in divorce. Marriage is forever."

Breathe. Try to stay calm. "You keep saying that—"

"Because it's true."

She pretended she didn't hear the interruption. "But at no point have you acted like you actually want to be married to me. You don't love me, and I'm pretty sure you don't even like me very much, either."

"That doesn't matter. You're my—"

"Wife," she finished for him. This was enough to make her want to tear her hair out. "Yes, I know that. But I'm not your damn property. I am a *person*, completely separate from you. This is about your ego, nothing more."

She could tell she'd scored a point, but Mark wasn't done yet with the guilt-tripping. "I can't believe you're going to turn your back on everything you were raised to believe."

"I already have." She lifted her chin. It wasn't going to work on her this time. "I quit living my life to please my family and my church when they turned their backs on me in my time of need."

"You weren't 'in need,' Marley." He sneered. "Stirring up drama for attention is not 'need.' Just because no one bought tickets to your theatrics—"

She couldn't believe she was having this conversation. Even after all that therapy, she'd still let herself be dragged back into his games. But it stopped now. She held up a hand to quiet him. "So did you come here just to embarrass me or is there something else?"

"Enough's enough, Marley."

"I agree. Sign the papers, and we'll be done with all of it."

"I will not. You need to come home."

I am home. "To a town where you've smeared my reputation? No way. And I don't know why you'd want me to. That would only be an embarrassment for you."

"It's less of an embarrassment than having my wife run off. You've had your fun, and now it's time to face the music."

"There's nothing for me to face." Something about the look on his face, though . . . "Wait. You seriously think I'm going to go back?"

He nodded.

There was shock. Then there was disbelief. Finally, there was just pity. "You know, all this time I thought you were just jerking me around as some kind of punishment. I never dreamed you were harboring some pathetic idea that I might actually drop the divorce proceedings. That's just sad."

His face reddened. "No one in my family has ever gotten a divorce. Yours, either. I won't be the first."

Nothing about love or their relationship—just his pride, his image. "Well, if you wanted to be married, you should have been a better husband."

"I've been patient, but I'm not going to let you hide down here forever."

"*Let* me?" Unable to hold it back, she laughed. "You don't get a vote."

Mark's face darkened when she laughed, and he took a step toward her. She refused to back up, widening her stance instead and dropping into the "ready" position they'd taught her in self-defense classes. "Seriously, I will drop you like the sack of shit you are. Last warning. You will not touch me ever again."

He was clearly shocked and a little unbelieving, but he wasn't brave enough to push her, either. "You're being unreasonable."

"I'm being honest. *You're* being a sore loser. Go home, Mark. Have your lawyer call my lawyer and end this." Turning on her heel, she wrenched open the door to Latte Dah. Mark made as if to follow her. "Oh, no you don't. This is *my* place of business. *You* are banned from the premises. Set one foot inside, and I'll have you arrested for trespassing." With that, she slammed the door in his face.

It was a buoying feeling, standing up to him, a thrill she'd never felt before. But knowing all those people who'd witnessed her humiliation were probably still out there, waiting for an explanation or something, deflated her pretty quickly. She sagged against the door and rubbed her hands over her face.

She had no idea how she was going to face all those people. How she'd face Tate. Well, Mark had been right about one thing: it was time to face the music.

Just not right this second.

Jane found her there a few minutes later. "Are you okay?"

"As much as I can be."

"Is he really your husband?" she asked carefully.

There was no denying it. The damage was done and everyone in town would know soon enough thanks to Mark's impeccable timing. What had she done to deserve such a karmic backlash? "Yes, much to my everlasting shame."

"I didn't know you were married."

"I don't want to be. And I'd kind of hoped the divorce would be finalized before anyone ever knew I had been." She could tell Jane didn't quite know what to think, much less say. While not proven a flat-out liar, she'd at least been proven as someone dishonest with secrets to hide.

And while this might be the twenty-first century, adultery was still definitely frowned on, and *oh dear God*, she'd been outed in front of the Grace Baptist Bible study group and the historical society—none of whom would likely shrug this off without some suitable condemnation.

She wanted to crawl in a hole and cry.

Jane patted her shoulder. "Why don't you let me mind the shop this afternoon. I'll call in Sam or one of the other girls to help. You go home, clear your head . . ."

The words *and figure out what you're going to do* hung in the air unsaid but understood.

Chapter 14

*M*olly was married.

Tate liked to think of himself as a modern, enlightened man, but there were some things that were just so ingrained as *right* and *wrong* it would be impossible to pretend they weren't.

Dating a married woman definitely fell in the *wrong* category. He hadn't known she was married, but that didn't really relieve much of the feeling for him. Ignorance wasn't much of an excuse, but it was all he had.

Of course, dating while married was very wrong, and Molly knew she was married. She couldn't claim otherwise. It wasn't exactly something a person just forgot about.

Good Lord, how long had she been married? She'd been in Magnolia Beach for over two years, so at least that long. Then he remembered her saying no one had asked her out since high school. Christ, it could be eight years or more. Maybe even a decade.

She certainly didn't act married, though, and she hadn't been glad to see her husband, either.

The shock had delayed any other reaction, but now the pain settled like a knot in his chest. *Molly was married*. He'd wanted to know the secret she'd been hiding, but he'd take the ignorance back gladly.

Standing in the middle of Latte Dah after that scene had him feeling like an exhibit at the zoo. Everyone in town knew they were seeing each other, and he could feel eyes on him, almost hear people asking themselves if *he'd* known, judging him as an accomplice. Once again, he was being judged for the actions of someone else. Something that wasn't his fault, done by someone he had no control over. But this was worse. He hadn't been an active participant in his father's drunkenness and violence, only a recipient. He was half of this couple, and people were going to assign half the blame.

Taking a quick glance at the room, he groaned. *Of course* some of Magnolia Beach's biggest busybodies just *had* to be here to see this go down. The very best thing he could do in this situation was to act as normal as possible and not make it worse. But how?

Then Quinn pulled him aside. "What the hell was that?"

"I have no idea," he answered honestly. "I'm just as confused as you are." How long had it been since Molly dragged her husband away? Five minutes? Ten? It seemed like an eternity. He looked toward the kitchen, but he couldn't see them in there. Molly must have taken him out through the back door into the alley. Should he go check on her?

"Do you think she's okay out there?" Quinn asked, the same thoughts obviously going through his mind.

"She didn't seem afraid of him, but . . ." There was something about that guy that just didn't seem right, regardless of who he was to Molly. He didn't like it.

He'd taken one step toward the kitchen when Quinn caught him. "I'll go. If that guy really is Molly's . . . well, you know, you might not be the best person to add to the mix. Why don't you say some good-byes and go back to the clinic. Play it cool until you can find out what's going on."

Quinn was a good friend and quick on the uptake. "Thanks."

With a nod, Quinn was headed out the front door, pausing just long enough to tap Todd West on the shoulder as he passed. Todd stood immediately and followed him, and the two of them disappeared around the side of the building.

Speak to a few people and head back to the clinic. That's what acting normal would look like, hopefully smoothing over some of this. If he didn't make a big deal, people might not think it was a big deal. Deep down he knew he was kidding himself, but it was worth a try.

So, as nonchalantly and unhurriedly as possible, as if this kind of thing happened all the time, Tate said his good-byes to the charity representatives, thanking them for coming. He was surprised at how normal he sounded, proving again how ingrained some things could be. A lifetime of pretending nothing was wrong finally seemed to be paying off. It was twisted. Then, very aware of the conversations in his wake, Tate pushed through the door and out into the street. Five steps away from the door, he ended up face-to-face with the man who'd just introduced himself as Molly's husband ten minutes earlier.

"So you're the home-wrecker," Mark said, leaning against a gray SUV parked at the curb. Anger radiated off him, a big change from the calmness he'd exhibited earlier. Whatever Molly had said to him, it wasn't what he'd wanted to hear.

Molly had lived in Magnolia Beach for nearly three years, he reminded himself. Regardless of anything else, Tate hardly considered himself a home-wrecker. Molly might be married to this guy, but it obviously wasn't a good marriage. Helena had suspected a bad relationship. It seemed she'd been right.

"Do you often sleep with other men's wives?"

Mark was a big square-featured guy, the ex-football

type who'd gone soft after his glory days. And regardless of his casual stance, he was obviously looking for a fight. Tate was pretty sure he'd be able to hold his own just fine, plus Quinn and Todd were hanging back unobtrusively at the corner, but still he didn't relish adding public brawling to the hot gossip of the day—with Molly's husband, no less. That was all this story needed.

But Tate's ingrained manners were failing him. What did one say to one's girlfriend's husband? "Molly never mentioned you."

"Her name is *Marley*," Mark gritted out. "Mary Marlene Lane. Not Molly."

Tate just shrugged, causing Mark's face to darken in anger.

"You're sleeping with her and you don't even know her name. That's pretty pitiful."

"No, pitiful is your wife choosing to sleep with someone else instead of you." It was a juvenile thing to say and would probably give Mark the excuse he was looking for to start swinging, but Tate didn't care.

"We may have some problems, but all married couples do. We're working on them. I'd appreciate it if you'd keep your hands off my wife while we do."

"Molly's lived here for a while now and no one even knew she was married. That doesn't sound like Molly's trying too hard to work out those problems."

"Don't presume you know anything about my marriage. We may have some problems, but there are other parts of it that are just fine." Mark cocked his head. "Oh, you didn't know she's two-timing you, too?" He snorted. "I suppose sleeping with your husband can't really be considered cheating on your lover, though."

It was an ugly, low blow, but untrue, he knew, since Molly simply hadn't had the time to sleep with Mark since she'd been with him. But the idea that she'd been keeping her marriage alive all this time still sat uneasy with him. It made him jealous, and he lashed out. "I wouldn't say that too loud, if I were you. People might think Molly took a lover because her husband wasn't enough for her."

That got a reaction. "You son of a bitch." Mark pushed out of his lean and stalked toward him, his hands clenched into big, meaty fists.

"Everything all right here?"

The overly casual voice came from behind him, and Tate glanced over his shoulder to see Adam and Ryan Tanner. Both Tanners were also former football players, but unlike Mark they still looked as if they could hit the field at any time. And by the way Mark froze, releasing his fists, Tate knew Mark wasn't willing to risk three-on-one odds—no matter how angry he might be at the moment.

Keeping his eye on Mark, Tate said, "I think we're all good."

Mark stomped back to his SUV and slammed the door.

"That guy really wanted to kick your ass," Adam said as Mark drove off.

"He was welcome to try."

"Okay, so who was that and what was that about?" Ryan asked.

So the news hadn't spread too quickly, but then, even the Magnolia Beach grapevine had a time lag.

Quinn and Todd were already closing the distance. Tate tilted his head in their direction. "They'll fill you in."

Both Tanners looked at him as if he'd lost his mind, but he just left them there and headed back to the clinic. He had patients waiting.

And he really didn't know what else to do.

Either the news was slow to spread—which he doubted—or else he could credit the "behind your back, not to your face" rule of gossip, but either way, no one mentioned the debacle at Latte Dah to him all afternoon.

For that, he was thankful, because he couldn't guarantee what he might say if he were pressed. Hell, he wasn't sure what he was even thinking right now.

He forced himself to focus on his four-legged patients—creatures who didn't lie or play mind games—but the thoughts kept randomly intruding.

Molly was married.

Molly had lied to him.

Okay, she hadn't *lied*, but she'd withheld a pretty important piece of information.

Molly was married.

Married.

To a real jerk, if first impressions were to be believed.

Married.

And she'd never bothered to mention it.

Christ.

Why?

Somehow, though, even with that litany running through his head, he managed to get through the afternoon. And somehow, he wasn't all that surprised to find Molly waiting on his porch swing when he got home.

He wasn't sure that was a good thing. He'd had time, yes, but not the opportunity to process the information, and he wasn't really ready to deal with Molly just yet.

She looked remarkably calm and clear-eyed, with only the way she was twisting a ring around her index finger giving him a clue she might not be.

"You deserve an explanation," she said without preamble, pushing to her feet.

"I'm not sure now's a good time."

"Please, Tate—"

"Fine. Are you married or not?"

She sighed. "Sort of. You see—"

"There's no 'sort of.' You can't be 'sort of' married. It's a yes-or-no question."

"Legally? Yes, I'm still married. But I don't want to be."

The odd pang he felt made him realize he'd been holding out a shred of hope that Mark had been lying, and Molly wasn't actually married. "For how long?"

"Does it really matter?" When he didn't answer, she sighed again. "I was a very naive, very stupid nineteen-year-old, so nearly eight years now."

"And you didn't think this was something I should know?"

"Yes, but . . . it's complicated."

"Not really. You're married, and I don't date other men's wives."

"If you'll just give me a chance to explain . . ." She dragged her hands through her hair, causing the curls to spring out crazily. Her big brown eyes were sad, her face pale and resigned when she finally looked at him. She was obviously miserable. At least they had that much in common. "Can we please go inside to talk?"

He opened the door and went inside, leaving her to follow if she wanted to. She closed the door carefully behind her. "I'm sorry you found out this way."

Not *Sorry I lied* or even *Sorry I'm married*. Just sorry that he'd found out. "It was certainly dramatic. And very public."

"And I'm so sorry about that, too. Mark couldn't have timed that better if he tried." She sat on the edge of the couch and took a deep breath. "Please know that I wasn't trying to deceive you by not telling you."

"You just forgot you were married?"

"No." An exasperated laugh punctuated her answer. "I wish I could. I don't *feel* married, though. Mark and I have been separated for a long time. Over three, almost four years now. I haven't even seen him or spoken to him since before I left Fuller."

That helped a little. "He seems to think you'll be patching it up."

"He's very wrong about that," she snapped. "I will eventually get my divorce. It's just been difficult."

"Really, Molly? Wait, according to your husband"— she flinched at the word—"your name's not even Molly. Is *anything* I know about you the truth?"

She met his eyes evenly and in a calm voice said, "Molly is a nickname my grandmother used to call me. Richards is my maiden name. I've never lied to you or anyone else about who I am or where I come from."

"You just left out the part about being married." *Which somehow colored everything else.*

The calm tone disappeared. "Because I thought I'd be divorced before it ever became an issue!" she shouted.

Good Lord. He leaned against the couch. "Guess not."

Visibly deflating, Molly rubbed her hands over her face. "Tate, please. You don't understand—"

"What don't I understand? It's not that hard to get a divorce if you really want one."

"In Fuller it is," she said flatly. "Mark's family is influential in Fuller. The way the Tanners are here, only the Lanes use their power and influence for evil." Her attempt at humor fell flat. "Our church doesn't believe in divorce, and my family practically disowned me when I left him. Then I couldn't find an attorney who'd represent me—they were either friends with the Lanes or not willing to make enemies of them. Mark wasn't going to give me an easy divorce—that was very clear from the get-go—so when I finally found an attorney willing to do it, he asked for a huge retainer, which I didn't have. Then my grandmother died and left me some money. I used that to pay the retainer, move to Magnolia Beach, and open Latte Dah."

It was a sad story, but it rang true enough. "So what's the holdup?"

Her mouth twisted. "Mark. His attorney covered me in paperwork until I ran through the retainer. The rest of my money was locked up in the shop, so everything was on hold for a while until I had more to spend. The judge plays golf with Mark's dad, so he keeps postponing and rescheduling. And every now and again Mark's attorney drops another request on me that requires me to pay more money and shuffle more papers around. I think Mark either thinks he'll wear me down or bankrupt me. So three years after filing for divorce, I'm still married."

"And you couldn't just tell me that?"

"When? When's the right time to tell someone that?"

"At the beginning. When I kissed you. When I asked you out the first time."

"I *tried.*"

She'd been walking a fine line between truth and lies the whole time. "You said you weren't 'there.' You made it sound like it was an emotional thing, like you were getting over a relationship."

"It's true. I was. I *am.* That didn't stop you from kissing me a second time, though," she reminded him.

"Don't try to turn this around on me. You kissed me, too. I had no way of knowing—"

Molly pushed to her feet and started to pace. "Do you think I'm *happy* about this? Do you think this is what I wanted? You're angry, yes, and you have every right to be. But I've also been humiliated in front of the entire town, and now Mark can amend the filing to include a charge of adultery."

"Well, that should at least speed things up."

She met his eyes. "You think the judge isn't going to use that against me?"

He didn't know much about divorce law, but he knew

plenty of divorced people and heard their stories. "He can't."

She rolled her eyes. "Maybe not outright, but judges have ways of being punitive when they want to. And now I'm the bad girl, an admitted adulteress. As soon as Judge Ramsey finds out, he'll make sure this drags on just to punish me. And if I ever actually get a hearing, I'm sure he will find a way to hold me accountable somehow."

He felt bad for her. Really. The situation sucked. But . . . "This is all very interesting, but it doesn't change the fact you lied to me."

"I didn't lie about it. I just didn't tell you."

"Don't split hairs, Molly."

"I hoped you wouldn't have to know. Do you not understand how embarrassing this is?"

"More embarrassing than what happened today?"

She flushed. "I know that was terribly embarrassing for you, and I'm so, *so* sorry you got caught in the fallout of Mark's drama. I'll make sure everyone knows that I was dishonest and you didn't know anything about it."

"If you'd simply told me the truth, no one would have been embarrassed."

"No one other than me." She said it quietly.

"If what you say is true, you wouldn't have had a reason to be embarrassed at all."

"No? I'm supposed to admit to you that I got married too young, and for all the wrong reasons, to a guy who turned out to be a bully and a jerk? That I'm estranged from my family and friends because none of them believe me, and I can't even go home now because he's trashed my reputation in my hometown and painted me to be an immoral, selfish jezebel?" Her voice, which had started out calm and dispassionate, was growing more agitated with each word until she was nearly shouting again. "That my grandmother had to *die* before I could even afford to do anything about it? And that while I've started over, I can't really get a fresh start because I can't even manage to get a damn divorce because Mark wants to jerk my chain? What's *not* embarrassing about that?"

"Things that are done *to* you are out of your control. You don't have to be embarrassed about them. It's how you react that matters."

She shook her head. "I'm disappointed in you, Tate. I thought you, of all people, would understand."

That sent his hackles up. "Sorry, but I've never been married."

Molly let the snark slide without comment. "No, but you know what it's like."

"To be married?" *Has she lost her mind?*

"To have someone you love hurt you. To have the people who are supposed to love and protect you turn their backs on you and let it happen. For them to deny it, to say it was your fault and you somehow deserved it. Not to mention the shame you feel for believing it, even for a minute, or not ending it sooner somehow."

He fought to keep his voice calm. He was not going to let her land that punch. "Don't go there. It's not the same thing."

"I didn't say it was. But I guess I really thought you'd understand. Or at least give me the benefit of the doubt."

He did understand—rationally, at least. "You could've trusted me with the truth. I could've helped." *That* was the kicker. The part that really hurt.

"How?" she demanded, angry again.

"Well . . . I don't exactly know."

"Oh, well, that's very helpful indeed," she snapped. "Look, I didn't *want* you to know. I didn't want *anybody* to know. I didn't want that part of my life touching my life here."

"So you were just going to let him pull your strings

as long as he felt like it? You just said he refuses to see the truth about your relationship. You were just going to let that go on indefinitely? You didn't see a problem with that?"

"I got myself in this mess by marrying him. That's embarrassing. Keeping huge parts of my life on hold because I can't divorce him is embarrassing. And it's frustrating as hell, too. And it'd gone on for so long . . . But I finally moved on. I decided to try to have a life and actually live it, which is the exact opposite of letting him pull my strings. And even though I knew it could blow up in my face, I risked *everything* to be with you. And now all the worst-case scenarios are coming true." She grabbed her bag and walked toward the door. Hand on the knob, she turned. "I'm sorry I'm married. I'm sorry I didn't tell you. I'm sorry you had to find out like you did and that you were embarrassed and hurt by it. But this is who I am, and this is the situation, and this is how I'm dealing with it. I'm sorry that it's not good enough for you."

With a shake of her head—apology or disappointment?—Molly left, slamming the door behind her.

He leaned back against the couch and closed his eyes. This day had gone to hell and he hoped to God there weren't any more hits coming his way. He wasn't sure he could handle anything else.

Not that he'd handled this particularly well.

For the first time in a really long time, he *needed* a drink.

She'd never actually watched a ceiling fan go round and round. It was boring as hell, but even after three hours of staring at it, Molly still didn't have the energy or desire to pull herself off the couch.

Nigel lay on her chest purring contentedly. She appreciated the company, but Nigel was probably just taking advantage of the fact she was lying still, rather than actually offering her any moral support in her deep blue funk.

She'd never taken a day off like this before. Unable to even contemplate facing people, she'd called Jane at five this morning and asked her to go open the shop. She had a sneaking suspicion Jane had expected that, as she'd sounded awake already and agreed to do it, no questions asked. It was pure cowardice mixed with a healthy dose of humiliation, and Molly fully admitted it.

To Nigel, at least.

She'd given up trying to figure out what to do late last night and was now just wallowing in self-pity, anger, and depression. In one fell swoop, she'd lost her dignity, the respect of her community, and Tate.

It sucked and it hurt and she wasn't sure which part of that was the *worst* part.

She had no one to blame but herself, really. Oh, she'd talked a good game. She'd even managed to convince herself that she'd done the right thing by moving on, and maybe she had, but she'd let fear and shame drive that bus without realizing it. She hadn't wanted to tell Tate the truth—not only to keep her past out of her present, but also because she wasn't willing to risk Tate's reaction. So she'd ignored it, pushed it out of her head, even sort of forgot about it, and now it was blowing up around her.

She'd unplugged the house phone, turned off the ringer on her cell phone, and put the laptop under the bed. She had nothing to say to anyone anyway. And she was staying inside for the same reason, with the added benefit of minimizing her risk of running into Mark somewhere in town and creating yet another scene for everyone's entertainment.

Early this morning, she'd toyed with the idea of leaving town for a day or two, only to be hit with the depressing realization that she really didn't have anywhere to go.

Good Lord. This was her worst nightmare come to life, and it was too depressing to even cry about.

Eventually, she'd have to start seriously thinking about what to do, try to come up with some kind of plan to mitigate the damage—if she even could—but that would be later.

She still had a lot of wallowing to do.

The knock on her door that became a pounding on her door when she ignored it wasn't all that surprising, considering she'd cut off all possible avenues of contact. Then she heard Helena's voice. "I know you're in there, Molly. Let me in."

Nigel lifted his head, ears twitching.

After a moment of silence, she heard keys in the lock. *Crap.*

"I'm coming in," Helena called as she opened the door.

"That key was supposed to be for emergencies," she grumbled.

"Since you're not at work, not answering your phones, and not answering the door, I'm declaring an emergency. For all I knew, you'd fallen and hit your head. You could have been bleeding to death on the floor."

Hadn't Tate jumped to a similar overdramatic conclusion? Those two . . . *Damn.* She didn't want to think about Tate right now.

"Well, I'm not." She draped an arm over her eyes as Helena turned on a light. "I love you, and you now know I'm alive, so could you please go away?"

"Not on your life. Here—" Helena appeared by her side, extending a Latte Dah to-go cup toward her. "Rocket Fuel."

Molly struggled to sit up, displacing Nigel, who shot

her a dirty look. "If I'd wanted coffee, I could have made my own," she groused, but took the cup anyway. It smelled divine, causing caffeine-starved nerves to twitch like a junkie in need of a fix.

Helena took the chair across from her. Leaning back, she sipped her own coffee. "So . . . what's new with you?"

The smugly casual question made her laugh, which felt weird in the middle of her carefully crafted depression. "You obviously know, or you wouldn't be here."

"I know what I've heard, but I also know better than to believe everything I hear. That guy . . . is he really your husband?"

"Unfortunately."

"Why did I not know this?"

"It was something I was trying to forget. Why would I tell people—even you—things that I would really rather forget?"

Helena nodded. "I can't fault you there. I know how that is."

"I know. And I like that about you. And by the way, thank you for never asking."

She shrugged a shoulder. "I knew there was something you didn't want to talk about. But now that it's not a secret anymore, do you want to tell me about it?"

She sighed. "I don't know where to begin."

"How about the beginning."

The story felt dusty—she hadn't told it in years, not since she'd first unloaded all of it in therapy. Helena, bless her, was as good as any therapist, listening without comment, her face neutral.

So Molly told her everything. The way her parents had rejoiced at the news she was dating Mark, seeing him as the steadying, calming presence needed after a rebellious adolescence—not to mention that being connected to the Lane family was quite the bonus. The arrogance that had led her to the altar, even though she was ignorant of what marriage would entail and had been oblivious to the warning signs of Mark's unstable personality. The belief system that had kept her trapped in an unhappy marriage because it must have been *her* fault Mark treated her poorly and how she deserved what she got because he was the man, the boss. The emotional abuse. The physical abuse.

The refusal of her family to believe her, much less help her.

Finally, she paused in her recitation and looked at Helena.

"Well, that sucks," she said.

The simple statement made her laugh. Trust Helena to skip all the platitudes. Helena had had her own set of troubles, and since she wasn't the type to want sappy sympathy, she wasn't the kind to give it, either. Which was somehow exactly what Molly needed right now. Nonjudgmental understanding without emotional baggage. "That it does."

Helena lifted her coffee cup in a toast. "Well, you've come a long way, baby. Why the hell aren't you divorced already?"

"Mark won't give me one."

Helena frowned. "It's not his to 'give.' Surely he understands he can't make you stay married to him."

"I don't know about that. It's worked so far for him. We're still married."

"That's just ridiculous. Like you'd go back to him. Like I'd *let* you go back." Making a sound somewhere between a snort and a growl, she added, "Right now I want to go find him and smack him."

That buoyed her spirits. It was nice to have a friend. "It's not worth the jail time, honey."

"I know the mayor pretty well. He could probably get the charges dropped. By the way," she added, "Ryan says Mark tried to pick a fight with Tate."

Oh dear God. "What? When?"

"Outside Latte Dah yesterday. It must have been right after he . . ."

"Humiliated me in front of God and everyone?" Molly supplied.

"Yeah. Look, I don't want to ask you anything you don't want to answer, but I do need to know one thing. Are you in any danger? I mean, this guy obviously has some serious problems. Any chance he's going to come after you? Or Tate, for that matter?"

The mention of Tate made Molly jump, but Helena seemed focused on the immediate issue. "No. I don't think so. Mark's a hothead and a bully, but like most bullies he's a coward at heart. He doesn't know what to do when someone actually stands up to him."

"Why don't you come stay with me at Grannie's for few days. Just to be safe."

"No. I'm not afraid of him, and I'm not going to let him disrupt my life more than he already has."

"But you'll be careful, though, right? No more taking him out into the back alley by yourself?" There was a touch of censure in her voice.

"I'm not worried. I could tell he wanted to slap me yesterday—"

"Molly!"

"Don't worry. I called him out on it and he backed down. He'll try to run his mouth, but— What?" Helena was making a face.

"Well, he's already running his mouth."

Molly cursed.

"He spent last night at the Bait Box bitching and moaning about you to anyone who would listen."

"Oh my God." She dropped her head into her hands. "He's already got all of Fuller believing I'm a terrible person, and now he's starting here?"

"Oh, don't worry. It's not like anyone believed anything

he was saying. It was all just butthurt and sour grapes. If anyone wanted to know why you left him, he made it pretty clear last night. In fact, it made a lot of people pretty damn indignant on your behalf." Helena smirked. "Peter the bartender kicked him out. Told him not to come back, either."

"You're kidding me." The thought made her smile.

"No. I just wish I could've been there to see it."

"You and me both. It's nice to know I have some friends."

"You do," Helena assured her. "I just wish you'd told me. You wouldn't have had to deal with this all alone."

"Honestly, it never occurred to me." She could see the concern on Helena's face. "It's just that I got so used to not having anyone since Mark turned almost all of our friends against me, that it never crossed my mind that I could."

"Well, you can, 'cause I've got your back now." Helena waited for her to smile, then added, "So, anything *else* you want to tell me?"

"No." She laughed. "You now know all my deepest, darkest secrets. You and the whole town. Jeez." Sighing, she dropped her head into her hands. "Considering what Mark is probably saying about me, the rumor mill is going to grind me up."

Helena waved a hand. "Honey, you know I've been grist in that mill plenty of times, but the fact of the matter is we protect our own. It's one thing for *us* to talk about you. It's another thing entirely for an outsider to try it."

"But I'm still going to be the talk of the town. And not in a good way."

"I figured that's why you were hiding today. I'm not going to deny that you've shocked a lot of people, and there will be some scandalized pearl clutching, but in this case the truth really will be your best defense. It might not be easy, but it'll pass and you'll be fine." She laughed. "If they're not running *me* out of town on the rails, *you're* in no danger at all."

That tiny shred of hope felt like a lifeline. "You really think that's true?"

"I know it is. And you know I'm not going to blow sunshine up your skirt about this town or the people in it. I'm fully aware of what they're capable of. But since they actually *liked* you to begin with . . ."

Oddly, this was cheering her up considerably. She didn't necessarily believe it a hundred percent, but the support was appreciated. "What would I do without you?"

"Mope. And wallow and worry, obviously." Helena pinned her with a hard look and Molly braced herself. "How is Tate handling all of this?"

"You haven't talked to him?" She'd assumed Helena would have gone to him first.

"No. I've been too worried about you. Why?"

Dangerous territory. "He's not real happy with me. I withheld pretty important information—"

"Yes, but that's understandable."

Oh, if only Tate agreed. "And I embarrassed him in a pretty spectacular way in front of everyone."

Helena waved that away, too. "Like he's never done anything embarrassing before. Hell, I've embarrassed him worse than that in front of way more people. Don't tell me he's giving you a hard time."

"It's complicated."

She seemed to understand. "I'll talk to him."

"No. Don't." Helena looked surprised, so Molly rushed to explain. "I don't want you in the middle of this. It's not fair to you. Be his friend. Give him a sympathetic ear like you gave me, but don't feel like you have to take sides or mediate."

"I'd make an excellent mediator. I know and like you

both and want everyone to be happy. That's even better than a disinterested one. If he's mad about something, I'm the best person to figure out what's stuck in his craw and Heimlich it out of there."

Typical Helena. "I'll be honest with you. I don't want you in the middle because I don't want this thing to affect us."

"How could it?" Helena looked genuinely offended, which warmed Molly's heart.

"If Tate made you feel like you had to choose—"

"I'd smack him silly," she said quickly. "Tate Harris is not the boss of me."

"That's why I didn't want to go out with him in the first place," she admitted. "I know you love me, but you've loved Tate longer. There's history there. You'd be right to choose him over me, but I don't want to lose you."

"If you'd done something to deliberately hurt Tate, that would be different. Why didn't you just tell him up front? He'd have kept your secret."

She sighed and leaned back. "At first, I thought I'd have to—that I *should*—but then I didn't want to. I didn't want him to think—well, less of me because of my baggage. Plus, I was afraid he'd have a problem dating a married woman." She snorted. "I guess I was right."

"It's weird, I'll grant you that."

"Then I was happy, and I didn't want to mess that up."

Helena looked at her carefully. "You care about him, then?"

Something squeezed painfully in her chest. That was the one question she'd been avoiding the whole time because it just hurt too much to think about. "I do. More than I realized."

"Then y'all need to talk this through." She made it sound so easy.

"I've tried to explain. He's not interested in listening."

"You're both hurt, you're both angry, and I know how

Tate gets when he's angry. You should hear him shout at me. He just needs a little space to calm down before he can be rational about it." She stopped and smiled crookedly. "But I want you two to work this out. I want to go on couple dates with y'all."

That panged Molly. Thinking about Tate was hard enough. It hurt to think she'd hurt him, and honestly, he did have a very good reason to be mad at her, but still . . .

She was also disappointed in him. Tate was a good guy, and deep down she'd hoped he'd understand. She hadn't really realized that she was counting on that until he hadn't. All that talk had just been talk, and his lack of follow-through let her down. It wasn't fair for her to blame him for not reacting how she'd hoped he would, but she could be sad about it nonetheless.

She was willing to admit she'd been in the wrong and that he deserved to be mad, but her feelings were hurt. It was irrational, but she wasn't feeling very rational right now. And while in a normal world discussing and dissecting boy problems would be the obvious thing to do with her best friend, it complicated matters quite a bit when it was the boy's best friend as well. She certainly couldn't tell Helena all that. She was going to have to have a long, hard think before she had any idea what to do about Tate. And that think couldn't happen until she got the rest of her life sorted out.

Ugh.

"What time is it?"

Helena smiled, understanding perfectly. "It's time for wine."

Things would have to look better in the morning.

Chapter 15

"I say we gather up a couple of guys and go kick his ass for him." Quinn stretched out on his lawn chair and threw a ball for Scoop to fetch. The dog took off like a shot across the yard and returned a second later, dropping the ratty tennis ball at Quinn's feet and staring up at him adoringly.

"It's tempting," Tate replied, mainly because that would be the expected response. He stretched his legs out, repressing a groan. Tonight was poker night, and he'd come early and scored dinner. Iona's jealousy had made his fridge a sad place recently, but maybe with this new development good food might return soon. It was the saddest search for a silver lining ever and he knew it. Sophie was an amazing cook, and he'd eaten way more tonight than he should have. He ought to be chasing that ball, not Scoop, but the thought of moving was a little too much.

"You two are supposed to be fine, upstanding citizens, role models for our youth and all that crap," Sophie said, coming out with fresh tea glasses for everyone. She'd obviously overheard. "You two end up in jail, and I'm leaving your asses there."

Quinn reached for her hand. "Aw, you wouldn't bail me out?"

"And waste perfectly good money I could spend on flowers for the wedding? Nope. You do the crime, you do the time." She threw Scoop's ball and the dog took off again. Sophie looked at Tate and sighed. "Are you sure Scoop's not some kind of retriever? She'll do this for hours."

Scoop was almost a textbook example of a boxer. "I don't see any in her, but you never know. I warned you she would be an active dog."

"I didn't believe you, but chasing after her has gotten me in the best shape of my life," Quinn said. "Molly's husband looked big, but I could probably take him."

Tate felt his eye twitch at the words "Molly's husband," but he was wearing sunglasses, so he didn't worry about Quinn or Sophie seeing it. "I thought the same thing."

"I don't know where he went, though. We'd have to find him first."

"Went?" Tate turned to Sophie. "I thought he was staying at your place?" Sophie's bed and breakfast was one of the nicest places on the beach.

"He *was*. I only gave him a room—and my owner's suite at that—because he dropped Molly's name. Once I heard about yesterday's foolishness, I told him he wasn't welcome in my establishment any longer," she said primly. "If he's lucky, that roach motel outside Bayou La Batre might rent him a room, but no one in Magnolia Beach will—even if they had one to spare."

"Ms. Marge turned him away today, too, when he tried to get lunch," Quinn added. "She told him to his face how she likes Molly and didn't appreciate what he'd been saying about her."

"Good for her," Sophie said.

Tate wasn't all that surprised. Everyone liked Molly, and Magnolia Beach stood by their own—even when they were in trouble. But he was amused. "Don't tell the tourism board. They've worked so hard to cultivate a reputation as a hospitable place."

Sophie threw Scoop's ball again and turned to go back into the house. Then, looking over her shoulder with a small smile, she added, "Who do you think sent out the e-mail?" With that, she went back inside.

Quinn shook his head. "From what I understand, Fuller's a pretty small town, too. You'd think he'd know how fast word can spread."

"Well, from what Molly told me, he's a pretty big deal in Fuller. I guess he thought his reputation would precede him or something."

"Is she okay? Sophie said she wasn't at the coffee shop today."

He didn't know, but it seemed he was supposed to. "I'm giving her some space."

"Oh."

There was a wealth of meaning in that word, but Tate let it pass and Quinn didn't push. He was still processing a lot of information, and some of the looks he'd gotten today hadn't helped his mood much. Sam's ringtone interrupted the conversation, and he debated answering it. He'd been avoiding Helena's calls and texts entirely—and those messages were getting downright testy now. Sophie's food hadn't been the only draw to coming early tonight. He didn't know what he'd do if Helena showed up on his porch, because he wasn't ready to talk to her about this yet. Escaping to Quinn's might seem cowardly, but it would keep him from saying something to Helena he'd regret later.

Sam, though, presented a different quandary. She might be calling about Molly—a conversation he didn't want to have—or their mother—something he didn't have the patience for tonight. But it could be about something else important. Bracing himself, he took a chance and answered.

As usual, Sam skipped over the preliminaries. "Do I need to quit my job?"

Molly, then, would be the topic. "What?"

"Well, am I going to get fired?" she demanded.

He kept his voice calm and toneless. "I don't know. What did you do?"

"I didn't do jack. I'm wondering what *you* did, though."

"Excuse me?"

"I know you. And I know Molly. Considering what happened yesterday and the fact Molly wasn't at work today, I can only assume *you've* done something stupid."

It seemed his sister was conveniently forgetting *he* was the injured party in this situation. "I have no idea how you've managed to jump to that amazing and erroneous conclusion."

"Like I said, I know you."

There was a challenge there, but he wasn't going to respond to it. Sam wanted information, and he didn't have any to provide, even if he felt so inclined. "Well, I sincerely doubt that Molly would take her anger at me out on you."

"So she *is* angry at you."

Damn, walked right into that. "You don't need to worry about it. This is between me and Molly."

"I like Molly. And I like you. I'm also pretty sure you really like each other. And y'all are awesome together." Her tone softened. "Fix it, okay?"

If only it were that easy. "Well . . ."

"Look, my divorce was relatively simple, but it's not an easy thing to go through. You have no idea what it's like. Even if you want the divorce and know it's the right thing, you still feel like a failure and a fool. I can't even imagine what it would be like to want out and not be able to get out. And to have it drag on so long? That's a beating no one's ego should have to take."

"Sam—"

She raised her voice and refused to let him interrupt. "Lord, just the thought of how much money she must have spent on this makes me want to cry for her. That's just insult on top of injury."

"Then Molly needs a better attorney. The rest of it really isn't your business, Sam."

"Molly's my friend, too. I get to be concerned about her. And you're my brother, so I can't help but make it my business."

"I'm not going to discuss my love life with you."

"Fine." She exhaled sharply, but her tone softened. "Look, try to be understanding. You wouldn't want to be in her shoes."

"I'll talk to you later, Sam."

He heard her sigh again, but he wasn't going to argue with her. Hanging up before he lost his temper and said something he'd later regret was the best idea. Yes, he knew he might be being a jerk, but it was hard to be rational right now. It was weird that Molly was married, but he was convinced it wouldn't have been as bad if she'd just *told* him. *That* was the part he just couldn't be rational about.

While his mood hadn't been what anyone would call "good" at all today, he'd now lost any interest in playing poker tonight. Not that the poker table was a particularly prime place for anyone to grill him about Molly, but he didn't really want to sit around with a group of people who wouldn't *ask* him anything but would most likely be wondering about it all the same.

He wasn't in the mood to deal with that tonight at all. Sliding the phone back in his pocket, he walked back over to Quinn. "I'm going to have to bail on tonight, sorry."

Quinn's eyebrows went up. "So we're going to go kick his ass after all? Do you need backup?"

He laughed. It was said as a joke, but Tate knew the

offer was sincere if he said the word. "I'm not going after Molly's ex. Sam just reminded me of some stuff I need to take care of. Tell Sophie I said thanks for dinner."

"Will do. And good luck."

"Thanks." He shouldn't need it, not for this at least, he thought, pulling out his phone again and looking for the number. But he appreciated it nonetheless.

He needed all the luck he could get these days.

Molly had dreaded today, fortifying herself with positive mantras while dragging her feet across town to open Latte Dah, hoping for the best but steeling herself for the worst.

The first surprise came with the morning pastry delivery from Miller's Bakery. Joe Miller normally did his mother's deliveries, so Molly was taken aback to see Joyce Miller herself arriving with the boxes ten minutes before she even opened the doors.

It was easy to underestimate Mrs. Miller. She was a sweet-looking, unprepossessing woman in her mid-sixties, the soft grandmotherly type, smelling of fresh bread and cinnamon and all the fabulous things she cooked in her bakery.

But underestimating her was a stupid move people only made once. Not only could Mrs. Miller rip someone down a size without even raising her voice, the woman had serious clout in this town. The Millers might not be as obviously influential as say, the Tanners, but Molly had the distinct feeling, if not the solid proof, that the Millers—and Joyce Miller, specifically—pulled a hell of a lot of strings in Magnolia Beach, and her "opinions" might as well be carved into Moses's stone tablets.

Her mouth went dry. She liked Mrs. Miller, but she was not ashamed to admit she was also slightly intimidated by her, and Molly was afraid of what this impromptu visit might bode. Plastering a smile on her face, she unlocked the door. "Good morning, Mrs. Miller. This is a lovely surprise. Joe's not sick, is he?"

"He's fine. I just had a craving for a good cup of coffee this morning and thought I'd kill two birds with one trip."

"Of course. I've got a fresh urn of dark roast ready—it's organic and fair trade—but I can easily start something else, or maybe I could make you a cappuccino? Or perhaps a cup of tea?" *Stop babbling.*

"The coffee is fine." She settled onto a stool at the counter as Molly got a cup. "How are you doing?"

She was not even going to pretend she didn't know exactly what Mrs. Miller meant by that. "I'm okay."

"You certainly gave us all a surprise."

"Trust me when I say that was *not* my intention." She placed the coffee in front of Mrs. Miller and busied herself getting milk and sugar.

"But goodness, Molly, that man . . . He's quite obnoxious."

She bit back a smile. "Well, now y'all know why I've been trying to divorce him."

"The bigger question is, why did you marry him?"

There was no judgment in Mrs. Miller's voice, and relief swept over Molly. "I was young and stupid?"

Mrs. Miller actually smiled at that. "We were all young and stupid once. Do you think you'll be getting that divorce soon?"

Molly refilled her own cup. "I remain eternally optimistic."

"Good." *That just seemed too easy.* "May I give you some advice?"

As if "no" was a possible answer. "Of course."

She patted the stool next to her, and Molly sat. "Don't hide. Don't slink. If you're going to try to keep a secret, you have to be prepared to brazen through once that secret comes out. And in small towns, secrets always come out eventually."

"I know. That's why I'm here today. I'm just going to have to face the shame."

"The shame?" Mrs. Miller's eyebrows knitted together. "I can understand your embarrassment, but shame? Why are you ashamed of yourself?"

"Because I lied to everyone."

Mrs. Miller's laugh caught her off guard. "Honey, no one has to tell the truth all the time. Imagine the disaster that would be. No one ever asked you if you were married, did they?" Molly shook her head. "Then you're not a liar."

"I've been told that's splitting hairs."

"So?"

Molly blinked in disbelief. Until just now, she'd have said Mrs. Miller had the strongest moral compass possible. Therefore her words seemed . . . surreal. "But dating Tate rather implied that I was single."

"True, but you've been separated a long time, right? And considering how unpleasant your hopefully soon-to-be ex-husband is, who can blame you for trying to find some happiness?"

"I figured most people would . . . I mean . . ."

"Expecting to wear the scarlet letter, are you?"

She sighed. "Yes, ma'am."

Mrs. Miller just laughed and shook her head. "And once again, each generation thinks they invented sex and all the possibilities therein. I've lived in this town my entire life, child. I know things you can't begin to imagine about people you'd never suspect. If I have to start handing out big red letter *A*'s to people, this town's going to look like the stands of an Alabama home game."

Molly clapped a hand over her mouth to stifle the giggle. "Surely not," she managed to say after a moment to control herself. "Not here."

"People are people, Molly. And throwing stones is a dangerous practice. Particularly in a small town where—"

"There's no such thing as a secret," Molly finished for her.

"Be easy on yourself," Mrs. Miller said, giving her a comforting pat on the shoulder. "It'll all be fine."

Molly spent a good portion of the morning reeling from that statement, and an equal amount wondering at the ongoing proof it might be true. Business certainly wasn't hurting, and while tourists could be credited with part of that, there were plenty of regulars coming in as usual. There were no ugly looks coming her way, only polite inquiries into her health as she'd been "sick" the day before, and a few whispered conversations when her back was turned.

And since good manners kept people from bringing up unpleasant topics directly, she was mainly able to carry on business as usual.

Then Sam showed up for her shift.

It was an awkward reminder that while the town in general seemed willing to if not *forget*, then at least outwardly *ignore* the entire situation, the one person who couldn't was Tate. And while Sam might like her, blood was always thicker than water.

And while she was trying very hard to not think about Tate right now, Sam's presence made that impossible. At the same time, this wasn't Sam's fault, and it wouldn't be fair to put her in the middle.

"Hi, Molly. I'm glad you're feeling better today."

"Thanks. And thanks for working overtime yesterday."

"No problem." She paused, twisting her lips as if she wanted to say something. Molly just waited, wiping down the counters. Finally Sam shrugged. "Tate's got a good heart. It just works against him sometimes."

And I hurt him.

Molly nodded.

"So is there a special today?"

And at that, the day was officially surreal. She'd expected . . . *some*thing from Sam. Granted, she was Sam's boss, so berating her wasn't one of Sam's options, but Sam must like her job a hell of a lot to not have *anything* to say about it. Not believing it, but not questioning it too closely either, Molly could only shake her head as she went to unpack the new coffee shipment that had arrived.

Not that it negated the utter humiliation and shame she felt at being exposed like that in front of everyone or the knowledge that people were gossiping about her behind her back even if they weren't calling her a harlot and a liar to her face, but it made things more bearable.

And honestly, she'd learned long ago to accept small favors for the blessings they were.

She let Sam go home early as a thanks for all the extra hours and stayed behind to finish the last of the cleaning up by herself. She moved quickly, ready to get home to the wine in her fridge that would reward her for surviving today.

Just as she went to turn off the lights, though, there was a knock on the door. Adam Tanner was peering in. Concerned, she went to see what he was doing there.

"Hey, Molly. I'm glad I caught you before you left."

"If you're after coffee, I'm afraid I've already poured everything out, and I don't have anything to offer. I could make you a cup of tea?"

"I actually came by to talk to you. Do you have a second?"

"Of course." She went to one of the comfy overstuffed chairs and sat, motioning Adam toward the other. "What's up?"

"I might be overstepping a line here into your personal business, but please don't shoot me for it."

"I think all my personal business is on display at the moment anyway, so I can't really take it out on you." It was weird, though, because Adam Tanner might have been one of the *last* people in Magnolia Beach she'd figure would have any interest in this.

"I'm not a divorce attorney—"

Molly jerked. She'd forgotten for a moment that Adam was an attorney of any sort, and this impromptu meeting took a scary turn.

"But from what I've heard, there's just something not right about what's going on with yours."

That was not what she'd expected. "What do you mean?"

"It doesn't make sense to me. It shouldn't be taking this long for it to happen. Can I ask you a couple of questions?"

A spark of hope lit in her chest. She wasn't going to fan that spark into a flame or anything, but it was nice to hear Adam say she should be divorced by now. "Sure."

"Is there money—a settlement, alimony—something like that you're fighting over?"

"No. At first, yes, I asked for alimony, but I didn't have a job then." It was weird to be discussing this so openly, but it was good, too. She wasn't hiding anymore. "But once this place started turning a profit, I decided I didn't need it, and it wasn't worth the battle. I withdrew the request a long time ago."

"Money and kids are the two things that usually slow down divorces. I don't see why yours would be stalled, then, if that's not an issue."

She gave Adam a few highlights of her divorce saga, but she trailed off when he started shaking his head. "No offense, Molly, but your lawyer sounds damn near incompetent to me."

She felt her jaw go slack, but Adam either didn't notice or was too polite to comment on it.

"If you're willing, I'd like to take a look at your paperwork. Do you have copies?"

"Of course. I've kept everything the lawyer sent me. It's all at home."

"I'll walk with you. I'll look it over tonight and, if you'd like, make a few phone calls tomorrow. I can't guarantee anything, but I think you need a second opinion." He shot her a small smile. "Assuming, of course, you want to be done with this. And him."

That spark of hope caught fire, and she pushed to her feet. "Let's go." Gathering her stuff, she said, "I'd really appreciate anything you could do. I'm thrilled you even want to try. I'm so tired of just sitting around *waiting*. I know Helena probably played a future-sister-in-law card for this, but I'm so—"

Adam was shaking his head. "Actually, Tate called me."

She stumbled a little. Way for Tate to prove her wrong. He'd said he would have tried to help, and sure enough, he'd come up with a way. She'd decided earlier today that she needed to call Mr. McCallan and try to light a fire under him, but she hadn't thought to simply get a second opinion. Maybe she would have, once she was thinking straight again.

He steadied her on her feet. "I told him it was a horrible violation of your privacy—"

"No, it's much appreciated. Just a little surprising."

"Why? He's got a vested interest in your divorce. I can easily see why he'd want to help you get it done and dusted."

Adam must not know how angry Tate was with her. But then why would Tate involve himself? "Maybe."

All this new, bubbly hope put a spring in her step, and the walk back to her house could not have been more different from the trip out this morning.

She'd dreaded today, yet it had turned out pretty darn good in the end.

Then, exactly like on her *last* really good day, Mark showed up to ruin it, his SUV sitting in front of Mrs.

Kennedy's house where she'd see it the moment she turned onto her street. She should have expected it, really, but she'd held on to the hope that since Mark wasn't hanging around Latte Dah or trying to contact her, that must have meant he'd left town. After all, she'd been clear she wasn't going home to Fuller, and he'd achieved his goal of humiliating her, so what was really left for him to do? "God *damn* it." Mark must have been watching for her, because the door opened almost immediately and he climbed out of his SUV.

Adam looked over at her. "He just shows up everywhere, doesn't he?"

"I'm going to kill him."

"I'm not a criminal attorney, either, but I will strongly advise you not to do that."

The levity helped, and she had to choke back a laugh.

Then Mark opened his mouth. "Another one, Molly? How many lovers do you have?"

It wasn't even worth addressing. "Why are you even still in town?"

"We still have a lot to talk about."

"No, we don't." She turned to Adam. "Can you get me a restraining order against him?"

Adam nodded. "First thing in the morning."

"Oh, you'd love that, wouldn't you?" Mark snapped. "It's not enough that I can't get a decent meal or a place to stay in this town?"

Confused, she looked at Adam.

He merely shrugged a shoulder. "A lot of folks have taken exception to some of Mr. Lane's comments and behavior. Many of the local businesses are exercising their right to refuse service."

It took everything she had to keep a straight face, but inside . . . *Oh, that was just too sweet.* She could picture Mark being turned away from places, stomping his feet and getting all bothered.

That giddiness, though, was quickly replaced by a surge of emotion that made her eyes burn. Mark was being turned away because of *her.* This was *her* town, *her* people, and they had her back. She might have screwed up, and they might be disappointed in her, but by God, they still had her back. Mark, her family, and Fuller, Alabama, as a whole could just suck it. "Maybe you should take that as a sign that you're not welcome here. Go home."

"Oh, I am. But I wanted to give you one last chance—"

"I don't want it."

"I'm glad you feel that way." His smile was smug, and that warned her she wasn't going to like what came next. "I've always wanted a coffee shop."

There was no way she heard that right. *"What?"*

"We're still married. I'm entitled to half of it in a divorce settlement."

Rage boiled through her veins. "You're insane." Adam put a hand on her—to calm or restrain, she didn't know, and she didn't care either way as she shook him off. "*My* inheritance from *my* grandmother provided the seed money for Latte Dah. You can't lay claim to a single freaking coffee cup."

"You left a loving marriage, selling joint marital property to move away with your lover—or lovers"—he sneered—"supporting yourself with the proceeds of those sales while you opened your business. *That* gives me a claim. My lawyer will be in touch."

This time, Adam's restraining hand was the only thing that kept her from flying at him. Mark merely smirked, pleased to have the last word, as he climbed back into his car and drove away.

"I'll burn the place to the ground first," she muttered.

"Calm down," Adam urged. "That's the most ridiculous claim I've ever heard. He won't get any part of Latte Dah."

"Oh, I know he can't touch it. My inheritance is mine and was never part of the joint assets. The only property I sold was jewelry purchased for and given to me. I've read the laws about joint marital assets, and I know I'm in the clear. It's just another threat and more stupid paperwork to fight, though. But that's the final damn straw. I'm done. He will *not* threaten Latte Dah."

She turned to face him. Still buoyed by the day's events, she felt stronger than she ever had. But Mark's petty, vindictive threats had also made her angrier than she'd ever been.

"It's time to end this," she said through gritted teeth. "Find me a lawyer who'll make it happen."

"One that can make him cry?" Adam teased.

She stomped up the porch steps. "That would just be a bonus."

Chapter 16

The worst thing about living in a small town was that it was damn near impossible to avoid someone. Short of locking yourself in and becoming a hermit, if your paths crossed before, the odds were very good they would cross again. And again.

While creating uncomfortable situations, those odds did tend to keep things from festering too long. There was no ignoring a problem until it went away.

But the fact that this *wasn't* happening—which had to be a first in Magnolia Beach—was making Tate tense and jumpy. He knew Molly was going about her business—Sam or Helena would have told him if Molly wasn't—but he never saw her. After a couple of days, he had to assume it was deliberate. At the same time, he wasn't exactly wandering into Latte Dah for a coffee, either. He wasn't quite sure yet what he wanted to say to Molly when he did see her, so while it was odd, it was also sort of a relief.

It was also amazing to realize how quickly he'd gotten used to a new status quo in just a couple of weeks. Fun texts for no reason, having someone to go to lunch or dinner with, and yes, wandering into Latte Dah for a coffee just because he wanted to see her. The depressing thing was how much he noticed that lack now and how much he disliked it. There was a hole, and he had nothing to fill it with.

The thing was, that hole had always been there; he just hadn't noticed it until now.

He wasn't sure how to fix it, though. And since thinking about the situation made his head hurt, he kept himself extra busy simply to avoid having to think about it.

Helena hadn't been hovering exactly, but she'd made herself very available. It was clear she wanted to talk to him, and he'd made it very clear that he didn't, so they'd spent the last few days in an awkward standoff. She might be his best friend, but he wasn't going to eat cookie dough and talk about relationships and girls and boys. That had never been their style and he had no interest in starting now.

So the days passed in what felt like an uneasy ceasefire, which was a crazy feeling since life had essentially gone back to its normal pre-Molly state almost instantly.

And that was another reason he didn't want to talk to Helena. He blamed her for this. *She'd* started it all by throwing him into Molly's orbit in the first place. If she'd left well enough alone, he wouldn't even have a pre- and post-Molly state of being to deal with at all.

So Molly was mad at him for being mad at her, Helena was mad at him for not wanting to talk about it, and Sam was mad at him for a multitude of reasons. At least Iona was happy with him again. She'd brought him *two* kinds of cookies.

He knew, though, that Helena wasn't going to put up with his silence for very long, so he wasn't really all that surprised to find her on his porch, unannounced and letting herself in like she owned the place after just a few days. She was not known for her patience—or her ability to butt the hell out, either. He was only delaying the inevitable by avoiding her, so they might as well get this over with.

And Helena was not one to mince words.

"I've held my peace, given you space and all that, but enough. I love you—you know that—but you're acting like a dumbass."

Only in Helena's mind could four days be considered "space." "And the space has been much appreciated. Could I have a little more?"

"No. This is ridiculous. If you ask me—"

"I didn't," he reminded her.

She frowned at him, but she wasn't backing down. "I'm not taking sides."

"Dumbass pronouncements notwithstanding, of course."

She met his sarcasm with snark. "I had no idea your ego was quite that fragile."

"My *ego*?" This had nothing to do with ego.

"So you were embarrassed. Are you honestly going to tell me it was worse than that time in tenth grade when you—"

"*Don't* bring that up. You swore you'd never speak of it again."

Her lips pressed into an angry line as she stared at him. "Well, is it?" she demanded.

On days like today, he wished she'd just stayed in Atlanta. "It's different, Helena, and has nothing to do with this situation. You're forgetting that I was publicly broadsided by information I really should have known going in."

"She said she tried to explain—"

"She's married."

"She's separated. Almost divorced."

Good Lord. "You're as bad as she is with the hair-splitting."

Helena slapped a hand against the couch. "He *hit* her."

Jesus. Molly had left that part out. Or glossed it over, at the very least. It made him ill, and not just because

Molly was about half Mark's size. "I'm not saying she shouldn't be divorcing him. It's just information she could have—*should* have—shared up front."

She sighed. "I agree with you about that—"

"Then maybe you see my problem."

Pinning him with a stare, she asked, "Would it have made a difference?"

Probably not. That was the one conclusion he'd managed to reach over the last couple of days. Now that the initial knee-jerk reaction to the word "married" had passed, he found his moral compass might not be as finely tuned as he'd thought. It might have taken him a little time to wrap his head around it, but he probably wouldn't have done anything differently. He just should have been given the option.

But he was apparently taking too long to respond, so Helena drew her own conclusions. "You're a good man, Tate Harris—maybe one of the best—but this isn't a black-and-white situation."

Only where it mattered. She hadn't trusted him with the truth. "All the more—"

"But," she continued, with a glare in his direction, "why don't you at least try to understand *why* she didn't share?"

He wanted to strangle her. "I understand that just fine, too. I don't particularly like it, and it doesn't make it right, but I do understand it."

"Then what is the problem?"

He sighed. *Bring on the cookie dough.* "She lied. She didn't trust me enough to tell me the truth, so she lied."

Helena nodded. "So that's the stick up your butt."

So much for sharing our feelings. "Wow, Helena. You're trying to pick a fight, aren't you?"

She cleared her throat. "I'm really not. That just came out harsher than intended."

"There's a nice interpretation of that statement?"

"I just think you're trapped in the 'she lied' and ignoring the '*why* she lied.' And I don't think it had much to do with trust. If she was worried you might not react kindly to the news she was married—well, it looks like she was proven right there."

That wasn't it at all. He knew why she lied. He couldn't get past the fact she felt she *needed* to. He wasn't sure Helena could be made to see that difference, though. So he didn't say anything at all. He'd rather be thought a jerk—but at least a jerk with strong morals and a grasp of right and wrong—than be exposed as someone his nearest and dearest didn't think they could trust or rely on.

Helena looked at him carefully. "You care about her, right?"

He could lie or even just brush off the question, but what was the sense? "Yeah."

"And I know you went to Adam."

He shrugged. "I'm actually surprised you didn't."

"I did. I just didn't think of it as quickly as you did." She sounded almost disappointed with herself. "I'm sure she's glad you thought of it, though. Adam seems to think things should start happening now, at least."

"Which she could have had happening ages ago if she'd just been honest."

Helena sighed. "You're going to have to let that go."

"Why?"

"Because you're thirty-one years old and pouting isn't attractive."

"I'm not pouting. I'm pissed. There's a difference."

Exasperated, Helena slumped back in her chair. "Well, keep it up, and you'll lose her permanently. Hell, you might have already."

Enough was enough. "Look, I appreciate what you're trying to do, and I know you mean well. But butt the hell out." Helena had started to smile, but that last statement wiped it off her face. "This is my business, and I'll thank you to leave me to it."

"You're a hard man, Tate. More so than I thought. But if that's how it is, fine. Be mad. Choose that over a wonderful girl who cares about you and makes you happy. I'm sure your ego is a lot of fun to snuggle with at night." Now he'd really pissed her off. *Great.*

Sighing heavily and muttering under her breath, she grabbed her stuff. At the door, she stopped and turned. "I'm not taking sides. Really I'm not. I think you both screwed up, and I hate that you're not together. But Molly needs support right now, and I'm going to give it to her. I'm not going to choose between the two of you."

He levered himself off the couch. "You don't have to. I know you love me. Even when you're being an nosy, harpy buttinsky."

"That's *why* I'm a nosy, harpy buttinsky." Her mouth twisted, and she wrapped her arms around his neck. Quietly, she added, "I just want you to be happy. You deserve it."

"I know." He returned the squeeze and let her leave with a wave. It was impossible for him to stay mad at Helena for very long. They had too much history for that—and too much dirt on each other to become enemies.

They'd get past it. They always had.

He just didn't have that same assurance it would work out with Molly.

Molly's legs were burning and she had a stitch in her side. She was very out of shape, which was all the more reminder why she needed to run in the first place and how long it had been since she'd done it last.

If she wanted a silver lining, this one would have to do: all that time in her schedule that she'd cleared out to be with Tate was suddenly empty, giving her time to run again.

It was the crappiest silver lining ever.

Of course, the hope was that endorphins would make her feel better. Plus, she was running off some of the frustration and anger, and she really needed the exercise, too. All good things.

It still sucked.

It also had the unfortunate side effect of giving her far too much time to think. She'd used her runs in the past as time to sort out problems—personal and professional— and her mind hadn't forgotten that habit. Pity.

At first, she'd been miserable, mopey and blaming herself. Then she'd gotten mad. And while anger helped carry her through her days, it didn't make this hurt any less.

And the fact it hurt made her even more angry.

But once the anger left, she had to face facts.

She'd been walking a very fine line, and she'd convinced herself she was safe doing it. And while it was true that this was her life and her business, she was the one who brought Tate into this without warning. He deserved to be angry, and there was no law that said he had to forgive her or even get over it.

She'd convinced herself that she didn't owe Tate an all-access pass into her personal life, but she also had to admit now that Tate didn't owe her unconditional acceptance of her actions, either. It would be nice, though, if he did, especially since she missed him so much it hurt to breathe sometimes.

She'd fallen, and she'd fallen hard. And she'd screwed it up.

But she'd apologized, and there wasn't much more that she *could* do to fix it. The ball was in Tate's court, and he seemed content to just let it lie there.

And so she would run, and she would concentrate on the pain in her legs instead of the pain in her heart.

When her phone rang, it was a welcome intrusion,

and seeing Adam's name on the screen was enough to get her hopes up even before she answered. "Hey."

"You sound out of breath. Am I interrupting something?"

"I'm running. I appreciate the interruption." She bent from the waist, panting for breath, and swiped an arm over her sweaty forehead.

"I have excellent news for you."

She didn't want to jump to happy conclusions, but that got her attention in a big way. "You do?"

"I finally heard back from my friend Amanda—she was out of town and just got back—and she wants you to call her tomorrow. I'll text you the number."

"She thinks she can help?"

"Her exact words once I explained the situation to her? 'Fuck that noise.'"

Her heart was already racing, but she could swear it picked up more speed. "You're kidding."

"No offense, but you have the worst divorce attorney in all of North Alabama. Amanda says he shouldn't be allowed to practice law at all. There's no reason this should have dragged out so long. And I promise you, Amanda doesn't play games. If she says she can make it happen, it will happen. You can trust her, too. She knows what she's doing."

She couldn't quite believe what she was hearing. "I don't know how to thank you. You definitely get free coffee for life at Latte Dah."

"I'll buy my own coffee." He cleared his throat. "I guess I need to warn you that Amanda's good, but she's not cheap. But," he added before she could panic, "due to the circumstances and the fact you're a personal friend, she'll let you work out a payment plan with her office manager."

"I don't know what to say. You're my hero." Adam's

office was only a few blocks away. She wanted to run over there and hug him.

"Just get divorced, okay? Helena is worried and she complains to Ryan and that makes Ryan grumpy and he takes it out on me—like I could actually do something about it."

"Well, you have done something about it. And I'm indescribably thankful." Hope was a happy bubble in her chest. "Let me buy you a drink or something to celebrate."

"It's not going to happen immediately. Amanda's not *that* good." Adam laughed. "It's still going to take some time."

"But things are looking up. And that's all that matters to me right now."

"Well, have fun divorcing that son of a bitch. Keep me updated."

She looked up at the clear blue sky and exhaled completely for the first time in years. "I will. I definitely will."

Magnolia Beach didn't go all out for the Fourth of July—mainly because two huge town-wide events a month apart would be more than anyone wanted to take on—but it wouldn't be the Fourth without a fireworks show. The tourists expected it, if nothing else.

And while Tate had come to watch fireworks at the Shore dozens of times, he couldn't help but compare this evening to Memorial Day just a month ago. That timeline alone was enough to depress him. Everything was too messed up to have been only a month in the making.

He hadn't wanted to come tonight, but not showing up wasn't an option, either. It beat staying home and moping—but not by much—and putting on a good face around a bunch of people who knew too much was getting old fast.

Sam came up beside him and handed him a drink. "She's not here," she said.

"Who?"

If Sam rolled her eyes any harder, she was going to sprain something. "Molly, of course. She told me she was going over to Pascagoula today to see a friend from high school who'd moved down here a few weeks ago."

What was he supposed to say? "Good for her. She needs more friends nearby."

"I just didn't want you to think she was off with Adam," she said, way too casually.

"Why on earth would I think that?"

"Well, she and Adam have been spending a lot of time together recently."

He didn't need the devil to come whisper in his ear. He had Sam. "He's helping her find a new attorney for her divorce."

Undeterred, Sam just shrugged. "People talk, you know. You wouldn't believe what I overhear at Latte Dah. I can't help but wonder if they might be onto something."

"That's all Molly needs right now. More gossip."

Sam looked at him over her beer. "She's going through an ugly divorce *and* a bad breakup at the same time. Rebounding would not be out of the question."

"Would you hush?"

Surprisingly enough, she did. For all of about thirty seconds. "You do know that Adam asked her out after she first moved here, right?"

He hadn't, but he wasn't surprised. "I'm sure a lot of men did."

"Well, now that the truth is out there, and people don't seem to mind, maybe Molly's ready to see what's on offer."

"Seriously, stop talking." He knew Sam was just trying to make him jealous, and it was working on him, as embarrassing as that was to realize. He'd said some pretty awful things and then immediately thrown a young, good-looking, ready-to-play-the-hero lawyer right into her path . . .

Not my smartest move ever.

Oh yeah, he was jealous as hell. Not that he'd admit that to Sam, though.

Sighing, Sam grabbed his arm and pulled him closer. "Look, if you ask me, you're running a huge risk here."

"I didn't ask you."

"Let me boil it down for you anyway. There are a lot of men in this town who are thrilled to discover exactly *why* Molly has turned them all down in the past. A not-quite-ex is much easier for them to get past than the thought that she just wasn't attracted to them. They're already circling like sharks at Latte Dah, looking for that moment when they can make *their* move."

He had to bite his tongue to keep from asking exactly who.

"They don't care that she's still married or that she kept it a secret all this time," Sam continued. "They know that Molly is amazing and beautiful, and they'd be happy to take your place since you don't seem to want her."

This was all very unpleasant. "I didn't say I didn't want her."

"Good. You should be flattered, you know. Molly's been living single all this time, but you're the one who finally broke through. You got to her and she wanted *you* bad enough to risk the exact shit-storm she ended up in. If you're really hung up on the fact she's techni-cally still married, tell her that. Tell her you'll wait until she's legally single, and just cross your fingers she's will-ing to wait for you. Otherwise . . . build a bridge and get over it. This is only major if you make it major." She sighed. "I've stayed out of this the whole time. I don't talk to Molly about you, and I haven't said a word to you about Molly—"

"And I appreciate that. Keep up the good work."

Undeterred, Sam ignored his interruption. "But this is insane and I can't believe you're acting like this. What is the deal? I mean, *really*? I want to trust that—"

"Then why don't you?" he snapped.

"Why don't I what?"

He sighed. He didn't want to go there right now, but since his ego was already in tatters, he might as well let Sam shred it the rest of the way. "Trust me."

"Because you're being an idiot." She started to roll her eyes again, but then paused and looked at him closely. "Wait. Is that a serious question?"

This wasn't exactly the right time or place, but . . . "Yes."

"Of course I trust you, Tate. More than I trust anyone in the world. What would make you think I don't?"

"You don't listen to me. You won't let me help you—"

She waved his words away. "Those are totally different things that have nothing to do with trust."

"How could they not?"

"Because none of that is about *you*." He started to protest, but she stayed him with a hand. "There are things I have to do for myself. Things that I *want* to do for myself and by myself, and things that I need to prove to myself. Taking care of myself—*doing* things for myself—is about me, not you. The trust is knowing you're there, and you've got my back if it all goes to hell. I'm sorry if I ever made you think otherwise, because there's no way I'd have the guts to do any of it if I didn't trust you to be there for me."

"I'm sorry I wasn't always there for you."

"You were. You always have been." With a depth of understanding he wasn't quite comfortable witnessing, Sam met his eyes and held his hands. "You think I'm holding some kind of grudge because you left? You going to school was my eventual ticket to freedom because I knew you'd come back and get me. That's trust, big brother. The old man just died before you had to rescue me, which didn't give you the triumphant moment you needed." She rose up on her tiptoes to kiss his cheek. "You're the best brother anyone could ask for, even when you're a big doofus."

It seemed too simple to be true, which meant he'd been beating himself up for no good reason. He certainly felt better. Even if he still wished she'd just let him help her, he no longer felt like it was a personal insult that she wouldn't. He squeezed her until she yelped. "Can't breathe."

He let her go and she fixed him with a stare. "Delightful healing moment of sibling solidarity aside, we're a long way off topic. What does any of that have to do with you and Molly?"

At that moment, the first firework streaked into the sky and exploded with a ground-shaking boom. It was fitting, really. "I'm not entirely sure," he finally said. "But it's something I need to think about."

Rainy summer days made Molly feel bad for the tourists. They'd come for the sun, sand, and water, and while Magnolia Beach did try to offer some indoor activities as well, those weren't what the people had planned for their vacation.

But rainy days were great for Latte Dah. She ran a ten-percent-off special and broke out the board games, setting up competitive Scrabble tournaments with prizes, kids' games like Candy Land and Chinese checkers—which one of her staff would play with the children, giving the parents a welcome break—and even a two-thousand-piece jigsaw puzzle set up on a table in the corner that everyone was welcome to work on. Sometimes, Mr. Yates would have one of his grandsons spring him from his assisted-living apartment and bring him into town, and the former chess grandmaster would take on all comers, regardless of age or skill. It made for a crazy, and often loud, day, but it beat sitting around in an empty shop because the tourists were hiding in their rooms, sulking over spoiled vacation plans.

And it kept her from sulking, too.

Staying busy was important, but wasn't all that hard. Keeping a smile on her face was also important—and that was terribly hard. Brutal, in fact.

Anger and indignation had lost most of their buoyancy powers, and while she could still dredge them up, they weren't keeping her from being plain old sad. She missed Tate, but she'd apologized and explained already, and if that wasn't enough for him, she wasn't going to compound the discomfort by doing it repeatedly. Then she'd get mad because he was being so obstinate about it.

At the same time, she wanted to be happy. However screwed up the situation was, and regardless of how it got that way, at least her divorce was moving along. For the first time in forever, she was feeling optimistic.

It was a very confusing vacillation of emotions, and since she couldn't quite choose one to stick with, it all gave her a great big headache, too.

And since Sam and Helena were being overly circumspect—as surprising as that was—neither of them even mentioned Tate in her presence—which was completely ridiculous. It wasn't as if she'd forgotten he existed. She was living in some kind of farce.

It was frustrating as all get-out.

She had to assume, though, that time would do its job, and all of this would settle into something reasonable and a new status quo would be established. Until then, all she could do was slap a smile across her face whether she felt like smiling or not and go on with her life. She'd have to see Tate eventually, and maybe when that did finally happen, she'd be over him.

She could hope.

If she could do it all over again, God knew she'd do it differently.

Or maybe she wouldn't. And that just made it all even *more* confusing.

Right now, she had a shop full of customers, and if nothing else, people needed coffee. That was her purpose in life until she figured the rest of it out.

Helena arrived then, umbrella-less and looking a bit bedraggled, as well as red-faced and out of breath, as if she'd been running. Grabbing a towel, Molly ran to meet her at the door. "What on earth are you doing?"

"You said you had news. I came to hear it." Helena took the towel and ran it over her face and hair, then shook like a wet dog.

She wasn't soaked to the skin, so that was a plus. "I meant for you to call me, not come running over. And do you not own a raincoat?"

Helena shrugged. "I'm wet, big deal."

"Well, come get something warm to drink and dry off a little before you catch cold. Do you want a dry shirt?"

"Lord, you sound like Grannie. It's like eighty degrees outside. So tell me—what's your news?"

She looked around, but no one was paying them any attention. "My new lawyer says Mark's ready to settle."

Helena let out a very un-Helena-like squeal and grabbed her in a hug. Molly could feel the dampness seeping into her, but she didn't care. "That's *awesome*. And so quick."

"I know. Amanda's amazing. I swear, she must know where all the dead bodies are buried. Either that or she's working black magic on these people."

"But how? I mean . . ."

After pouring two cups of coffee, Molly set one in front of Helena and kept the other as she settled onto the stool next to her. "It turns out my former lawyer wasn't just incompetent. He's stupid, too, and was totally cowed by Mark's lawyer."

Helena wrinkled her nose. "When you told me what a hard time you had finding one to represent you, I was afraid of that."

"It took her less than two days to find out that Mark has at least one, if not two, girlfriends in Huntsville." Molly couldn't keep the disgust out of her voice.

Helena's lip curled into a small snarl. "Making it very hard for him to play the lovelorn husband wanting his wife back."

"And definitely not news he wants spread around Fuller. Especially since both of the ladies in question take their clothes off for a living. Frequenting strip clubs would be an impediment to him becoming a deacon in the church like his daddy." She snorted. "My former lawyer told me things like that wouldn't make a difference, but it seems even the threat of exposure has Mark singing a new tune. I told you he was basically a coward who didn't know what to do when someone stood up to him."

"So you'll be divorced soon?"

"Wow. I knew Amanda was a miracle worker, but that seems a little too miraculous, even for her," said a voice from behind her.

Molly spun to see Adam. "What are you doing here?"

He shrugged, then shook his head, spraying raindrops at her. "You texted and said you had news."

"And neither one of you think to use the phone? Especially when it's raining buckets and you're dripping all over my floor?" She grabbed another towel and handed it to Adam.

He shrugged, but duly dried off. "It gave me an excuse to get out of my office. So things are going well?"

"Really well." She went and got him a cup of coffee, too. "There's still a lot of paperwork and motions and things that have to be withdrawn, but there's light at the end of the tunnel. Mark isn't contesting anymore at least, so Amanda may be able to sort it out without too much hassle. Worst-case scenario is we have to go to mediation, but it's happening."

"I'm so happy for you," Helena said, giving her another hug.

"Me, too," Adam added. "That's really great."

"I cannot thank you enough." She lifted her mug in a small toast.

"We should celebrate," Helena announced. "And with something stronger than coffee. I think we should take you out and get you knee-walking, dance-on-the-bar drunk—"

"Those are two completely different states of inebriation."

Helena didn't seem bothered by that issue. "Well, we'll do one kind now and one when it's final."

Molly felt herself smiling. After the last week or so of faking smiles, it felt a little strange, but good, too. "I am not against that idea."

"Am I invited?" Adam asked. "I want to see Molly dance on a bar."

"Someone will need to hold her purse," Helena said.

"As long as I don't have to hold her hair back if she yaks."

Helena agreed with a nod. "That'll be my job. Ryan will drive."

Molly could barely keep up. "Shouldn't you ask him first?"

"*I'll* drive." Jane edged her way into the conversation. "I can't drink anyway," she said, rubbing her bump. "There's a great club in Mobile we could take her to."

"I was thinking the Bait Box," Adam said.

Jane shook her head. "It's a dive and this calls for better than that."

"Do you want to invite your friend from Pascagoula?" Helena asked.

Before she could answer, Adam interrupted. "We'd need two cars, then."

"I can borrow my sister's SUV. It seats eight, I think."

"So me, Molly, Adam, Jane, Ryan, maybe Molly's friend . . . there's room for two more."

Molly just shook her head as the conversation took off without her. They obviously didn't need *her* help planning this. It was funny, really. The celebration for finally getting her life back under control had rapidly spiraled *out* of her control. *Oh, the irony.*

But she didn't mind. These were her friends. The truth was out, and they liked her anyway. She hadn't realized how much her secret had weighed on her every day until that weight had disappeared.

They were so intent on planning this event, none of them noticed when she walked away to get the coffeepot. By the time she'd returned, the additional guests had been decided, as had the location.

"We'll need to do this on a Saturday night," Jane reminded them. "Molly can't be expected to open the shop if she's hungover the next morning."

"So Saturday night, then?" Helena asked her.

"Whatever works," she said, pouring refills. "I'm leaving this entirely in your hands."

Helena grinned. "Oh, *excellent*." She turned to Jane. "We need strippers."

"Hey, now," Adam protested, even as Jane nodded wholeheartedly.

"Um . . ." Molly started to say something, but Helena waved her away.

"Shoo. Go run your business. We've got this."

Laughing, she left them to it. She'd just wait to be surprised, obviously. As she put the coffeepot back on the warmer, shaking her head at the scene behind her, she realized she was finally done with the past.

She trusted these people—Jane to run her shop, Adam to help her sort out legalities, Helena to watch her back. Hell, hadn't the whole town rallied behind her, claiming her as one of their own and sticking by her? *I have people.* She'd been telling herself that she needed to get rid of her bad habits—shouldering the blame, carrying the guilt, hiding behind a smile, doing everything alone because she just didn't really trust anyone—but she hadn't really done it. At least not until now.

This was both the best and worst couple of weeks ever.

She was finally the Molly she wanted to be.

It just sucked she'd lost Tate in the process.

Chapter 17

After more than a week of no contact from Molly, Tate was knocked a little sideways to see her name on his appointment list today. Nigel was due for his annual visit.

Maybe he should have spent more time thinking instead of spending all that time trying not to think about her and how badly he'd screwed this up. It hadn't helped that Sam had given him so much to think about the other night—which might have been good stuff to think about, but Molly wasn't Sam and the situation didn't exactly apply equally to someone *not* his sister.

He wasn't sure what he was going to say, and he needed to think fast. Sally, his tech, had already gone into the consultation room to get Nigel from Molly, bringing him to the back for his shots and exam.

Nigel behaved nicely enough for Sally, but as soon as he stepped in to get a look, Nigel turned half snake, hissing and twisting out of his grasp.

She laughed. "I don't think Nigel likes you very much."

"That much I knew already." *Of course, neither does Molly these days.*

Sally had to hold Nigel while Tate examined him. She cooed nonsense at him—"Who's a pretty boy?" "Don't you have such a sweet face?"—while Nigel growled a warning low in his throat. "You're a good kitty. We're almost done. Aw, you can trust Dr. Harris."

That last statement had him snorting. Another trait of Molly's that Nigel had adopted. Or maybe it was the other way around. Nigel had never had any use for him.

Wow. He was losing it. Nigel was a pet, not Molly's familiar.

He let Sally wrangle Nigel back into his carrier while he took a deep breath. Ignoring the ominous noises coming from inside the cage, he carried it into the consultation room, where Molly was waiting. She stood as he entered.

God I've missed her.

"Hey," she said quietly.

"Hi." He set the carrier on the counter and Molly stuck her finger through the opening to pet Nigel. "He's great. No problems at all. Jenny will give you his vaccination certificate when you check out."

"Good. Glad to hear it."

"Do you have any questions for me?"

Molly's head jerked up. He asked the same question of everyone. It was part of his spiel, and it had come out by habit. He hadn't realized how loaded a question that could be in some circumstances.

She shook her head. Then she looked at him evenly. "No questions about Nigel, but there a couple of things I need to say. I know it's not the best time, but . . ." She took a deep breath and sighed it out. "First, I wanted to thank you for calling Adam. I hadn't thought of getting a second opinion, but he has hooked me up with a friend of his up in Huntsville. She's a real shark."

Her voice was flat, emotionless, and it bothered him. "Good. I hope she's able to help you out."

"She already has."

He wanted to follow up on that, but it wasn't his business now, so he just nodded.

"And I want you to know that I'm moving Nigel to that vet up near Bellfontaine. It's nothing personal—I really do think you're a great vet—but I'd feel . . . It's just . . ."

She didn't finish the sentence, but he was rather glad. His professional ego was smarting—he was a better vet than Hugo Malcolm—but it felt like a personal slap, too. Which it obviously was. Molly's sweetness hid a core of unforgiving steel. He could understand her silence and her avoidance, but removing her cat from his practice was a deep cut and underscored how bad this had gotten. "Jenny can copy his records and forward them."

"I'd appreciate it." Molly cleared her throat. "I'm sorry that things went so horribly wrong. I really didn't mean to . . ." She shrugged instead of finishing that thought either.

"Molly—"

She held up a hand. "It's all right. I won't bring it up again, and we'll just try to move on. I realize that we probably can't be friends, but I'd like to think we don't have to be enemies, either. For Helena's sake, if nothing else."

Damn it. "Look—"

"You have every right to be angry with me, and you don't have to accept my apology. That's fine, too. But I do want to say that it was fun while it lasted, and I thank you for being the catalyst that got me out of my rut."

He'd been seconds from apologizing, and was now very glad she'd interrupted him when she did. He didn't know what he'd expected or hoped to hear . . . but a *catalyst*? To get her out of a *rut*? He didn't quite appreciate being reduced to such a functional role. "Glad I could be of service."

Molly's head snapped up. "Excuse me?"

All of his vague plans of remaining calm, cool, and detached suddenly failed. "Was any of it actually about me or was I just part of some twelve-step recovery program for you?"

"I have no idea what you're talking about."

"Was this recommended in one of your self-help books or something?"

"Don't be an ass."

"What? I'm glad you got your empowerment or your groove back or whatever it was I was the 'catalyst' for. It's just you could have been up front with that, too. It would have saved us both a lot of embarrassment."

Molly blinked. "Wow. I meant that in the best possible way, and you've twisted it into something unrecognizable. I wanted you—I wanted to *be* with you enough to take the risks I'd been hiding from for years. I did what I thought was best at the time—primarily for me, yes, but also for you. I'm terribly sorry it all went to hell, but you've taken a bad situation and made it a lot worse. I expected better of you."

The words felt like a slap. "Well, I expected better of you, too, so I guess we've let each other down."

Molly's eyes widened, letting him know he'd landed the hit. Quietly, she said, "I was doing the best I could, and I thought it was the right thing. I can't apologize more than I already have, Tate."

"I don't want another apology."

"Then what do you want?"

"I want to know . . ." *Jesus, this was tough.* "I want to know why you didn't think you could tell me."

"Because it wasn't about you!" Molly's shout echoed off the tile. "It was about me."

"I'm sorry, I thought there were two of us involved in that relationship."

"I didn't really realize until right now how important

it was for me to try to do it on my own. Yeah, it backfired in my face, and yes, you are right and everything would be different and easier if I'd told you and let you help." There was a moment of silence—broken only by the increasingly impatient yowls emanating from the depths of Nigel's carrier. Then Molly's jaw tightened. "You know, the real kicker is that I wanted to tell you—and I nearly did—but didn't. At first, it was too early—there was no good reason to tell you when we might not be more than just a weekend fling. At the same time, it was too late, because we'd already slept together." The heat had gone completely out of her voice. "I guess after that, I thought it wouldn't matter. I just put my faith in us, thinking that you might be upset, but you'd understand. I thought you'd have my back."

Molly seemed calmer, but then she grabbed the handle of Nigel's carrier and grabbed her purse with jerky movements that told him her temper was barely being held in check. "You know, if you want to know how to learn and grow from this experience so you can be a better person, have Sam loan you my book. I think you'd find it quite helpful. Maybe you could learn to trust people the way they trust you."

With that, she was gone, slamming the door behind her.

Tate really wanted to hit something, and if he'd had something in his hands other than his tablet, he might have thrown it against the wall. He was reeling from the bombshells Molly had been dropping and frustrated because he'd let the conversation get out of hand—and then end like that. But her words kept pounding into his brain.

I wanted you.
I took the risk.
I thought you'd have my back.
Trust people the way they trust you.
It wasn't about you.

He was seven kinds of a fool.

Jerking the door open, he found himself in the waiting room with eight sets of wide eyes on him. They were certainly good at making scenes, and this one, while not as juicy as the last, had at least been louder.

Molly should have been at the desk, checking out with Jenny still, but a quick glance showed no sign of her. Jenny spoke quickly. "She's gone. I'm sure she'll be back, though, to settle up."

That wasn't his worry, and Jenny—along with everyone in the waiting room—knew it.

"God *damn* it," he said, wanting to pull his hair out. The blasphemy got him a reproachful look from Mrs. Jackson, who looked ready to clap her hands over her corgi's ears.

Turning on his heel, he stormed back to his office.

"Um, Tate?" Jenny called after him. "Mr. Martin and Patches are in room two."

"They'll just have to wait."

The dark clouds in the sky and the threat of rain perfectly mirrored Molly's mood. So much for staying calm. She was a complete idiot, causing *another* scene and storming out like—

Oh hell. She'd stormed out without paying. Damn it.

Slinking back in after such a dramatic exit would be excruciatingly embarrassing, but exactly what she deserved after behaving like that.

It would have to wait, though, as the first raindrops landed on her windshield as she pulled up next to her house. Sam was on her own at Latte Dah, and the rain would bring customers in soon enough, easily overwhelming her. Grabbing Nigel's carrier, she ran inside and let him out, only for him to give her a dirty look and immediately stalk off to the bedroom to sulk on her bed.

She dashed back to Latte Dah in the increasingly

heavier rain, tossing her purse into the office and quickly tying on an apron. The crowd wasn't too bad, but it was building even as she stood there, and Sam seemed relieved to see her. Helena, she noted, was in her usual Thursday place, earbuds in and hunched over her laptop, a forgotten cup of coffee gone cold at her elbow. Molly took a deep breath and tried to put a neutral look on her face, because God knew she didn't want Helena questioning her right now about what might be wrong.

Forcing herself to smile so wide her cheeks hurt, she greeted the next customer in line, letting her brain check out as the familiar routine took over.

She had the container of soy milk in one hand and the steamer pitcher in the other when she heard Sam mutter, "What is he doing here?"

She looked up and saw Tate in the doorway, water dripping off his hair onto his shoulders. He scanned the crowd and the counter, his eyes passing over her before coming back to land on her with some weight. Molly couldn't look away.

Then Tate started walking toward her.

Ah hell. She wasn't emotionally ready for round two, and she certainly didn't relish the idea of entertaining her customers with it, either. But she didn't know what to do, and she seemed unable to move under the weight of that stare.

The locals, familiar with the whole sordid story, seemed to know something was about to go down, and conversations died off as heads swiveled to follow Tate's progress. The tourists also began to fall quiet—they might not know exactly what was going on, but they knew something certainly was. The air turned tense, expectant.

That change in atmosphere must have penetrated Helena's "zone," as she jerked out her earbuds and jumped up, intercepting Tate by stepping directly into his path. She put a hand on his arm and spoke quietly to him.

Tate finally broke eye contact with Molly to look down at Helena briefly, shaking his head as he spoke and then stepping around her. He walked straight to the counter.

"I need to talk to you," he said without preamble.

She swallowed hard. "Now's not a good time—"

"It can't wait."

"I've got a full house of customers, and—"

Tate kissed her.

Leaning right across the counter, in front of a roomful of people, Tate grabbed her face and kissed her.

She nearly dropped the soy milk.

The kiss was equal parts frustration and hunger and hope, and as suddenly as it started it was over, and Tate was standing there looking at her, an unreadable look in those blue eyes.

Her lips were tingling, but she didn't need to move them anyway—forming words out of the swirling mess in her mind was out of the question. But she had to do *something*. Not only was Tate staring at her, but so was a large portion of the clientele of Latte Dah, and as the shocked silence grew, everyone's head was turning their way.

What that *something* she needed to do actually was, though . . .

"I'll take those," Sam said brightly, removing the milk and the pitcher from her hands. She'd forgotten she was holding them in the eternity she'd been standing there.

Then Helena was beside her, steering her none too gently toward the kitchen, Tate in tow. "I've got customers," she protested.

"I'll help Sam," Helena countered, nearly shoving them through the door. "I've watched you enough to pick up the basics."

The door swung shut in her wake, leaving them standing silently in the bright kitchen while the noise returned to its normal level on the other side.

She couldn't make sense of anything right now, and she took it out on Tate. "What the sweet hell do you think you're doing? Do you not think we've both been embarrassed enough in public recently? Did you really have to make it worse?"

Tate had the decency to look a little ashamed of himself at least, putting his hands in his pockets and hunching his shoulders. "That wasn't what I intended, no. I just got carried away." He looked adorable and self-deprecating and her heart gave a little flip, but after everything she'd been through recently she wasn't making any decisions based on heart flips. And the complete one-eighty his mood had taken was unnerving.

She was feeling plenty of things, even if it was hard to identify any *one* emotion out of the melee inside her. The annoyance finally broke through, as it was the easiest to deal with. She was very tired of putting on a show for the population, and the longer she was back here, the more curious people would be. Just because he was ready to talk, that didn't mean she had to be. "Then maybe you'll believe me that now isn't a good time—for either of us—to have this conversation." She turned to leave.

"Molly, wait—" He grabbed her hand but let it fall once she turned around. "I'm sorry I was so dramatic out there. It's just that I finally got my head screwed on straight, and I couldn't wait to tell you."

"To tell me what?"

"That I'm sorry and I miss you and I'm hoping you'll give me another chance."

Part of her had expected something along those lines. He *had* just kissed her, after all. And while it was nice and everything, and another part of her was turning cartwheels . . . she sighed. "Nothing's changed, Tate. I'm still married."

"I know. But I'm okay with that. I've actually been okay with that for a while now."

"What?" Then why had he been so angry with her?

The corner of his mouth quirked up. He found this amusing? "We've been arguing about two different things. And they've got nothing to do with your divorce."

She actually felt herself blink in shock. "Say again?"

Maybe he shouldn't have come here like this. There were a lot of things that needed to be said, and a lot of discussion that needed to be had, and the kitchen of Latte Dah was not really the right place to be doing either. But he was learning that he had a real problem being rational when it came to Molly.

And since he'd already created scenes in two different locations today—in addition to walking out on a waiting room full of people—he might as well see this through.

"I've been a complete and insufferable ass. And I sincerely apologize."

If Molly kept blinking like that, she was going to get airborne. At least he had her attention.

"And it is about me." As her eyes widened, he quickly clarified his words. "Just not in the way it seemed."

She shook her head. "Tate—"

"Let me finish, please." He waited for her nod. "Your decisions were yours, made in order for you to do what you needed to do. That's the part that's not about me. I understand that—now," he admitted. "My reactions were about me, though. I thought you didn't trust me enough to tell me the truth."

She shook her head. "That wasn't it at all."

"I know that. *Now* at least," he added. "I thought that if you trusted me, you would have told me everything up front, asked me for help."

"I didn't need—I didn't *want*," she corrected, "someone else involved. I wanted to get out of this mess by myself.

Which, as we've discovered, was stupid because I *needed* advice from someone else," she muttered.

"It's understandable. It's just that my feelings—and my pride—got a little dinged."

He took a deep breath. *Cards-on-the-table time.* "I like to fix things. Save the damsel from her distress and all that."

She nodded. "Considering your childhood, it's not surprising." She paused for a moment, thinking. "I have a hard time remembering that I'm not on my own anymore. That I have friends I can turn to and count on. That I don't have to do it all myself," she finished quietly.

It was his turn to nod. "Considering your past, that's not surprising, either." He reached for her, not pulling her in, but just letting his hands gently stroke her arms. "That's a problem."

Molly raised an eyebrow at him.

"I mean, what's a White Knight to do when the damsel doesn't require his assistance?" he asked.

Her mouth twitched. "He reins his horse in and guards her back until she *asks* for help. The damsel, of course, promises to keep him informed and accept his support. People shouldn't have to fight battles alone if they don't have to."

The knot in his chest finally relaxed. "Sounds like a solid plan."

He hooked her apron pocket with his finger, tugging her toward him a step. She didn't resist, and his breath came a little easier. Another small tug and her thighs were almost touching his. "I guess we both needed to learn something from this experience," she said.

"I didn't need to borrow the book from Sam, though," he added. "I figured it out myself."

"It's a good book," Molly insisted. "You should read it. I think—"

Unable to resist any longer, he dropped his head to hers and kissed her. Molly's hands came to rest on his shoulders as she kissed him back, and everything seemed to fall into place for him. She sighed as the kiss ended, leaning her head against his cheek. Putting his hands on her hips, he pushed her back a few inches so he could see her face. "If I promise to read that book, can I back up a bit?"

It took her a second to figure out what he was saying, but then she carefully schooled her face and asked, "How far?"

"To the last big scene we were a part of in Latte Dah. Pretend Mark just left, and I've pulled you back here so you could explain."

She shot him a look. "Do I pretend you didn't just kiss me?"

That could be a trick question. "Whatever makes you the least angry."

That got him a small laugh.

"So." He cleared his throat. "That was your husband? He's a real jerk. I assume you're trying to get a divorce?" He waited for her to nod. There was a small smile tugging at the corner of her mouth, and it gave him hope. "I'm very sorry you're married to a jerk. I'm sorry you didn't think you could tell me about it before now."

"And I *am* sorry you had to find out this way. I should have told you. I know you would have understood."

"I'll survive. You do what you need to do and let me know if there's anything I can do to help." He brushed her hair back from her face, then settled his hands on her hips again as she leaned into his chest. "I'm sorry I was a jerk," he mumbled into her curls. "I love you and I don't like being without you—"

Molly's head snapped up, only barely missing his chin. "What?"

"What what?"

Her brown eyes were huge. "You're in *love* with me?"

"Of course. What do you think I've been saying?"

"A lot of stuff, but not that."

"Well, it was implied."

She shook her head. "That's not the kind of thing it's safe for someone to try to infer. It needs to be spelled out."

"I L-O-V-E Y-O-U. *Ouch*," he added when she smacked him.

Then she rose up on her tiptoes to kiss him, wrapping her arms around his neck and pressing against him, chest to toes. It took a long, lovely while, but when it finally gentled, Molly pressed her forehead against his and sighed. "I love you, too."

He didn't realize he'd been waiting—*wanting*—to hear it until she said the words, and the feeling settled into his chest.

He leaned down to kiss her again but was interrupted by a banging on the door. A moment later it opened about eight inches. Sam stuck her head around, a hand covering her eyes. "I hate to interrupt—and I hope I'm interrupting something good—but I *need* Molly out here. The line is really getting backed up, Helena is not much help, and I'm afraid she's going to break something."

Molly laughed as Sam disappeared. "I gotta go. I've got customers."

"And I really need to get back before all those people I left sitting in the waiting room decide to find a new vet. One who *doesn't* ditch them to go chasing after a girl."

Brushing her hair back and straightening her apron, Molly smiled at him. "All things considered, I think they'll understand."

"I'll see you tonight?"

"You bet." With one last quick kiss, she followed in Sam's wake.

The door immediately swung back open as Helena rushed in. "So?"

"We're good."

"Oh, thank goodness." She put a hand on her heart. "I couldn't take much more of it."

"Yes, you were truly the one suffering over this." He patted her shoulder. "You poor thing."

Helena leaned against the wall and crossed her arms over her chest. The relief on her face turned to triumph. "I told you so."

"Excuse me?"

"Just wanted to get that out there. I called it, you know. I told you that you and Molly would be great together."

He'd spent enough time blaming her lately for her interference, but he was feeling magnanimous right now. "Fine, fine, whatever."

Helena wasn't going to give up her moment just yet. "I'm so proud of me," she crowed. He tried to walk away, but Helena followed him out of the kitchen. "You owe me big."

He stopped to give Molly a quick kiss on his way out. A small cheer went up from the customers, causing Molly to blush. "You didn't actually do all that much—you do realize that, right?" he tossed over his shoulder at her.

Helena caught up. "I nudged. I encouraged. And look, here you two are. Exactly where I wanted y'all to be." At the door, she poked a finger into his chest. "You owe me. Remember that."

He looked back at Molly, who was laughing with a customer. She looked up, saw him, and smiled. He looked down at Helena. "Thanks."

Epilogue

Molly blinked against the bright sunlight as she emerged from Adam's office. Nearly blinded, she dug one-handed into her purse for her sunglasses. Then she looked up at the sky and let out her breath.

It was over. Done.

She was free.

Funny, it didn't feel all that different. She'd felt more divorced than married for years now. But *knowing* it was true—really, honestly, true—was damn nice nonetheless.

Turning to go back to Latte Dah, she saw Tate leaning against a streetlight. "You're supposed to be at work."

He shrugged that off. "How'd it go?"

He'd offered to come with her today, even offered to sign as her witness. It would have been a very nice poke in the eye to Mark to have Tate's name on their divorce papers, but very juvenile. She hadn't wanted him to come, though. She'd wanted—needed—to do it by herself, and Tate had understood. "It went very well actually."

His eyebrows pulled together. "I'm not seeing much excitement and jubilation. I was expecting a happy dance, at least."

"Oh, I'm jubilant. It was just a little anticlimactic after three years of nonsense and fighting. I always figured we'd end up in a courtroom shouting at each other, forcing me to literally claw my way out of that marriage by my fingernails. Instead, I went and signed a few papers." She shrugged.

"I would think that's the better scenario."

"It is. That doesn't make it less anticlimactic, though," she grumped.

"But you're now divorced, right? It's over?"

She nodded. "Adam notarized the papers and will send them to the judge, who will sit on them for thirty days—in case I change my mind, I guess." She snorted. *Like that would happen.* "It's not officially final until then, but yeah. It's done."

"Congratulations." He opened his arms and she walked into them without hesitation. "I thought I'd take you out to dinner tonight to celebrate. How about Bodine's?"

"Helena promised me an evening of drinking and carousing to celebrate my first night as a single woman." Tate raised an eyebrow at her. "I've denied myself a lot over the years, you know," she said in her defense.

"I'm not saying you haven't. And I'm not even bothered if you'd rather go party with Helena tonight. *I'm* concerned by your use of the word 'single.'"

"You're right. I'm not single until it's final," she teased.

He frowned. "Still not the point."

She wiggled out of his arms and grinned as she stepped away. "You're not forbidden fruit anymore. I'm worried it won't still be as hot and exciting now that we're not breaking any rules."

Tate growled as he pushed out of his lean and grabbed for her. "I'll show you hot and exciting." He swept her into a dangerously deep dip and kissed her soundly, the blood rush to her head and the hunger in his kiss making her equally dizzy. He broke the kiss but didn't set her back upright immediately. She could hear hoots and shouts of encouragement from a group of teenagers across the street—upside-down teenagers, due to the view from her rather precarious position. "That was definitely exciting," she confessed, fanning her face. "Pity we have an audience."

Tate grinned at her, then stole one last quick kiss before setting her back on her feet. He held her around her waist as she wobbled momentarily, both from the head rush and the kiss, and waited for her equilibrium to return. "I'd take you home and really show you how single you aren't, but I've got back-to-back appointments all afternoon."

"Jane's waiting for me to get back, too." She sighed. "See? I told you it was rather anticlimactic. Coffee and critters. Nothing has changed."

Tate pulled her close again, and the look in those blue eyes made her light-headed and swoony. "*Everything* has changed, Molly. Give me a chance, and I'll prove it to you."

She'd never quit believing in happily-ever-afters.

And it seemed she was going to get one.

At last.

Read on for a sneak peek at
the next book in Kimberly Lang's
charming Magnolia Beach series.

Available from Berkley Sensation
in December 2016.

Phone calls after midnight never brought good news. Shelby Tanner knew that, which made being woken out of a sound sleep—and a really good dream—even worse. She groped for her phone on the nightstand, but the phone was dark and silent, confusing her. She stared at it blankly until she heard another ring, then rolled out of bed cursing, and ran downstairs to the office to answer the landline.

"Marina. This is Shelby." *And this better be important.* She blinked and rubbed her eyes to clear them as she turned on the big desk lamp and peered at the caller ID. It wasn't a local number, and she didn't recognize the area code.

"This is Declan Hyde and I need some assistance. I'm . . . um . . . Well, I seem to be . . . floating. Out on the water."

This guy sounded a little too old to be making crank calls, but not everyone outgrew their adolescence. "It's the middle of the night, and I'm really not in the mood for pranks, so—"

"This is not a prank," the man said quickly. "I'm supposed to be at the dock, yet I'm . . . not." There was a frustrated sigh. "I've been staying on a boat in slip seven.

I woke up a few minutes ago, and I'm not in slip seven anymore."

That got her attention. Balancing the phone on her shoulder, she raised the blinds on the window and looked out, scanning the boats below. Sure enough, slip seven was empty. The *Lady Jane* hadn't moved from that spot in more than six weeks, so the absence was glaring. She didn't see the *Lady Jane* anywhere. "Well, where *are* you?"

"As I said, I seem to be adrift."

Okay, now I'm awake. While the man seemed to be frustrated, he did not sound afraid or freaked-out, so that was good. Whatever had happened to the *Lady Jane*—and she'd riddle that out later—it couldn't have been more than a few hours ago, so there was a good chance he wouldn't be more than a couple of miles offshore, max. That was good news; it would make the search easier.

But she could tell by the way he talked that he wasn't a very experienced sailor—which wasn't all that uncommon in Magnolia Beach. They had a lot of tourists with an overestimation of their skills coming to town, and a dark night and unfamiliar waters could easily lead to disaster, even close to land. Adrenaline rushed through her. "Don't hang up. I'm going to get the Coast Guard on the radio—"

"I was assuming you could just come get me."

"What?"

"It shouldn't take you long," he said in the most ridiculously reasonable-sounding voice she'd ever heard. "I mean, I can almost make you out in the window, so I've not made it all that far out yet."

She nearly dropped the phone. "You can *see* me?"

"Well, not clearly, no. But I assume that's you. The light in that building did come on about the time you answered."

Last time, she'd only looked to see that the *Lady Jane* was actually out of her slip. This time, Shelby looked out toward the bay. A cloudy sky shrouded everything beyond the marina's entrance in darkness, but, sure enough, there were lights bobbing just beyond. It would be unbelievable without confirmation. "Can you flash your lights for me?"

"Um, sure. Hang on."

Suspicions growing and her irritation barely held in check, she drummed her fingers against the windowsill as she waited. A moment later, those lights in the not-very-far-at-all distance flashed off and back on again.

"Do you see me now?"

"Oh, I see you." That probably sounded snarky, but *jeez*. Thank goodness she hadn't called the Coast Guard. She'd have never heard the end of it. Reminding herself that Mr. Declan Hyde was a paying customer and shouting at him would not be good for business, she took a deep breath to steady her voice. "Sir, is there something wrong with your boat?"

"No, not that I know of."

"Then why don't you just come back?" she said carefully.

He laughed. He actually laughed, causing Shelby's hand to curl into a fist. "That would make sense, except I don't know how. I've never driven a boat before. I wouldn't know where to begin."

The number of wrong things in those few sentences made Shelby's head hurt. He'd been living on that boat for six freakin' weeks. That boat cost more than some people's houses.

And he didn't know how to operate it.

Who the hell lives on a boat when they don't know how—

She took a deep breath to calm herself. Even if she walked him through it, step by step, he'd probably ram the thing into something on his way back. Maneuvering space was limited in the marina, and there was no telling how much damage he could do—both to the *Lady Jane* and to every other boat in the place. And, not to mention, it would be illegal if he didn't have a boating license. It would just be quicker, safer, and involve fewer insurance claims to just go get him.

Oh Lord, deliver me from idiots.

"Miss? Are you still there?"

She sighed. "Yes. I'm on my way. Just sit tight." *And try not to fall overboard.*

Grumbling, Shelby headed back up the stairs to her tiny apartment. It had just been a storage room until she'd converted it three years ago—shortly after she'd pretty much taken over the day-to-day running of the marina. Her parents hadn't liked the idea at all, claiming worry about her safety being there alone at night, but Magnolia Beach wasn't exactly a hot spot for crime—or for anything else, for that matter.

She'd always wanted to live near the water, but since Magnolia Beach was a tourist location, all the waterfront property was either too expensive for her to purchase or was designed for tourists to rent. Living here at the marina was both convenient and cheap, allowing her to save money for later. The apartment was small but cozy and, thanks to her cousin Ryan's handyman skills, comfortable and perfect for her needs—which weren't all that many.

A glance at the clock told her it was close to three, and that only made her grumpier as she pulled on shorts and a sweatshirt and slipped into her shoes. She took a minute to pull her hair back and braid the ponytail to keep it out of her face—Mr. Hyde wasn't going to drift out to sea or anything in that extra minute; hell, he was still in the No Wake area, for goodness' sake—then grabbed the keys to the dinghy and stomped down the stairs. There was even an eighty percent chance that he'd end up on the sandbar in another hour or so, where he could safely wait until a reasonable hour to be fetched back. But she couldn't ignore that twenty percent chance he wouldn't.

Cupid woofed at her questioningly as she got off her doggie bed and followed Shelby outside. Shelby patted the shaggy head. "I know. It's crazy to be up at this hour."

Crazy or not, it was a beautiful night. The clouds blocked the stars, but they also kept the temperature from dropping too much, making the October air a little warmer than usual. Everything was quiet—only the wind making the rigging on the sailboats sing—and mostly still except for the gentle movement of the boats. And while she would much rather be asleep in her bed, at least going out wasn't going to suck.

Cupid sat on the wooden dock, a little miffed she wasn't going as well, as Shelby untied the dinghy and started the small motor, which sounded unnaturally loud in the quiet.

This wasn't the first time she'd had to go help a tourist out of a jam. It just came with the territory, and normally she didn't mind. People came to Magnolia Beach to enjoy the water that surrounded the town on three sides—Mobile Bay to the east, Heron Bay to the south, and Heron Bayou to the west. It was a quiet, almost-stereotypical small town and very family friendly, perfect for water-centric vacations.

She was quite used to people with more enthusiasm for boats than with skill at operating them, but never in her life had she heard of someone living on a boat when he had no idea what to do with it. Aside from it being just *wrong*, it didn't seem safe, either. It simply hadn't occurred to her to check that the inhabitant of the boat possessed that minimum level of skill.

The *Lady Jane* belonged to Mr. Farley's cousin's nephew—or something like that—and was normally docked in a marina over near Laguna Beach. But that marina didn't allow live-aboards, so Mr. Farley had asked if the *Lady Jane* could dock at their marina for a few months. Had it been summer, Shelby would have had to turn down the request, but she'd figured it would be okay this time of year. It wasn't something they allowed often, as live-aboards often turned out to be sketchy and dubious situations, but Mr. Farley had given his personal guarantee that Declan Hyde wouldn't be a problem.

And until right now, he hadn't been.

A college-aged kid had brought the *Lady Jane* in and gotten everything settled, and at some point shortly after, the occupant had arrived and the kid had left. Shelby had been in Hattiesburg at her cousins' for a couple of weeks, so her father had been the one to get Declan settled in. By the time she'd gotten back from Mississippi, their new resident had established himself as a bit of a ghost—to the extent that Shelby often forgot he was even there. She'd see lights on at night, and his car would disappear from the parking lot on occasion, but aside from her servicing the water and waste tanks, he might as well *not* have been living aboard, for all the extra effort it had caused her.

It was odd, sure, but not odd enough to even ping on her radar as concern. This was Magnolia Beach; they had plenty of odd ducks in town. And most of *them* were far more interesting than some Yankee—the SUV in the parking lot had Illinois tags—who was probably just suffering through a Jimmy Buffett–inspired midlife crisis.

The *Lady Jane* was starting to take shape in the dark in front of her. It really was a damn nice boat, the kind a lot of people only dreamed of owning one day. Built for serviceable, but not overly luxurious, comfort, it was easily big enough for one person to live aboard reasonably well for an extended but limited time, as it was really designed more for weekend excursions and deep-sea fishing.

The hermit in question came into view, standing near

the rail of the cockpit. In the dark and from this distance, it was hard to tell much beyond that he was tall and broad-shouldered. She cut the engine on the dinghy and let it glide the last little bit, sliding easily alongside the bigger boat until she could catch hold.

It only took a second to secure her dinghy to the *Lady Jane*. Then she was climbing aboard, ignoring the hand extended to help her.

"I'm very glad to see you."

Her earlier assumption was proven wrong immediately. Declan Hyde was not some middle-aged former salesmen in an existential crisis. In fact, he probably wasn't much older than she was, maybe in his early thirties or so. It was hard to tell due to the darkness and the wild overgrown "I've been living on the sea" hair-and-beard combo he sported. He was wearing jeans with the knees ripped out and a T-shirt that once upon a time might have been blue.

"I'm Declan Hyde," he continued, offering his hand again. "Welcome aboard."

"Shelby Tanner," she replied, returning the handshake briefly while biting back the snarky but deserved comment she knew she'd probably regret later. He seemed about to say something else, but she knew she would not be able to manage polite chitchat right now. Not under these circumstances. "The keys?"

Declan nodded and opened the door to the cabin, giving her a glimpse inside. Papers and books were scattered around, and a laptop graced the center of the mess. A writer, then. She'd seen that before, too.

Please don't tell me about your book.

She accepted the keys and tried to start the boat, but the engine wouldn't turn over. "Great," she muttered, praying for patience.

"It looks like I would have had to call you regardless." The voice came from right behind her, causing her to jump. He'd followed her up and was now eyeing the controls with a shake of his head. "I certainly don't know anything about engine repair."

Of course you don't. He seemed to find this slightly amusing, but Shelby was unable to share in the humor. "Well, it's a good thing I do. There's a small toolbox under the seat in the dinghy. Would you mind?"

Declan went to get her tools as she assessed the situation. There was a flashlight stowed inside the engine door, and she held it between her cheek and her shoulder as she checked the most obvious culprits, hoping it would be something easy.

"Maybe we should call the Coast Guard," Declan said, returning with her tools and setting them beside her.

"I don't think that will be necessary." She'd have to be on fire or sinking before she'd call the Guard. She knew every one of those guys, and she'd never be able to hold her head up again if they had to come get her for anything less than a bona fide maritime disaster. And probably not even then.

"Should we drop the anchor or something? We're still drifting."

The fact he hadn't tried already meant he probably didn't know how. "I promise we won't drift far. We're fine."

He squatted beside her. "Can I hold the flashlight for you?" he offered. She must have looked at him funny because he added, "At least that way I won't seem completely useless in this time of need."

Declan's self-deprecating smile told her he saw the ridiculousness in the situation and his part in it, and that finally helped tamp down her irritation. "It's hardly desperate times." But she put the flashlight in his hand anyway and adjusted him so it would point where she needed it.

As if he knew she was not in the mood, Declan didn't try to make conversation while she worked. Thankfully, the problem was easy to find—and would be easy to fix. "It's just a bad wire. Won't take me but a minute," she told him.

Declan was quite large and the space was not, so his head was right over her shoulder. Contrary to what his hair and clothing said, he wasn't doing the unwashed-hippie thing. He actually smelled nice, kind of woodsy. "You're very capable," he said after a minute or two of watching her.

She snorted. "We are a full-service marina."

"I think this situation is a little above and beyond the usual offered services."

He sounded sincere, which took the edge off. *A little.* "It's a first—that's for sure."

"I'm sorry I had to wake you up. I honestly have no idea how the boat got loose. I worked until after midnight, then went to bed. I don't know what woke me up, but I realized it was a lot darker than normal and there was a lot more movement. I was rather surprised to find myself out here."

It would be disconcerting, to say the least. "Well, I'll tell you all about it later."

"You know how this happened?" He sounded surprised.

"I have my theories, but I also have video surveillance of the entire marina. It won't be hard to find out." She reached for the electrical tape, thumping Declan in the chest with her elbow in the process. He grunted. "Sorry. I'm not used to working with an assistant."

It wasn't the cleanest of repairs, but it wasn't terribly bad, either, for three something in the morning. Declan moved aside as she stood and tried again to start the boat. This time, the engine came to life easily.

"I'm impressed."

He was obviously easily impressed, then, but since it wasn't often that she was able to impress people, she took the ego boost happily. "It's holding together with tape and prayer, but it'll get us back to shore. I'll fix it properly tomorrow—I mean, later today."

"There's no real rush. I don't exactly have plans to take her out or anything."

The smile on his face told her he thought he was being funny, but she didn't see the humor this time, either. She stowed the flashlight and closed the engine door. "It's a safety hazard, though. Any particular time you'd prefer I come?"

He finally took the hint and quit trying to be cute about it. "At your convenience."

That would be a nice change. Yawning widely, she turned the boat toward shore.

Shelby Tanner was not happy with him—that much was very clear. Declan couldn't exactly blame her, though. No one liked being dragged out of bed in the small hours of the morning, but what else could he have done? Thomas had loaned him the *Lady Jane* with a laugh simply because he *didn't* know anything about boats. He'd have plenty of time to study and catch up on all those books he said he wanted to read and all the movies he'd missed—and he'd get to catch up on all the sleep he'd lost in the last few years, too.

And, Thomas had added, he needed to start finding his sea legs. Miami was a boat culture. A few months in Magnolia Beach would be an easy introduction.

Shelby, though, obviously knew a hell of a lot about boats. It was to be expected, of course, since she worked at the marina, but there was an ease and confidence to her movements that told him this was second nature to her. Even the matter-of-fact way she'd fixed the problem with the engine spoke to a level of competence unusual in someone so young.

And she was young—maybe early or mid-twenties—

which seemed very young to be in charge, yet she was the one answering the marina's phone in the middle of the night. She must have had some level of responsibility. *Interesting.*

The same ease with which she handled the boat was almost a rebuke to his lack of skills. It wasn't a slap to his ego or anything—he was well aware of his skill set and had no need to get into a pissing contest over it—and he could see her side of things. In a broader sense, yes, someone living on a boat should at least know how to start the engine.

And he'd had every intention of learning.

He just hadn't found the time, yet. The movies and books and sleep—and the amazing antebellum architecture in this part of the country—had proven to be far more attractive.

She still would have had to come and get him—the engine *had* been broken, after all—but the event wouldn't have had that farcical overlay, adding insult to injury.

It wasn't going to be a long trip back to shore since he hadn't drifted that far, but he wasn't sure what he should do during that time. He had nothing to offer in the way of helping—not that Shelby seemed to need it—but it seemed rude to go below into the cabin as if Shelby were some kind of chauffeur. At the same time, it seemed rude to stand there and hover like he needed to supervise her.

He settled for leaning back against the console, out of the way but still nearby, and scanned the shoreline. Magnolia Beach was a poor substitute for Miami. It was just a tiny Southern town, smaller than even one of Miami's suburbs, and without any of the culture or excitement. Yes, both towns were on the water, but he wasn't sure this interlude was going to transition him from life in Chicago to life in Miami in any meaningful way.

But he couldn't take possession of his apartment in

Miami until January second, and Suzanne had been very clear that he couldn't continue live in their apartment in Chicago. He had too much pride to couch surf at his friends' places for the next couple of months, and with winter setting in, leaving Chicago seemed to be a good idea anyway. He was sick of the snow.

So one drunken night, two weeks after he'd lost his job and Suzanne had kicked him out, he'd let Thomas convince him that living on his family's boat in Backwater, Alabama, was an excellent idea. To someone who hadn't had an actual vacation in more than five years, four months on a boat had sounded like paradise.

And while the last six weeks had been restorative, he wasn't sure he would make it all the way through December.

Shelby wasn't one for small talk, it seemed—whether it was her personality or the fact she was peeved at being pulled out of bed, he didn't know. If it was her personality, that trait put her in the minority of people he'd met down here. He'd never had so many small-talk conversations with strangers in his entire life as he'd had recently. But even if that was her preference, he felt he needed to say *something*. He settled for "How long have you worked at the marina?"

"My whole life," she answered. "My parents own it."

That explained not only her familiarity with boats, but also with the dock area, as she maneuvered around buoys and navigated without so much as crinkling her forehead with the effort. So while he doubted she needed full concentration to work, he took her lapse back into silence as a hint.

After killing the engine, Shelby quickly jumped to the dock and the *Lady Jane* slid back into her spot with a gentle bump. Within moments, the boat was secured in place and Shelby was plugging it back into the main power, bringing the lights on the boat back to full strength. The whole adventure had taken less than an hour from start to finish. A mere thanks didn't seem like enough, but Shelby merely shrugged when he said so.

"You're safely back, and that's what matters. We'll sort everything else out in daylight. Try to get some sleep." Then, without even waiting for him to respond, she was untying her little dinghy from the *Lady Jane* and puttering over to the main dock, where the large shaggy dog that roamed the property came out to meet her.

Shelby stopped to pet it briefly, and then the dog followed her back to the main building. A moment later, the light downstairs went out.

No other lights came on, meaning Shelby was doing exactly what she'd told him to do: getting some sleep. But he was awake now; the adrenaline in his system was not quite flushed out yet. Back in the cabin, he shot a long look at the bed visible through the open bedroom door and sighed.

Another episode of Breaking Bad, *coming right up.* It wasn't like he *had* to get up in the morning or anything.

He opened his laptop and took it over to the couch.

Out of habit, he opened his e-mail client first, but only a few e-mails had landed in his in-box since he'd last checked a little before midnight. Most of it was spam, so he started tagging it for deletion.

One subject line caught his attention, though: NO BETTER WAY TO SAY 'THANK YOU!' THEN WITH FLOWER'S!!

Unnecessary exclamation points and poor grammar notwithstanding, the message did ping his conscience. Hadn't he just been thinking that a simple thanks wasn't really adequate enough for Shelby's assistance tonight? Flowers would be a nice gesture, and might help smooth over her irritation with him. Hell, it had always worked with Suzanne. If he'd irritated her and *hadn't* sent flowers, he'd have been asking for the silent treatment.

Suzanne had required large flower arrangements, sized

in relation to the magnitude of the transgression committed. Waking her up in the middle of the night to come get him? He snorted. He didn't know if they made arrangements *that* large.

A small bouquet for Shelby, though, should be enough—just a token of his appreciation for going above and beyond in customer service.

It took less than ten minutes to find a local florist with an online-order function and to arrange for delivery to the marina office tomorrow—or later today, actually.

Oddly pleased with himself, he shut down the computer, grabbed a bottle of water out of the fridge, and stepped out onto the deck of the *Lady Jane*. The sky was just starting to lighten, even though sunrise was probably another hour or more away. It was quiet and peaceful now, and the view would be beautiful as the sun came up.

When was the last time he'd watched the sun rise?

So, instead of staying inside with his laptop, he sat on one of the benches, propped his feet up on the rail, and relaxed back with a sigh.

Soon enough, he'd be back in civilization and all that entailed. He should enjoy the peace and quiet while he could.